Drinking Deep

WHISKEY WARS

DYLANN CRUSH

Cheers!
XO,
Dylann Crush

To Kelly Greer ~
the right hand I didn't know I was missing

CHAPTER 1

THE GORGEOUS BLONDE at the end of the bar shut down another hopeful Romeo looking for a hookup. I hid my smile as I drained my glass of whiskey. Watching her turn down the guys who offered to buy her a drink might be even more entertaining than the hockey game playing on the big screen behind her. The way her lips curved into a sympathetic smile while she shot them down one by one almost made me feel sorry for them.

They should know better than to make a play for a woman so clearly out of their league. I couldn't blame them though—if I was a guy who hit on women in noisy hotel bars, she'd be exactly the type of woman I'd go for.

I should have been sitting at my brother Vaughn's place watching the battle on the ice in high def with surround sound. Instead, the meeting I'd had with a big law firm ran long, and rather than make the three-hour drive back to Beaver Bluff, I was stuck at a hotel in downtown Knoxville for the night.

"Ready for another?" The bartender gestured to my drink.

"Not yet." I was pacing myself. The bar's selection of

bourbon and whiskey wasn't awful, but I was used to the best of the best. As part owner of one of the biggest whiskey distilleries in Tennessee, I had access to a tasting room even a lifelong collector would envy.

"Stop being such a snob and try something from the competition." My cousin Deacon nudged me in the ribs. He'd been working as in-house counsel for the family distillery for the past year, ever since my brothers and I convinced him to move back to Beaver Bluff. I should clarify—in-house counsel for *my* family's interest in the distillery.

Unfortunately, we shared ownership with two other families. We got along great with the Devines. The Stewarts were a different story. My family had been embroiled in a feud with theirs for the better part of the past hundred years. Whoever said keep your friends close and your enemies closer had no idea what it took to stay one step ahead of the Stewart siblings.

"How do you think the meeting went today?" I winced as a shot bounced off the goal post. Then another hopeful businessman approached the blonde, blocking my view of the replay.

Deacon followed my gaze. "Do you want to move so you can see the game?"

"Nah, it's all right." There wasn't anywhere to go, thanks to a busy happy-hour crowd. Plus, if we switched seats, I might lose my secondary entertainment. The guys were like minnows circling a shark.

"I was hoping for better news this afternoon, but we shouldn't give up just yet." He loosened his tie and downed the last sip of amber liquid in his glass.

Since he'd joined the business, my siblings and I had been hoping he'd figure out a way for us to break off from the awkward three-way partnership our great-great-great-grandfather joined when he settled in the mountains of Tennessee. I wondered if he would have made the same decision had he known then how the relationship between the families would dissolve.

"You really think this firm can help us?" I trusted Deacon completely, but it wasn't the first time we'd tried to extricate ourselves from the partnership. We were on the brink of celebrating the distillery's 150th anniversary next year. I couldn't imagine my descendants having to spend the next hundred and fifty years navigating a generations-long family feud.

"If anyone can handle all the complications, it's them." Deacon nodded toward the TV. "How much have you got riding on the game tonight?"

"Fifty bucks."

"Those are some pretty high stakes," Deacon joked. "Do you and Vaughn still donate your winnings to charity?"

"Yeah. If I win, he has to give it to the wildlife rehab center. They just rescued some baby beavers and could use the extra funds." Deacon didn't need to know I'd already given them a couple hundred. I had a special place in my heart for organizations that worked to protect the place I called home.

"And fifty bucks is going to cut it?"

I shrugged. It wasn't the amount of the bet I made with my brother, it was the thrill of seeing who'd come out ahead. We'd been competing against each other since the day we were born. As identical twins, we were a pretty even match, though Vaughn held it over my head that he was born first. He thought the extra few minutes of life made him the one in charge.

Technically, since he was also the general manager of the distillery, he was. Though he had to share the title with one of the Stewarts, since neither family trusted the other to act in our joint best interest. I was tired of constantly butting heads, especially since I had to share my title of co-master distiller as well.

If we could somehow untangle ourselves from the partnership, we could start doing things our own way. For me, that meant honoring our roots and not forgetting where we came from.

"You know I'm not much of a gambler," I admitted.

"It's not really gambling when either way the money goes to a good cause." Deacon clamped a hand to my shoulder. "You're taking a gamble by looking into breaking off from Devil's Dance."

"I prefer to look at that as a calculated risk." The idea of gambling with my family's share of the business sent a chill racing up and down my spine. I was a man who considered my moves carefully—in business and in life.

Deacon pulled out his wallet and tossed some cash on the bar. "I'm ready to turn in. Do you care if I head up to my room to call home?"

"Of course not. I'll just finish watching the game and probably turn in early myself."

Since Deacon had moved back to Beaver Bluff and gotten engaged, he'd been living life a lot more low key. It was the kind of future I wanted for myself someday. But living in Beaver Bluff, where the whole town had divided into either Team Bishop or Team Stewart, made it difficult to find someone who hadn't been affected by the stupid feud.

Deacon abandoned his stool, and I motioned the bartender over. There was still another full period of hockey to go. May as well try one of our competitor's latest whiskey releases. I'd consider it research. One of the other Tennessee distilleries had been experimenting with using a few strains of wild yeast in the fermenting process, and I'd been thinking about trying it on a batch or two we'd be bottling later this season.

While I waited for my drink, a brunette walked to the end of the bar. The blonde got up, and I took a better look at her.

She was petite, probably no more than an inch or two over five feet tall, but with curves a guy could lose himself in for days.

The game was between periods, so I shifted my attention to watching the two women. They hugged, probably friends meeting up for a drink—too familiar to be coworkers but not friendly enough to be a couple. The blonde glanced around the crowded bar, probably looking for an empty table. Finding none, she eyed the empty seat next to me that Deacon had abandoned.

"Excuse me, are you using this stool?" She walked toward me, her front even more appealing than her back. Gazing up at me, her green eyes wide, a hint of a smile spread across her full, pink lips.

"No, my friend just left." I pushed the stool away from the bar. "It's all yours."

"Thank you." She shifted her gaze to the drink the bartender set in front of me. "Is that whiskey?"

I wrapped my fingers around the glass and lifted it to my nose. "I hope so, since that's what I ordered. Are you a fan?"

"I don't know much about it, but I'd love to learn." She lingered, her head tilted, eyeing my glass like she might reach out and take it from me.

Instinctively, my fingers gripped the tumbler tighter. "What would you like to know?"

"You think you can teach me a few things?" She arched a brow, and I picked up on the flirty vibe. At least, I assumed that's what she was going for. Hard to tell, since it had been so long since I'd put myself in a position where I might be the recipient of a woman's interest.

"I know a thing or two and would be happy to share my knowledge." With another ten minutes before the start of period three, I had some time to kill, and that would be just long enough to give her some basics before her eyes glazed over.

She scooted the stool back to its original position next to me and settled on the seat. "Okay, what do I need to know?"

Her friend joined, and my gaze shifted between the two women. "Maybe we can start with a name. I'm Cole."

"Nice to meet you, Cole. I'm Danica, and this is my friend Jolene."

I shook Jolene's hand first. She looked less than thrilled to have me intruding on their girls' night. Then Danica leaned close and slid her hand into mine. A hum of electricity buzzed through my fingers while a trace of pineapple and coconut scented the air around her and made me instantly crave a piña colada. I didn't even like rum.

Danica let go first, giving no indication of whether she'd felt the same buzz. "Now that we've got that out of the way, why don't you tell me why you drink whiskey?"

I leaned against the back of the stool. "How much time do you have?"

"Is it that complicated?"

"Honestly? Yes." I wasn't about to unload a hundred and fifty years of history on a stranger I'd just met at a bar. Instead, I racked my brain, trying to come up with one of the sound-bites I'd shared during one of the many interviews or podcasts I'd been on over the years.

She moved her hair off her shoulder, drawing my attention to the smooth column of her neck. My gaze zeroed in on the spot where her pulse beat. "Did your dad drink whiskey?"

"Yeah. And his dad before him, and his dad before him." I wasn't sure what she was going for, but I'd play along for a few minutes. "I suppose that's part of the attraction—the history behind the spirit. You don't get that with a lot of other types of alcohol."

"Interesting." Her eyes narrowed slightly. "What do you suggest for a newbie like me?"

I loved and hated that question. As someone who'd lived his entire life in the shadow of the family business, introducing my family's work to a potential new whiskey lover was an opportunity to draw someone in. But there were so many options. Not knowing anything about the intriguing woman next to me, I had no idea what to recommend.

"What do you like?"

"I don't know. That's why I'm asking you for a recommendation." A slow smile spread across her mouth.

Attraction simmered low in my gut. "I need to know more about you to decide what to suggest."

"What, like my sign? I'm an Aquarius, does that help?"

"Not exactly." I didn't have time to get too deep into the flavor profiles of different grains, not going into the third period with the Predators tied with the Ducks. "Do you prefer things sweet or spicy?"

Her eyes widened for half a heartbeat, then she leaned forward and bumped her hand against mine where it rested on the bar. "I'm not sure we know each other well enough for me to answer that type of question."

The same buzz I felt before vibrated through my limbs, radiating out from the spot where her slim fingers brushed mine.

I was so out of practice at engaging in the banter two single people might volley back and forth from a barstool that I didn't want to embarrass myself. "Maybe we should play it safe, then. Go for a middle-of-the-road, everyday whiskey."

"What if I said I prefer things sweet?"

That was easy. "Then I'd recommend a corn-based Tennessee whiskey that's been aged at least four years."

Her friend leaned over and bumped shoulders with

Danica, knocking her hand away from mine. "Don't let her fool you. She might look sweet on the outside, but this one's all about the spice."

Danica lifted a shoulder in a dramatic shrug. "What would be a spicy choice?"

The third period started, but I was more mesmerized by the vibe flowing back and forth between the two of us than keeping my eyes trained on the screen.

"If you like spice, go for something rye based. It's got a little more kick to it."

"Are those my only two options?"

"That's just the beginning. Whatever grains you choose sets up the mash bill. From there you can play with the yeast, the distillation process, how long you age it in the barrels... Even where you store the barrels in the rick house has a direct effect on what you pull out of the barrel years down the line."

"I had no idea there were so many things to think about when deciding on a whiskey." She eyed me for a long moment. "What would I get if I said I want it exactly how you like it?"

CHAPTER 2

WHAT WAS I DOING? Jolene was the flirt, not me. I was the one who usually sat on a stool by her side while she bantered with multiple men begging for her attention.

There was something in the air tonight. It might be the full moon, or possibly the shot of confidence I'd received by lining up my first consulting gig. Whatever it was, flirting with the hot-as-Hades guy with the broad shoulders and mesmerizing brown eyes was turning out to be a lot of fun. Plus, I was learning a little about whiskey—info that would come in handy when I started my new job next week.

I didn't know much about whiskey beyond the fact that my grandpa used to keep a bottle in his kitchen cabinet and take nips from it when he thought my grandma wasn't looking. But over the past decade or so, the business of making whiskey had exploded and distilleries were popping up all over in my home state of Tennessee.

Cole got a super sexy grin on his face. The kind that sent heat zinging straight to my core. "I prefer it balanced. A little sweet, a little spice. I like it to start off strong, then go down easy with a nice, smooth finish."

"That sounds good to me." Were we still talking about whiskey? I needed a fan to cool myself off after hearing him describe his perfect drink.

Jolene turned her back to him and rolled her eyes. She'd been in town for a seminar and tomorrow she'd be heading back to Charlotte. We'd planned on enjoying a last girls' night out, but thanks to a meeting that ran over, she'd shown up late. She had an early flight, and I could tell she was ready to turn in.

While Cole called the bartender over, Jolene leaned close and whispered, "Do you want me to stick around for a bit or are you going to pump the whiskey guy for info for a few more hours?"

"You look beat. I can take care of myself if you want to get to bed."

"How lame is it that keeping my eyes open until nine has become a challenge?"

Cole leaned forward. "Hey Jolene, did you want in on the whiskey tasting too?"

"Thanks, but I'm going to head out. Danica will have to let me know what she thinks." Jolene turned to me, her eyebrows raised. She tilted her head toward Cole and mouthed, *I like him for you.*

I shook off the idea that anything might happen between me and the bearded stranger. Jolene might joke, but she knew I didn't do one-night stands. "Come here, girl. It was so good to get to see you over the last few days."

"Likewise." She pulled me in for a hug.

"Thanks so much for referring me to your friend." When Jolene asked if I'd be interested in taking on a consulting gig for a friend of hers, the opportunity arrived just in time. I'd been unemployed for the past three months and was running out of savings. If I didn't get something lined up soon, I might have to seriously consider moving back in with my parents—every twenty-six-year-old woman's dream.

"You're so welcome. I can't wait to hear how it goes." Jolene squeezed my shoulders and let me go before she turned toward Cole. "Hey, take good care of my friend tonight. She's starting a new job next week."

Cole grinned. "Congratulations. We'll have something to toast."

"When do you need to be there again?" Jolene asked.

"Monday. I'll drive down Sunday night and spend the week trying to figure out exactly what they need."

"You'll blow them away." Jolene slipped her purse strap over her shoulder and leaned forward, lowering her voice so only I could hear. "I told you things were changing for you. Have a little fun with the whiskey guy tonight. You deserve it."

"Cut it out." I got back up on my stool as the bartender set a glass in front of me. "It's just a little research."

"Yeah, well, remember, a little research can go a long way." She backed toward the entrance of the bar and blew me a kiss before reaching the door.

So much had changed since our high school days. Now she was climbing the corporate ladder at a medical device manufacturer in North Carolina and I was unemployed, unable to find a job since my last boss had pretty much blacklisted me in the small marketing circles of Knoxville. He quoted poor performance reviews as grounds for termination, but I knew better. It had more to do with the fact I wouldn't sleep with him than it did about my success at my job.

This new opportunity Jolene had passed on would be my chance to change my luck. I could already sense it shifting since I'd sat down next to someone who knew so much about whiskey.

"You ready to give it a try?" Cole picked up his glass and swirled the amber liquid around.

I mimicked his action, putting a little extra swivel in my wrist. "Just waiting for you."

"It's too bad your friend couldn't stay longer."

"She has an early flight tomorrow. I'll probably head out after you show me how to taste this right." I lifted my shoulder in a slight shrug. Even though I was enjoying his company, it would be best if he got the signal loud and clear that this wasn't going anywhere.

"Well, then, I'd better take my time."

Heat sparked in my lower belly at the comment. Before I had a chance to come up with a snappy comeback, he held the glass up to his nose.

"Tell me what you smell."

I took a whiff. "Alcohol."

One side of Cole's mouth ticked up. He was hot. So much hotter than the guys I usually met at a bar. Not that I frequented bars, and I'd never gone by myself. Maybe Jolene was right. Maybe I needed to put myself out there more. Take more chances. I shoved that idea away almost as quickly as it popped into my head.

"Underneath that. Do you pick up anything?"

I tried again, taking a deeper breath. "I've got nothing. Is this like wine tasting? Because I failed the wine appreciation class I took out in Napa. Maybe my sniffer is broken."

Cole put his hand on my chin and tilted my head from side to side. "Looks fine to me."

My stomach tightened at his tender touch. It had been so long since a man had put his hands on me, I wasn't prepared for the kick to my nervous system. "How can you tell from just looking?"

"How else am I supposed to check?" He leaned forward,

peering over the bar. "I don't see any lemons or anything. Hey, I know. See if you can smell me."

I laughed for what had to be the first time in months, ever since the shitshow with my ex-boss had started. "Excuse me?"

"Give it a shot." He shifted closer to me and held the collar of his shirt away from his skin. "Tell me what kind of undertones you pick up."

I took in a deep breath. Even though it was barely April, his skin was already tanned to a delectable shade of bronze. Maybe he worked outside. Though the crisp, collared button-down made an office job more likely. I scooted to the edge of my stool and gripped the bar with one hand.

He moved even closer, his Adam's apple bobbing up and down as he swallowed.

My mouth went dry, and I inhaled, just a quick breath to see if he smelled anywhere near as good as he looked. I picked up the faint scent of a campfire and something else underneath. Closing my eyes, I tried to figure out what it was. Soap, maybe. But it was sweet. He didn't look like a man who shopped for scented shower gels, so I chalked it up to just being his signature scent. Whatever it was, being so close to him, drawing in the scent from his skin, made me want to be bold. Made me want to take a chance like Jolene suggested.

"Well?" He shifted back, and I forced my eyelids open.

"Campfire. I definitely smell something woodsy though I'm wondering how that's possible since it looks like you spent all day in an office."

He gave me a grin that made me think he was about to tell me a closely guarded secret. "I had to meet with lawyers today, so I dragged my suit out of my closet. Usually I'm a T-shirt and jeans kind of guy."

My heart ricocheted around the walls of my chest at the image. If he looked this good in a suit, I wondered what a nice, snug pair of hip-hugging jeans would do for him. Mmm. It was almost too delicious to imagine. I hadn't even had a sip of whiskey yet, but somehow felt a little tipsy from being so close to him.

It was a good thing Jolene had gone upstairs. She would have pushed me deeper into the testosterone-induced fog clouding my judgment. I couldn't explain it, but Cole felt safe. Which was ridiculous because I'd just met him, and I knew absolutely nothing about him except for the fact he seemed to know a lot about whiskey.

But it had been a long time since I'd felt safe anywhere, especially with a man. I was leaving next week, and he obviously wasn't from around here or he wouldn't be staying in a hotel. Maybe this was my chance to find out if I could enjoy a man's company with no expectations and no regrets.

"Damn. There goes fifty bucks." Cole shook his head at the TV screen where the Ducks just scored against the Predators.

"You bet on hockey?"

"Just against my brother. It's not really about the money, but it makes watching the game more interesting." He nudged his chin toward my glass. "You ready to try your whiskey?"

"Let's do it." I picked up my glass and swirled it around again.

"Here's what I want you to do. Breathe it in, but keep your mouth open."

"You want me to breathe with my tongue?" I bit down on my lip to keep from laughing. This was starting to sound like the woo woo mediation class Jolene had dragged me to a couple of years ago.

Instead of laughing, his eyes got more intense. "Yes, exactly."

He was really into this. I'd been planning on quizzing the guy at the local liquor store to teach me everything he knew before I had to head down for my meeting next week with a distillery, but with Cole willing to share his knowledge, it might save me a few hours of time. Plus, he was at least twenty times more attractive than the grizzly older man who'd been running the family liquor store for the past forty years.

"Can you demo for me? I'm not exactly sure I know how to breathe through my tongue."

"Why do I get the feeling you're giving me shit?" His eyes crinkled at the corners, but he picked up his glass, swirled it around, then held it up to his nose with his lips slightly parted.

My entire reproductive system shimmied as I ran my gaze over the sexy scruff on his cheeks, the strong hand currently wrapped around the glass tumbler, and the sight of the tip of his tongue. I could think of so many other things he could use that part of his anatomy for beyond breathing in a beverage.

"There." He lowered the glass and glanced at my hand. "Your turn."

Mmm. I cleared my throat and brought the glass close to my mouth. With my lips parted, I took in a breath. The alcohol sent fire racing across my tongue, followed by a wisp of something smoky. I shifted my gaze to Cole. The intense way he studied my mouth made heat hurtle toward my belly.

Then lower.

"You ready to get your first taste?" His voice went low, rough around the edges like a piece of sandpaper lightly scraping against my skin.

I was more than ready for my first taste... of him. "Yeah, let's do it."

He lifted his glass. "Let it roll over your tongue, hold it in your mouth for a few seconds, then let it slide down the back of your throat. Okay?"

My chest rose and fell as I took in a breath. "Got it. Roll, hold, slide."

"That's right." He lifted his glass, and I couldn't tear my gaze away as he sipped, tipped his head back, and slowly swallowed.

Since when did watching someone take a simple sip from a glass make my panties damp? Eager to find out what might happen next, I copied his movements. A slow burn traced its way over my tongue and down my throat, all the way to the bottom of my belly. In that moment, I could feel appreciation for why so many people were drawn to whiskey. It was so much more than taking a nip from a hidden bottle.

It was romantic. It was sexy. It was a whole new world opening up to me.

My mind spun with possibilities for the meeting I had next week.

"What do you think?" Cole asked, liquid fire burning in his gaze.

"I think it was a bit of a religious experience." For someone who made a living at communicating, I was temporarily at a loss for words. "What do you think about what I think?"

He rested his arm on the back of my stool and held my gaze for an extra-long beat. "I think I'd like to kiss you right now. What do you think about that?"

My stomach clenched. I wasn't a woman who kissed strangers in bars. Then again, where had that gotten me? Jolene's words pounded through my head. Take a chance. You deserve it.

Swallowing my hesitation, I tilted my head and met his gaze. "I think I'd like that very much."

CHAPTER 3

HER GAZE DARTED BACK and forth from my eyes to my mouth. Her back stiffened as I moved closer. She was nervous. The last time I'd picked a woman up in a bar was... Okay, never. I didn't know how this was supposed to work. The only thing I knew was that if I didn't kiss her right then and there, I'd regret it for the rest of my days.

So I leaned in, cupped her cheek with my palm, pulled her face closer to mine, and pressed my lips to hers. Her lips were soft and full and yielding. She tasted like the perfect blend of cherries and my favorite whiskey—an irresistible combination.

At the risk of her pulling away, I took the kiss deeper, pressing against the seam of her lips with my tongue. They parted, allowing me entrance. Tentatively, I slid my tongue against hers, testing, teasing, taunting her with my mouth.

A tiny moan vibrated through the back of her throat. I lifted my other hand to cup both of her cheeks between my palms, angling her head to better slant my mouth against hers.

She shifted her hips on the stool, sliding her knees between my parted thighs. Her hands went to my shoulders, her fingers pressing down hard.

"Do you want to come upstairs?" I whispered the words against her mouth, silently begging her to say yes.

She hesitated, pulling back to meet my gaze. Doubt clouded her eyes.

Shit. I'd fucked up already. "Sorry, I got a little carried away."

"It's okay. I think I'd like that."

"Really?" I didn't want to talk her out of it, but I was operating out of my comfort zone.

She nodded, a move that made her blonde hair fall over her shoulders. I wanted to smooth it back from her face and tilt her head up so I could ravage those plump pink lips. Instead, I pulled a few bills out of my wallet and tossed them down on the bar. With my fingers twined with hers, I tugged her toward the elevator, eager to find out where the night might lead.

The elevator door had barely closed behind us when she turned toward me. I wrapped her in my arms and pressed my lips to hers. The scent of whiskey surrounded us as she rose onto her tiptoes and took the kiss deeper.

The elevator stopped. We parted, but I held her tight to my side. An older couple entered, and the man pressed the button for the first floor. Danica had me so distracted, I'd never hit the button. Desperate to taste her again, I held back, not-so-patiently waiting for a chance to be alone again. Once the couple exited into the lobby, I pushed the button for the fifteenth floor.

She rounded on me again, her gaze focused on my lips. "Jolene made me promise not to go into a stranger's hotel room."

"I'm not a stranger, remember?" I held out my hand. "I'm Cole. Nice to meet you, Danica."

She laughed. "I'm not sure that will cut it."

"So if you can't enter my room..." I put my hands on her

curves, that spot just past a woman's waist where her body flares out to her hips. "Let's see. I've got three brothers and a sister and I bleed UT orange."

"Why didn't you start with that? I'm a fellow Volunteer. That means we're practically best friends already." Danica reached over to pull out the stop button on the elevator, then raised her brows in a challenge.

I liked her line of thinking. Liked it enough to nuzzle my nose into her hair, chasing the scent of piña coladas behind her ear.

She wrapped her arms around me and backed against the wall. I wanted her. Wanted her like I hadn't wanted a woman in far too long. Shit like this didn't happen in Beaver Bluff, especially to a guy like me.

Her fingers toyed with the hair at the nape of my neck while I tasted the sweet skin just below her ear. Her scent made me think of a tropical island: coconuts, sunshine, and sipping cocktails on the beach. Somewhere far, far away from springtime in the mountains of Tennessee.

Maybe something far away was what I needed. In that moment, all I wanted—all I needed—was her. Desire pounded through me, the proof rising to attention in the front of my boxer briefs.

"Do you think there's a camera in here?" She glanced over my shoulder.

I took a quick look around, not seeing anything that looked like a camera. "Most of these old buildings aren't retro fitted with them."

She untangled her arms from around my neck and reached for the waistband of my pants. "We'd better hurry then before they send someone to check on the elevator."

"You sure about this?" I'd had a couple one-night stands,

but they were with people I knew to some degree. We didn't get many strangers passing through Beaver Bluff.

"Yes. Are you?" Even while she asked, she pushed my pants down my thighs so they pooled around my ankles.

Instead of answering with words, I slid my hands under the hem of her short skirt and hiked it up her legs. "Condom?"

"In my purse." She fumbled with the bag at her hip and pulled out a packet.

"Impressive."

"Do you mind if I..." Her gaze shot to the bulge in my briefs.

"Go ahead." I trailed a finger along the waistband of her panties while she freed my erection. She fisted my cock in her hand and slid up and down my length a few times, taking me from hard to hardly able to control myself before unrolling the circle of latex over my raging erection.

"Now that's impressive." Smiling, she peered up at me through dark, long lashes, her fingers still gripping the base of my cock.

Time was short, and I was ready. I dipped my finger into her panties to find out if she was the same. My finger slid through her slick heat. Her chest rose and fell as I circled the bundle of nerves at the apex of her thighs. I wanted to slow down, enjoy the moment, take my time.

My cock had other plans. It would be easy enough to stand here, her back pressed against the mirrored wall of the elevator and get each other off without even losing our clothes.

But I wanted more.

Slowly, I dragged my finger away.

She slipped her panties down her legs and stepped out of them. Then she braced herself in the corner of the elevator, her ass resting on the handrail. She dug her fingers into my shoulders, her breasts heaving with each breath. Damn, I wished we had more time so I could explore every inch of her with my mouth.

I bent over slightly to accommodate for our difference in height and hoisted her up against the wall. My dick notched at her entrance, ready to slide into her welcoming heat. Dipping my head, I got my first taste of the skin at the base of her neck. Her hips shifted, tilting back to give me better access, and she moaned.

Knowing we were short on time, I thrust into her. She bit down on her lip mid-moan, cutting herself off. I pulled out almost all the way, then plunged into her again. She felt good. No, better than good. She felt fucking amazing. Her tight core gripped my dick like it didn't want to let go. I braced my free arm on the wall next to her head and pulled out again.

Her hold on my shoulders tightened, and she pulled me closer by crossing her ankles behind my waist. She wanted more. I grunted, heaving into her with everything I had.

Desperate to taste her, I pulled the top of her shirt apart with my teeth… so eager to lavish some attention on her breasts that I didn't care that her button popped off and bounced across the elevator floor. My tongue slid down to sweep along the cleft between her breasts. Her hand went to the back of my head and she held me there. I flicked my tongue out, sliding under the cup of her bra to tease her nipple into a tight bud. She arched her back, straining, like she was chasing down her release and had almost caught it.

"Right there, oh God, don't stop." Her breath brushed against my ear.

I had no intention of stopping. I was too far gone myself. What the hell was I doing? I was thirty years old, not some horny teen who couldn't keep his dick in his pants. Somehow, knowing the elevator could start up at any minute and the doors might open made me even hotter for her. Any second I'd come inside her, this stranger who'd gotten me more turned on in the past hour than I'd been in the past year.

As she dug her nails into my shoulder, she paused, her naked ass pressed against the wall. I watched as she let herself go, falling headfirst into her release, wringing every bit of pleasure from riding my cock.

The way her mouth parted, the slightest smile playing at the corner of her lips, sent me hurtling after her. I pulled back and pumped into her one final time. My ass clenched, my balls tightened, and I free fell into my own orgasm, coming so hard my knees shook.

Danica pressed hot, wet kisses against my cheeks, my eyelids, my mouth. Then she unwrapped her legs from around my waist and slid down the wall until her feet touched the ground.

I pinched off the condom and tied a knot at the end. With nowhere else to put it, I slid it into my pocket. That was better than getting caught with it in my hand when the doors opened.

Danica adjusted her shirt, unable to fully close the top since I'd pulled the button free. Then she released the stop button, and the elevator lurched before slowly beginning to rise. My fingers fumbled to button my pants and redo my belt buckle. As the elevator door opened, I tucked my shirt into my pants.

That's when I saw them.

Her lacy black panties had landed on the floor on the other side of the elevator. I stepped over to the corner and covered them with my size fifteen dress shoe. I only wore them once or twice a year, usually at weddings. At least they'd come in handy today.

"Ladies first." I blocked the elevator door with my arm while she stepped out. "Do you think we're still strangers?"

"I'd say we just became fast friends." She tilted her head to the side, her lips curving into a teasing smile.

I'd probably never see her after tonight, the woman with the smart-ass mouth who smelled like sunshine and tasted like two of my favorite things. I wasn't ready to let her go yet. As a couple stepped onto the elevator, I bent down to pick up the panties, sliding them into my pocket before anyone noticed.

"So, friend… any chance you want to join me for a late-night cocktail?" I reached for her hand, then lifted it to my lips to kiss her knuckles.

She wrinkled her nose, making her look like the perfect mix of sweet and sexy. "Only if we can skip the cocktail."

Resting my hand on the small of her back, I guided her down the hall to my room. I had no idea where she'd come from, but she'd pulled me out of a deep, narrow rut I'd been living in for the past eighteen months. Hell, I didn't even know her last name. Didn't even know if she'd given me her real first name.

It didn't matter.

I pressed the key card against the door, a smile on my face and a spring in my step that hadn't been there before.

WHEN I WOKE the next morning, she was gone. Not that I expected us to linger over coffee and breakfast in bed after the night we'd shared. But I at least thought I'd have the chance to get a last name. Maybe a phone number. I rolled over and inhaled the lingering scent of the tropics from her pillow.

She'd been here. I hadn't just imagined the gorgeous woman who'd reminded me of what had been missing in my life. Needing more proof that it hadn't all been a dream, I reached for the pocket of the pants I'd tossed on the floor and pulled out her underwear.

Hell, I might need to come to Knoxville more often. Wanting nothing more than to lie back in bed and relive every moment I'd spent exploring Danica's curves, I closed my eyes.

My phone buzzed on the bedside table. I cracked an eyelid. The screen lit up with my brother Vaughn's text.

Vaughn: *What time will you be home?*

It was already seven-thirty, and I had a three-hour drive ahead of me.

Me: *Probably around noon, why?*

Vaughn: *You'll never believe the shit the Stewarts are pulling now.*

A ball of dread gathered momentum as it rolled around in my gut, just like a snowball multiplied in size on its way down a hill.

Me: *I'm almost afraid to ask.*

Vaughn: *They've got a meeting on their calendar for nine on Monday morning.*

Me: *So?*

Vaughn: *It's with a marketing exec. Some out-of-town consultant.*

I thought we'd reached a place where we could pause in the feud between our two families. Things had been uneventful over the past couple of months. I should have known they were working on something behind the scenes.

Any tightness in my shoulders that had been relieved by my time with Danica faded away.

Looked like I'd be working all weekend, trying to figure out what the Stewarts had planned, and how I'd be able to beat them at their own game.

CHAPTER 4

Danica

I CHECKED my lipstick in the rearview mirror. Hopefully, I looked every inch the professional business expert Jolene had made me out to be. Summoning my inner boss babe, I flung the car door open and set my foot on uneven ground. The gravel parking lot at the Devil's Dance main offices was going to be tricky to navigate in the three-inch heels I'd chosen to wear today. With my ego badly bruised from my last job, I needed every boost of confidence I could gather.

I'd be lucky if I didn't twist my ankle on the rocks. Hopeful that no one was watching me through one of the windows facing the parking lot, I let go of the hood of my car and teetered toward the door. Today's meeting was a chance for me to get to know more about Devil's Dance, so I could help them figure out where to take their business from here.

I didn't like to go into a potential new client meeting without doing tons of research, but this had been a last-minute opportunity. Except for the whiskey lesson I'd received from the hottie I met at the hotel last week, I hadn't had time to deep dive into the history of Devil's Dance. Though I had bought a bottle of Devil's Dance Deluxe, the whiskey Cole had me try.

I'd sipped on it most of the weekend while I scoured the internet on information about the brand. The burn sliding down my throat reminded me of the hot time we spent in the elevator and the hours in his hotel room that followed. That was the most out-of-character move I'd made in my entire life, and I couldn't get him out of my mind.

Enough of that. I needed to focus. If this meeting went well, I could secure my first client and start making progress on my dream to establish my own agency. I stepped onto the concrete sidewalk in front of the building, grateful to have survived my trek through the minefield of gravel.

The building spoke to the history of the distillery. Weathered wood covered the exterior, and two giant barrels overflowing with bright-colored flowers flanked the double front doors. Feeling like I was traveling back in time about a hundred years, I pushed the door open and stepped inside.

It looked like an old general store with wooden plank walls and weathered floorboards. A reception desk sat directly in front of me, and bottles of the distillery's offerings lined the shelves running along the walls.

"Welcome to Devil's Dance Distillery. Can I help you?" The woman wore a T-shirt with the distillery logo on it and sat behind an antique wooden counter.

"Hi. I'm here for a nine o'clock meeting with Mr. Stewart." Comfortable to be on more level footing, I crossed the room to stand next to the desk. The scent of whiskey floated through the air, another reminder of my weekend encounter with Cole. Thinking about him and the confidence I'd felt when I was with him made me straighten my back. I could do this.

"Which one?" The woman offered a patient smile.

"Oh, how many are there?"

"Two. I'm assuming you're meeting with Davis. He's the co-manager of the distillery, along with Vaughn Bishop, of course."

Jolene hadn't said anything about there being co-managers. It was a little too late to gather more details now, so I nodded. "Yes, Davis, the manager."

She tapped on her headset. "I'll let him know you're here."

"Thank you." While I waited, I walked over to one of the displays on the wall. A black-and-white picture showed the front of the distillery, slightly different from the entrance I'd walked through a few moments ago, but still the same. This building must be the original office. It sure felt like it based on the antique look and feel of the place.

"Ms. Watson, thanks so much for coming all this way."

I turned away from the photo to face the man with the deep, rich voice. He had on a pair of khaki pants and a long-sleeved shirt with the sleeves rolled up. His lips parted in a wide smile while his eyes drank me in.

"Thanks for having me." I took the hand he extended.

"I'm Davis Stewart, manager of the distillery. We've got the conference room set up for our meeting this morning. You said it would be best to start off by talking to a just a few of us, so I invited my sister Harper to join in on the conversation."

"That sounds great." He let my hand go, and I followed him through the door behind the reception area. I always liked to start a job by gathering info from just a couple of people. Getting too many opinions involved early on only complicated things.

The conference room decor mimicked the lobby. Rough wooden slats covered the walls, and the table was a wide slab of wood. Bottles of whiskey sat on shelves along the walls, along with memorabilia and framed photos showing the history of the place through the years.

"Ms. Watson, meet my sister Harper. She's the master distiller here at Devil's Dance."

Harper stood and reached across the table to take my hand. "It's nice to meet you."

"Please, call me Danica." There wasn't anything formal about the distillery except me in my dark gray suit and red high heels. "It's nice to meet you, too."

She sat down and scooted her chair closer to the table. "You come highly recommended by our mutual friend."

I took the chair directly across from her and reminded myself to breathe. "Jolene thinks the world of you. I'm thrilled we were able to connect."

"Can we get you anything to drink? Coffee? Water?" Davis asked.

"I'd love a coffee. Black, please."

An attractive man with light brown hair and broad shoulders entered the room. There must be something in the limestone spring water the local distilleries bragged about around here. All the guys I'd seen so far were at least elevens on a scale from one to ten. His brow furrowed and his lips curved into a frown.

"Miller,"—Davis let out a loud sigh—"before you get all bent out of shape, we're just having a preliminary meeting with—"

"A business consultant?" He held my card in his hand. The receptionist must have given it to him. "Why do we need a branding and business consultant?"

"I never said we did." Davis met the intruder's dark look with one of his own.

Harper got to her feet. "We're looking into possibilities, that's all."

Something about the man with the broad shoulders and flash of anger in his eyes seemed familiar, though I couldn't quite place him. I'd never set foot in Beaver Bluff before last night, and the only person I'd spoken to beyond the team at the distillery was the proprietor of the bed-and-breakfast where I was staying.

"Hi, I'm Danica Watson." I pushed back from the table and stood, offering a hand on my way out of my chair.

He ignored me, not even bothering to toss a glance in my direction.

"Jesus, Miller. Be pissed at me if you want, but you don't have to be so rude to our guest." Davis shook his head.

Instead of backing down, Miller moved to the doorway. "Cole, get in here. There's someone I want you to meet."

Cole... the realization plowed into me. The man speaking had the same broad build, the same electrifying brown eyes, the same strong hands as the man I'd lost myself with in Knoxville.

The same man who walked in the door.

"What's going on?"

My cheeks flamed as I laid eyes on the hottie from the hotel. The hottie I wasn't ever supposed to see again.

I had to grip the edge of the table to keep from falling over. Breathing proved too difficult in the moment, and I struggled to take in some air.

"You heard him. What's going on?" Miller repeated.

Cole hadn't looked over at me yet. Who was he? Why was he here? Questions piled up faster than I could process them. The only thing I could comprehend was that the man I'd lost my panties to last Thursday night, the man I never thought I'd see again, was standing right in front of me.

"Nothing. It's a preliminary meeting to get some ideas. If something comes out of it, y'all will be the first to know." Davis rolled his eyes.

My gaze volleyed back and forth between the two sides of

the table. There was something else at play here, something a lot bigger than me.

"Ideas about what?" Cole stepped next to the man named Miller.

Except for the difference in hair color, the two of them looked like they could be related. Like brothers. I almost smacked myself upside the head at the realization. They were brothers. Two pairs of identical intense eyes drilled into Davis.

"The anniversary is coming up next year, and it's a good time to pivot." Davis stepped to the side and nudged his chin in my direction. "That's why we brought in an expert. Danica will be able to look over our data and tell us if she thinks we're missing opportunities."

Cole ran his gaze over me, his eyes sending sharp daggers my way. I wanted to duck down to avoid the piercing look, but I made myself stand tall while I waited to see if he recognized me.

A quick flicker of heat passed through his eyes before he snuffed it out. "Danica?"

"Danica Watson." I offered my hand, unsure whether to acknowledge our brief but intimate prior acquaintance. Deciding no good would come from that, I pasted a smile on my lips and tried to pretend I hadn't been digging my fingers into his naked ass a mere four days ago. "It's nice to meet you."

He gripped my hand firmly in his. "It's nice to meet you, too."

Looked like we were both up for playing the "let's forget our one-night stand-ever-happened" game.

"Danica's an expert in her field, and—"

"An expert at whiskey?" Cole's lips ticked into a slight smirk. Unlike the other night, when his teasing had made me laugh and grip tighter onto his broad shoulders, this type of teasing held an undercurrent of malice.

"No, an expert at business. We know whiskey." Davis crossed his arms over his chest.

I still had no idea what was going on. Why did I feel like I was caught in the middle between two warring factions? Weren't they all in this together?

"Now you're implying we don't know business?" Cole glanced over his shoulder at where his brother leaned against the door. "Miller's got his MBA and is a certified CPA. What degree did you get again, Davis? Forestry services, was it?"

A muscle ticked along Davis's jaw. "We don't have time to do this right now. If you'll excuse us, I'll be happy to update you later."

"Or we could sit in and save you the time." Miller slid a chair away from the table.

"We're not trying to pull one over on y'all." Harper stared at Miller for a few moments, then shifted her gaze to Cole.

"Then you won't mind if we listen in for ourselves." Cole dropped into the seat next to his brother.

With the two of them right next to each other, it was impossible to miss the resemblance. Though there was something about Cole that made my toes curl in my heels. Looking at his brother didn't have the same effect.

Toe curling. No, toe curling didn't belong in a conference room. If I got hired on by Devil's Dance Distillery, there would be no allowance for toe curling in my future. I needed this job and the paycheck that went along with it. More than that, I needed the win.

If I could figure out how to help the distillery, I'd have a testimonial I could use to get more business. No matter how much seeing Cole again made me want to find the nearest coat closet and offer a repeat of Thursday night, it wasn't an option.

Davis Stewart brought me in. My only chance at success meant making him the happiest client a consultant could wish for. The only thing standing in my way stood about six-feet-four inches in those snug jeans I'd imagined, with a scowl on his face and enough negative energy he could knock out power to the entire state of Tennessee.

Ignoring him might not be easy, but it was the only strategy I had at my disposal.

Besides, how hard could it be?

CHAPTER 5

Cole

SHE LOOKED out of place in a feminine suit that accentuated the curves I'd run my hands over the other night and a pair of red fuck-me heels. Good. I was glad to see her hand shake slightly as she pulled out a notepad and pen. I wasn't going to call her out in front of everyone, but I couldn't wait to get her alone so I could find out what she'd hoped to gain by playing me for a fucking fool. She had to be after something.

Today she was all business. The long blonde hair I'd fisted in my hand was piled up on top of her head. I liked it better down, though she could totally rock a sexy librarian look if she had a pair of glasses. I'd never spent too much time between the bookshelves of our local Beaver Bluff library, but if there'd been a librarian who looked like Danica Watson, I might have reconsidered.

A silky blouse dipped into a V at her neck, revealing just enough creamy skin to give me some semi-wood. That had to be a first for me...sporting a hard-on in the conference room. I shifted in my seat to alleviate the building pressure. For a brief moment, I caught a whiff of coconut. I tried to chase it down, taking in a deep breath through my nose, but it was either a figment of my imagination or had already dissipated into the air.

She was supposed to be a one-night stand, not a consultant hired by the opposition. No wonder she wanted to know all about whiskey the night we met. The walls of my chest squeezed tight. Had she planned to show up at the hotel to get some intel? I tried to recall what we talked about before I dipped my head down to press my lips to hers. If I'd divulged any of our plans, I'd never forgive myself.

Davis took the seat at the head of the table, and I waited to find out what he and his sister had been working on behind our backs. "Thank you, Ms. Watson, for coming all this way to meet with us."

She looked up from her notepad. "Please, call me Danica, and it's my pleasure. I've never been to Beaver Bluff before. I'm looking forward to getting to know the area."

I crossed my arms over my chest, wondering how long they were going to exchange pleasantries before they got to the point. We were supposed to be receiving a big grain shipment this afternoon, and I had work to do.

Miller must have read my mind. Though he was the youngest of my brothers, thanks to hours spent at the gym, he had the biggest build and looked the most intimidating. He'd taken over managing the books since our parents officially retired. He didn't look like a typical number cruncher, but he handled the finances with the same care I might handle a hundred-year-old bottle of whiskey.

He leaned forward and rested his elbows on the table. "What exactly is the purpose of this meeting?"

Danica shot him a quick glance before turning her attention back to Davis. She seemed to be avoiding looking at me. Either she was just as surprised to see me this morning as I was to see her, or she felt guilty for trying to get insider info the other night.

Fine by me if she couldn't look me in the eye. It gave me a chance to study her from across the table. She didn't look like someone who'd do what it takes to get the job done, but my bad judgment in women had cost me in the past. I wasn't really the best guy to try to get a read on a woman's intentions.

"Ms. Watson goes way back with one of Harper's college friends and comes highly recommended. We invited her here today to provide some background on the distillery. With our anniversary coming up next year, it makes sense to use the opportunity to pivot." Davis turned to his sister. "Do you have anything to add to that?"

If I were a superhero, Harper Stewart would be my archenemy. Though technically we were supposed to work together as co-master distillers, she diabolically opposed me at every turn. If I said we needed to swap out a mash bill, she'd insist on keeping things the same. When I identified the barrels I thought we should use for our single barrel and small batch bottles, she always picked something different. Now I had another reason to vehemently dislike her—she and Danica seemed to have a history together.

Harper drummed her fingers on the table, one of her more annoying habits. "That sums it up. We have the chance to do something special with our anniversary. Maybe introduce a new blend, or even expand our offering to include other spirits under the Devil's Dance umbrella. I think we're leaving a lot of money on the table by not considering other options."

I clenched my hands into fists. They'd been pushing their agenda since before my grandfather died and my dad signed over his interest in this distillery to my siblings and me. The Stewart family had always made profit their top priority and had no regard for the foundation our predecessors set.

Miller signaled me with a slight shake of his head. He knew how I felt about preserving the history of the distillery. Our other siblings felt the same way, though probably not to the same degree. If they'd been responsible for losing pieces of it like I had, maybe they'd be more vocal about it. My great-grandfather made me promise before he died that I'd preserve what he and his business partners started.

That was back when the Bishops and Stewarts considered each other family, before the feud created a divide so wide neither side would ever be able to cross. It didn't matter that no one alive today could remember those days.

"You think it's a good idea to bring in outside counsel instead of handling things between us?" Miller asked.

The door to the conference room opened, and a peace-keeper arrived in the form of Charity Devine.

"Sorry I'm late. I didn't know you had a meeting scheduled this morning." Charity took a seat between Miller and Davis. That's where she always sat—directly in the middle. According to my grandfather, being in the middle was literally her job. Like all of us, she'd inherited her position from the line of Devines who came before her.

"Charity, this is Danica Watson. We invited her here to get some background info on the distillery and see if she can come up with some suggestions for us on how to take the business into the next hundred and fifty years," Davis explained.

The two women exchanged polite smiles.

"Charity is the glue that holds this place together. She's assistant manager of the distillery and keeps us all in line." Davis smiled as he said it, and I could feel the sincerity in those words. The Bishops and the Stewarts could only agree on one thing: Charity Devine was the only reason we all hadn't killed each other yet.

"How do you suggest we get started?" Davis pressed, putting Danica on the spot.

She flipped open the embossed portfolio in front of her. "Why don't you give me a little history of the distillery? I'd love to learn more about how your families started working together."

I settled back in my chair and waited for Davis to give his take on things. This ought to be good. No doubt Miller or I would correct him if necessary.

Davis handed her a glossy piece of paper that outlined the timeline of the business. It had taken us two years to put together a history that all of us could agree on. "Here's a general timeline. You'll see the distillery was established back in 1871 by a member of each family: a Stewart, a Devine, and a Bishop."

"Oh, I assumed it was a partnership between two families." Danica jotted down a few notes. She wasn't the first one to jump to that conclusion. Ever since the feud divided my family from the Stewarts, the Devines had fallen out of the limelight.

"Our ancestors settled here from England and Scotland and started doing the one thing they knew best—making whiskey. Business was great until Prohibition, and in 1910, the distillery was almost shut down. They were able to continue production, but only for medicinal purposes. The next twenty years were tough until Prohibition was repealed in 1933."

I could remember my great-grandfather talking about those days. He'd been born right at the end of Prohibition but grew up hearing his dad and granddad talk about how grateful they were the day the law was rolled back. A pang of regret twisted in my gut at how much more we'd know about that time if it hadn't been for me.

Danica's pen flew across her notepad, capturing every word as it fell from Davis's mouth.

"Of course, the 1940s brought war, which meant we had to shift production to help with the war effort. After returning to making whiskey in the 1950s, the distillery enjoyed a period of prosperity up until the eighties, when attention shifted to clear spirits like vodka and rum."

"Why did attention shift?" Danica's pen paused, and she glanced up.

I would have told her it was because the kids who grew up in the seventies wanted something new. They rebelled against the idea of drinking a spirit steeped in history like their dads and grandfathers did.

Davis presented a more watered-down version. "There were shifts in culture along with some groundbreaking advertising campaigns that gave vodka a huge boost. Lucky for us though, today the whiskey industry is on its way back up."

"What do you attribute that to?" She tapped the tip of her pen against her lip, drawing my attention and reminding me how it felt to press my lips against hers.

"There's a sense of nostalgia when it comes to whiskey." Davis slid his gaze to meet mine. He knew respecting the history of our company and the industry was a hill I was willing to die on. "But who knows how long it will last? That's why we think it would be in our best interest to diversify a bit."

"By 'we' you mean you and your sister," I clarified, tired of sitting out on this conversation.

Danica glanced at me, her eyes barely meeting mine before color stained her cheeks.

"I mean the Stewart family, including my brother and sisters," Davis said.

"You know he's right." Never one to hold her tongue, Harper spoke up. "It takes years to make a good batch of whiskey. We can crank out thousands of bottles of vodka or gin in the amount of time it takes to produce a fraction of that in whiskey."

This was an argument I'd never back down from and the reason I needed to find a way to separate my family's interest in the distillery from theirs. "You want to sell out. When our great-great-great-grandfathers went into business together, they set out to make the best American whiskey they could. They carved out a place for us in this industry that would stand the test of time. You want to throw it away so you can try to weasel your way into a crowded and competitive market?"

"Cole." Miller shook his head, his way of telling me to shut the fuck up.

I was tired of being quiet. Tired of being shut down for wanting to do what was right, what our ancestors would have wanted.

"What?" I turned toward my brother. "That's what they're talking about doing."

Charity cleared her throat, drawing everyone's attention. "I have a suggestion, if you're willing to entertain it."

Davis nodded, so I did the same.

She steepled her fingers under her chin and rested her gaze on each of us in turn. "This isn't the first time the families haven't been able to agree on which direction to take. With the anniversary coming up next year, it's the perfect time to eval- uate what's been working well and what we might want to change. Since you're coming at it from different directions, I'd like to propose that you each come up with a plan and we put it to a vote."

"That's asinine," I mumbled under my breath. "You know we all vote along family lines."

With granddad gone, we'd lost our one vote advantage, so anything we put to a vote would end up in a tie.

Charity narrowed her eyes and lifted a brow in my direction. "Since it's pretty much guaranteed there aren't any impartial parties here at the distillery, I think we should put together an impartial advisory board to listen to both sides and decide which direction makes the most sense."

"There's a major issue with that." Miller pushed back from the table. "First, no one in Beaver Bluff is impartial. Everyone's been affected by the feud and will vote for whichever family they like best."

Charity shook her head, dismissing his concerns. "We can create a group of business owners or professors or some other group who can be impartial and base their choice on the facts."

Davis and Miller sized each other up from across the table like two generals meeting on a battlefield who were negotiating the terms of war.

"We come up with our plan and they come up with theirs?" Miller asked.

Charity nodded.

"Works for us, as long as we're able to get Danica's input and you allow her access to any info she needs," Davis said.

Harper tapped something into her phone. "Assuming we want to move on this as quickly as possible, we've got a scheduling issue. We're all supposed to be out of town starting next week for that family cruise Nana booked us on."

I didn't try to hide my smile. I'd been looking forward to having the Stewarts out of the office for an extended vacation for months.

"I guess we'll have to postpone then," I said. Too bad for them. Now that we had an idea of what they were up to, it would give me and my siblings a chance to put together some ideas of our own.

"Not so fast. We've got some time this week. If Danica needs anything after that, I'm sure one of you can answer her questions and show her around." Davis's gaze landed on me. Hit me square in the chest like he'd made a fist and slammed it into my breastbone.

"Oh, no." I shook my head and waved my hands in front of me, palms out, the universal sign of "no way in hell."

"What's wrong, Cole?" Davis narrowed his eyes at me. "You not up for it?"

Exactly the opposite. I couldn't get caught up with Danica Watson. Not when the last time I'd allowed myself to get distracted I'd almost lost everything.

CHAPTER 6

I SENSED I was in over my head by the way the testosterone in the air pressed down on me—thick and heavy and suffocating enough to choke me. Whatever bad blood flowed between the Bishop and Stewart families might be too dark and too deep for me to fix, no matter how much I needed this win.

Cole glared at me, not even trying to hide his dislike. It shouldn't have bothered me as much as it did. I hardly knew the man. Though I'd known him in the biblical sense, we hadn't exactly spent a lot of time in deep conversation or shared our most intimate secrets.

"You want to hire her, then she's your problem." Cole narrowed his eyes as he glared at Davis Stewart. Then he crossed his thick forearms over his chest. Had it only been a few days since I'd been wrapped in those strong arms?

The hair on the back of my neck rose and prickles raced along my skin as I remembered the way his mouth felt on my neck, my chest, my lips. Even now, though five feet of conference table separated us, I caught a whiff of his smoky campfire scent.

Davis shook his head, his mouth set in a smug smirk. "If you want to give up now, we wouldn't mind making the plan for the next five to ten years."

Cole stared straight ahead. "Fine. We'll make sure she gets whatever information she needs."

I wasn't some sort of problem who needed to be managed. This wasn't going to work, no matter how much I wanted to prove myself. I flipped my portfolio closed and slid my pen into the holder. "Gentlemen, I don't think I'm the right person for—"

"Yes, you are." Harper interrupted me. "Jolene told me about the work you did for the Sidney Seltzer Company. They were on the verge of shutting down, and you helped them evaluate what was working, where to focus their efforts, and how to breathe new life into their brand. You're exactly the right person to help us."

I risked a quick glance at Cole. The deep furrow between his brows let up a smidge, making him look a little less pissed and a tad more curious.

"Ms. Watson, I know we have a lot of work to do here at Devil's Dance to get all of us on the same page. With your help, I hope we can do that." Davis got up from his seat and moved toward one of the shelves attached to the wall behind me.

I shifted in my chair so I could track his movements. He was an attractive man. Not nearly as burly and grumpy as the brothers sitting across the table, but with thick, wavy brown hair and the build of someone who probably played varsity sports in high school, he was definitely easy on the eyes. But looking at him didn't send waves of heat rolling through my limbs like a quick glance at Cole Bishop did.

Davis picked up a ceramic jug with a cork on top. The front was marked with three large Xs in a row. "This is one of the first bottles Devil's Dance ever produced. The whiskey's been gone for years, but all the founders touched this bottle, all had a say in what they filled it with, and how it reached the market. That's what we're trying to do today. Times have changed and Devil's Dance has done little to change with it. Please help us find a way to move forward."

Maybe it was because it had been so long since someone asked for my help, or maybe it was because I needed a win as much as they did. Whatever the reason, I nodded. "Okay. Let's see what we can come up with."

Cole grunted and rolled his eyes before pushing back from the table and leaving the room. My gaze followed. A mixture of relief and disappointment lodged in my chest.

"Don't worry about him." Davis held out a hand like he wanted to seal the deal and commit me with a handshake. "Either he'll come around or—"

"Or what?" Miller asked.

Davis swiveled his head to make eye contact with Cole's brother. "Or we'll move on without him. You and I both know something needs to change or we're going to get steamrolled by the new distilleries popping up all over."

"We'll see about that." Miller followed his brother out, leaving me with Davis, Harper, and Charity.

"Their bark is much worse than their bite." Charity swept her notepad up in her arms and stood. "Just let me know if anyone gets out of line."

"If they do, Charity is the only one who can yank them back in." Harper grinned. "I'm happy to have you on board, Danica."

Based on the animosity I'd just witnessed, I wasn't sure I shared her enthusiasm. Having Devil's Dance as a client would be a great way to kick off my private consulting business, though. I'd do whatever it took to give myself the best shot at success, starting with figuring out how to smooth things over with a pissed-off Cole Bishop.

"I can show you around the distillery this afternoon. Do you have plans for lunch?" Harper asked. "If not, I'd love to get together to talk about some ideas and also get the lowdown on what's been going on with Jolene."

The only plans I had were to do as much research on the Devil's Dance Distillery as I could. Maybe Harper could give me some additional background information, along with some intel on Cole Bishop. I'd have to be discreet. If word got out that the two of us had hooked up, I may as well kiss any chance at success goodbye.

"I'd like that a lot."

"Great. I'll circle back with you to make plans. Until then, I'll leave you with my brother. See you in a bit," Harper said as she and Charity disappeared through the door.

Davis held the jug out to me. I took it, surprised at how heavy it felt in my hands. Unlike the Sidney Seltzer Company, who'd only been in business five years before I got involved, Devil's Dance Distillery had layers and layers of history that I couldn't hope to understand in just a few days.

"It blows my mind to think about how many years it's been since my family started this place." Davis shifted his gaze to the jug. "I'm sure they had no idea way back then what it would turn into today."

"Maybe not." I appreciated the history of the distillery, but it was my job to look toward the future. If I wanted to make a go of setting myself up as a legit business, I needed to get all the information I could on where the distillery stood in today's landscape of beverage offerings.

"I'll take that." Davis set the jug back on the shelf. "Do you really think you can help us?"

His voice held an underlying hopeful tone that called out

to my heartstrings. I was a sucker for a comeback story. How could I not be when I was trying to stage the same kind of tale for myself?

"I sure hope so. I'm going to need to do some research on the industry and also get a good understanding of your current offerings to see where you fit in the marketplace. When do you and Harper leave on vacation?"

"Friday morning. The timing couldn't be worse, but Nana invited the whole family on a seven-day cruise to the Caribbean to celebrate her eightieth birthday." His mouth quirked into a half-smile. "She booked it over a year ago."

"Don't worry about me. I'll be fine here. When would you like me to have something ready to present?" It would usually take me a month or more to pull together a big project like this. I had a feeling Davis didn't have that kind of time. At least I didn't have other clients who'd be battling for my attention.

"As soon as possible," he said. "We need to get the ball rolling now if we want to tie our vision to the anniversary celebration next year."

"Assuming I can get what I need, I'll try to have a preliminary plan ready to present when you come back from your vacation."

Davis nodded and gestured for me to head out of the room first.

All of my eggs rested in the Devil's Dance Distillery basket. Too bad one of the men in charge looked like he'd rather crush them than help me hatch a plan.

CHAPTER 7

Cole

"WHAT THE HELL are they trying to do to us? A consultant? Isn't that the kind of thing we ought to make a decision about together?" I paced the short distance in front of my twin brother Vaughn's desk, possibly wearing an actual groove in the wide plank flooring. He'd been out in the warehouse when everything went down. At least I'd had Miller there with me.

"Settle down. She'll come up with a plan for them and we'll present one we're all comfortable with. Everyone around here knows how important the history of the distillery is. They won't let it get erased." Vaughn tapped the tip of his pen against his desk—a nervous habit he'd inherited from our dad.

"I'm not worried about it being erased." Devil's Dance had too big a hold on the local community for that. I was worried about becoming obsolete, unimportant, disregarded.

"What the hell were you going on about in the conference room, then?" Miller asked. He might have the head for numbers, but Vaughn always had the big picture in mind.

It was hard to explain, but I'd do my best. "We've always

heard about the history of Devil's Dance. How the families got together and decided to make something out of nothing."

My brothers nodded. Tales of the distillery's history had been drilled into our heads since the day we were born.

"I think we need to lean into that. Our success is going to come from sharing our story, not from coming up with another trendy flavored vodka."

Vaughn leaned forward in his chair and set his elbows on his desk. "That's the plan we need to present to this impartial board Charity is proposing. The Stewarts are selling an idea of what's hot now, chasing trends and looking into the short-term future. We want to honor the past and build on what our families started. I like it."

I liked it, too. Being named master distiller, even though I had to share the title with Harper Stewart, meant being entrusted with something precious. I was one man in a long line of my ancestors to take on the role and would always be a part of the distillery's history, just like the others who'd come before me.

Whiskey had been a part of Tennessee's history, too. People around here appreciated that. I just needed to find a way to spread the word and get people outside of Tennessee to understand how integrated into American history the beverage was.

"How long do you think you'll need to put some ideas together?" Vaughn asked.

"Me?" I'd assumed he would take the lead on this project since he was in the management role.

"Yeah. You're the history buff. If that's our angle, you should be the one to take point. I'll back you up and pitch in, but with Davis being gone for the next two weeks, I'm going to have my hands full trying to keep things going."

With the Stewarts gone, we'd all have a lot more on our

plates than normal. As much as I resented having to work with them day in and day out, it was easier sharing the workload.

"I can get something started," I said.

"Get Ruby to help." I figured Vaughn would rope our little sister into this. She handled marketing and had the most face time with customers.

"I'll pitch in, too." Miller rubbed the back of his neck. He was already trying to balance a full-time job while helping part-time at the distillery and raising his son on his own.

"It's going to take all of us to pull this off." I swiped through my phone to look at a calendar. "Why do you think there's such a big rush on their part? We've got over a year until the anniversary."

"Who knows?" Vaughn shuffled a few papers around on his desk, his signal that he had work to do. "Hey, I've got a few errands to run this afternoon. I'll probably just meet you at the softball field for the game tonight."

"Got it." We usually had a standing appointment on the calendar for Monday night softball. We'd play after work, then hit Pappy's Last Call for a burger and beer before heading home. It was the one time the Bishops and the Stewarts were able to put their differences aside and join together in an effort to beat the other local businesses in our softball league.

"I need to confirm plans for when they all go out of town," Vaughn said. We were both competitive by nature, but my brother eclipsed me with his constant need to come in first.

"You have subs lined up?" Usually we could get some guys who worked part-time in the warehouse to cover for us, but we'd never had all the Stewarts leave at once before.

"What about asking the new consultant to play?" Miller suggested.

"Danica?" My voice came out sounding strangled on the tail end.

Vaughn peered up at me over the top of a piece of paper he held in his hands. "Is there something going on there?"

Doing my best to fake surprise, I made my eyes go wide. "Where? Me and the consultant? No. Hell no."

"Okay, just checking." Vaughn gestured toward the door. "Miller and I need to go over some reports this morning. Let's catch up later?"

"Sounds good." I left my brother's office, pulling the door closed behind me as I exited.

"So we're pretending to be strangers?" Danica's voice hit me from behind.

I whirled around to find her leaning against the doorway of the empty office across the hall. My gaze drifted lazily over the way that tight gray suit hugged her curves. The irritated look on her face put an end to my subtle appreciation of her figure.

"How else did you want me to play that?" I asked. Seemed faking ignorance was better than admitting exactly how well we'd gotten to know each other last week.

"I don't know. That was a first for me." She pushed off the doorframe.

Maybe it was the way the natural light hit her as opposed to the dim lights we'd met under at the hotel bar, but she looked even younger than she had the other night. She barely had on any makeup, yet her cheeks were flushed and her lips were as pink as the damn flowers one of the Stewarts had planted all over the distillery grounds.

"You could have told me the reason you knew all about whiskey was because you owned a damn distillery." Color rose on her cheeks, though she kept her voice low enough that her words stayed between us.

"Isn't that why you targeted me with your innocent 'I know nothing about whiskey' act? So you could try to get me to slip up and give you something that might help your new employers make their case?" Even though I was pissed, I kept my voice steady. It wouldn't do any good for someone in the office to get wind of what had gone down between us.

"Are you kidding me?" Her eyes narrowed. "What makes you think I had any clue who you really were?"

"Who I really was? I didn't pretend to be someone I'm not the other night." I needed to get to the warehouse to check over that grain shipment, but five feet of simmering anger that looked like it was about to boil over blocked my way.

Her finger jabbed me in the center of my chest. "If you're implying that I was pretending to be someone I'm not, we've got a big problem."

Voices came from around the corner. I grabbed her hand and pulled her into the empty office, then shut the door. My chest pressed against hers, putting her back against the wall.

Someone knocked on Vaughn's door. I put a finger to my lips, signaling Danica to keep quiet. We couldn't afford to get caught like this. I should have just backed away from her in the hall. There hadn't been a need to pull her into an empty office with me, back her up against a wall, and press into her curves.

She put her palms on my chest and pushed me away. "What's wrong with you?"

"Shh. Quiet," I whispered.

"Why?" She adjusted her blouse, pulling my attention to where her top button had come loose, revealing a sliver of lace.

My dick hardened like I'd caught a glimpse of the Victoria's Secret catalog Vaughn and I used to swipe from the mailbox and take turns poring over when we were kids.

"Because I don't want to get caught."

"Get caught doing what? Having a conversation in the hallway?" Her eyes flashed with annoyance. "Stop being ridiculous."

"Would you please be quiet?" I wasn't sure what was more annoying: that she was right about me being ridiculous or that she was going to give away our hiding place.

Davis's voice came from the other side of the door. He was saying something to Vaughn. If Danica opened the door now, we'd have a hell of a lot of explaining to do.

"You're being irrational." Her hand went to the doorknob.

There was no time to think. I reacted to the immediate threat of discovery. That was the only reason I pressed her body against the wall and dipped my head down to touch my lips to hers. Her arms went up to wrap around my neck. My hands found the sweet spot at her waist. I inhaled, breathing in the scent that had evaded me since the last time I held her in my arms.

Her lips parted, and I tasted the same hint of cherries, this time mixed with a bit of mint as if she'd been sucking on a peppermint earlier. She arched into me, her breasts pushing against my chest. I skimmed a hand under her jacket and over her silky blouse while she pulled my head down and swept her tongue into my mouth.

My brain screamed at me to put on the brakes. Now that I knew who she was, this couldn't happen. But my cock had put up an out-of-office message and didn't respond. It had experienced her sweet heat before and knew what kind of treat was in store.

"Okay then, good luck." Davis's footsteps sounded right outside the door, then grew fainter as he walked away.

The coast was clear. I should let her go, apologize, and take a blood oath to never touch her again.

Then she palmed my cock through the front of my jeans, driving that thought clear out of my head.

CHAPTER 8
Danica

NO, no, no, no, no. The one syllable word pounded through my head, even as I ran my palm along the length of Cole's erection. I knew what he had to offer, and I wanted it.

I didn't just want it, I craved it. I was desperate for him to fill me like he had the other night.

But I couldn't. I tore my mouth away from his, my chest heaving. "We can't."

His palm rested on my breast. My nipple was so tight, so ready for his touch. I circled his wrist with my fingers and pulled his hand away. The orgasm I turned my back on wept at the loss of his touch. Why did the only man who could take me from zero to ready to kick off my panties in ten seconds or less have to work for the company who had just hired me?

Not only was it a breach in my own personal ethics to hook up with a client, if word got back to my ex-boss about this, he'd ruin my business before it even got off the ground.

"We have to stop." I repeated the sentiment, more determined this time.

"You're right." Cole backed away and funneled both hands

through his hair. "I don't know what got into me. You were about to open the door, and I guess I lost it."

Knowing I had the power to drive this man to do things he didn't want to provided a bit of a rush. Then the all-knowing voice of reason raised its hand and spoke up, reminding me that Cole was just as likely to stick his tongue down any available woman's throat if he found himself in the same situation. There wasn't anything special about me. Wasn't that what experience had been teaching me my entire life?

"It can't happen again." Even as I said the words, a tiny part of me hoped they wouldn't come true.

"It won't." The look of determination in his eyes was the only proof I needed that I represented nothing more to him than a walking vagina.

I refastened my top button that had come loose and straightened my jacket. Nothing like failing fast on the first day. I glanced down and reached for where my bag had fallen on the floor. "I'm going to—"

"Yeah, here." He held the door open while I stepped into the hall, then closed it right behind me.

It probably made sense for us to leave separately. At least no one was standing in the hallway. I clutched the straps to my computer bag and tried to find my way back to the foyer. The offices appeared to have been pieced together as the company grew, so there were mazes of hallways and doors. I might need someone to draw me a map so I could navigate on my own. That would also tell me where Cole's office was, so I could make a point to avoid it.

"There you are." Davis approached as I found my way back to the conference room where we'd met earlier. "I've got our tech guy setting up a laptop you can use to work on Devil's Dance business. It should be ready this afternoon."

"Oh, I've got a laptop." Though I'd been working on the

computer I'd used in college, it was still functional. Once I completed this job, I could afford to get the brand new Mac I'd been eyeing.

"It's no trouble. Using one that's already set up on our network will make it easier while you're here. Harper and I were hoping the three of us could grab lunch together and talk about some ideas we have for next steps."

"Of course." My pulse still beat an erratic tempo thanks to Cole Bishop's kisses, so I tried to take a few calming breaths through my nose.

"There's a barbecue place downtown, or if you're in the mood for something lighter, we can grab a sandwich or salad from the café at the distillery."

"I'm flexible." It didn't matter to me where we went; I probably wouldn't be able to choke down more than a few bites. The run in with Cole had me more flustered than I expected.

"Let's go into town. It'll give us a chance to show you around, and we won't have to be careful about someone from the other side catching wind of our plans. How does that sound?"

"Sounds good to me." It didn't matter how much my traitorous body responded to Cole, Davis was the one who'd hired me. My loyalties should lie with him. That's where the money was coming from.

TWENTY MINUTES LATER, I took a seat at Jackie Jay's, a crowded restaurant spanning two stories of a building that was listed on the national registry of historic places. The tantalizing scent of spices and sauce danced through the air, and my stomach gurgled in anticipation. Now that we were here, I figured I might eat half of my own weight in authentic Tennessee barbecue.

"You just pick your main dish and the rest is served family style," Davis explained. "This place has been around almost as long as the distillery. You can't go wrong with anything on the menu."

He and Harper didn't bother to take the menu the server offered, which left me to scan the front page of the simple paper menu alone. My mouth watered as my gaze drifted over the offerings. The hickory-smoked ribs sounded delicious, but I didn't trust myself to be able to eat them without getting sauce all over my jacket. I'd be better off with something that would require a fork. The smoked chicken would be my best bet.

We placed our order, and I glanced around the cozy space. It looked like it could have been lifted straight out of the early 1900s based on the period decor.

"This place has a colorful history in Beaver Bluff," Davis said. "It's been a funeral home, a brothel, and for the past seventy-five years, a boarding house and restaurant. You can still rent rooms upstairs, but now they rent by the night, not the hour."

I took a sip of the sweet tea our server just set down. For some reason, it tasted sweeter here in Beaver Bluff than it ever had in Knoxville. Though I'd traveled extensively around Tennessee during my years as a consultant, I'd never visited such a small town with such larger-than-life character.

"You definitely have your fair share of colorful history here." Hoping Davis or Harper would provide a little more background info on the distillery, I forged ahead. "I had no idea there was a longstanding feud between the partners at Devil's Dance."

Harper frowned. "It's been going on so long that no one can even remember exactly what caused it in the first place."

That didn't make sense. "If you can't remember what caused it, then why not just let it go?"

"We might not remember what caused it, but the Bishops definitely do their part in keeping it going." Davis tipped his glass toward me before taking a sip.

"How? I don't mean to overstep, but isn't it in your best interest to mend fences so you can all focus on your business?" A feud that lasted over a hundred years sounded like something someone made up. Even the Hatfield and McCoys—the most famous family feud the world had probably ever seen— had reached a truce.

"One would think." Harper's lips stretched into a tight smile. "It sounds easy, but we've been hating on each other for so long, it's just the way it is."

"Except for Charity," Davis said.

"She's from the third family, right?" I was still trying to wrap my head around everything.

"Yes." Davis sat up straight and glanced around like he wanted to make sure the conversation wouldn't be overheard. "As I mentioned during our meeting, Devil's Dance started off when our three families started doing the only thing they knew and began making whiskey out of the corn leftover from their harvest. Business was great and as far as I can tell, everyone got along just fine up until Prohibition hit."

"We don't have a lot of records from before that point. They were lost in a fire about twenty years ago," Harper said.

"During Prohibition, there was a difference in opinion on how the distillery should move forward. The Stewarts were in favor of running moonshine to keep the money coming in while the Bishops preferred to stay on the other side of the law and only produce what they were allowed to as a medicinal distributor." Davis slid his napkin into his lap as our server delivered huge platters overflowing with home-cooked goodness.

My eyes widened at the sight of so much food. There were only three of us, but the plates of creamed corn, yeast rolls, collard greens, and mashed potatoes could have fed a group five times our size.

"I hope you brought your appetite," Harper commented. "I always end up taking enough home for dinner for the rest of the week when I come here."

"I can see why." My stomach rumbled, and I couldn't wait to dig into my lunch.

Davis waited until our server made sure we were all set before he picked up where he'd left off. "We're still arguing over that basic issue. Our family thinks we need to take advantage of the branding we've built over the years and expand into other spirits. The Bishops want to stick with what we know—Tennessee whiskey—and dive deeper into producing more of the same. That's where you come in."

I'd just slid a big bite of the most delicious smoked chicken into my mouth. Rather than talk around it, I chewed, swallowed, and then had to swallow again before attempting to respond. "You want to figure out if it's more profitable to go wide or go deep."

"Bingo." Davis grinned as he sliced into the brisket in front of him.

I'd done similar work before and what they were asking sat squarely in the middle of my wheelhouse. Once I gathered the industry data, I'd be able to do some forecasting and make a recommendation on which way the data pointed.

"What do you think, Danica?" Harper asked, her fork suspended in mid-air, halfway between her plate and her mouth.

"It's absolutely delicious. Best barbecue I've ever had, hands down."

She laughed. "I meant about the business."

"Oh." I swiped at my lip with my napkin. "I think you're in a great position to even be able to consider different options. Most of the companies I've worked with in the past were forced to take action either from new competitors entering the market or a decline in business."

"We'd like to maintain our great position." Davis scooped up a serving of potatoes and added it to his plate.

"Of course." I knew how to do a job like this. Confidence should be oozing from my pores. But something told me it wasn't going to be as easy as doing my research, coming up with a plan, and making a recommendation. A tall, broad-shouldered, bearded distiller who happened to be an excellent kisser stood in my way.

He didn't seem like the type who'd step aside and let someone else decide his fate.

CHAPTER 9

IT HAD BEEN two days since I kissed Danica, and I couldn't stop thinking about her. It didn't help that Davis had set her up with an office at the distillery's headquarters. Every time I turned around, she was there, looking up at me with those deep green eyes, usually with a hand planted above the curve of her hip and a hint of a frown on her mouth.

I'd fucked up. First, I'd fucked the consultant, which was really fucking up. Then I'd kissed her, which meant I was for sure, well, fucked. I couldn't let her get under my skin. She'd aligned herself with the Stewarts and picked her side. That meant she was the enemy.

My only hope was to beat her at her own game. Vaughn and I had been chatting about what kind of plan we could come up with to pit against the Stewarts' idea of expanding our product offering. I didn't want to discuss it at the office. The risk of word getting back to the opposition was too great. Instead, we'd made plans to meet at the coffee shop down-town this morning. They had a back room where we could have some privacy.

The line was long for a Wednesday morning, so I set my things down on the big table in back to save a spot. Vaughn came in as I stepped into line, and I almost fell over when I saw the woman behind him. He held the door open for her, a strained smile on his lips. Danica grinned up at him and said something I couldn't make out.

Seeing my brother so close to the forbidden object of my desire lit a fire in my gut. I pulled myself together as the two of them headed my direction.

"Good morning." Danica's eyes lit up when she saw me. Maybe it was due to the industrial lighting hanging down from the ceiling. It couldn't be because she was thrilled at the coincidence of running into me.

I shouldn't read more into it than what was there, but damn, she looked delectable today. She had on a just-above-the-knees dress that belted around her waist and left her arms bare. I wanted to wrap my hands around her upper arms and pull her into my chest. Instead, I forced a grin and made eye contact with my brother.

"Look who I ran into in the parking lot." Vaughn let his backpack slide off his shoulder and hefted it into his hand.

"I heard this is the best place to get coffee." Danica's gaze shifted from Vaughn to me.

I couldn't hold back my smile. "It's the only place to get coffee."

"Did you get the table in the back room?" Vaughn asked.

"Yeah. I'll pick up the drinks. You want the usual?" I asked.

"That would be great. Thanks." He nodded toward Danica. "See you at the office later."

"Have a good day." She gave him the kind of smile she'd given me at the bar—the kind that sparked heat in my belly and made me wonder what it would feel like to kiss those perfect lips. Jealousy clawed at my gut, but I shut it down fast as she turned toward me. "What's your standard coffee order?"

In my opinion, there was only one way to drink coffee, and that was black. "Straight up black. No sugar, no creamer, no nothing."

"Why doesn't that surprise me?" She joked. "You're very much a traditionalist, aren't you?" The tone in her voice came across as dismissive.

"You say that like it's a bad thing."

"Oh, no, I don't mean it that way. It's just easy to see why you and Davis are always standing on opposite poles."

I took a step forward in line. "Because he's so progressive?"

Her forehead wrinkled, and I fought the urge to smooth it out with the pad of my thumb. Nothing good would come from touching her. I'd learned that the hard way already, and I wasn't a man who needed to learn that type of lesson twice.

"You're saying that like it's a bad thing." Her brow lifted like she was challenging me to deny it.

I shoved my hands in my pockets and rolled my shoulders. "Sometimes I feel like it is. We've been at each other's throats for so long, it seems like he's lost sight of where we came from."

"He only wants what's best for the distillery." She shifted her gaze to the chalk menu board hanging on the exposed brick wall.

"I'm calling BS on that. He only wants what's best for the distillery's bottom line. He doesn't give a shit about maintaining quality or flavor profiles. His short-sightedness could cost us everything." I clamped down on my lower lip with my teeth. When would I learn not to divulge information to a stranger? That's what Danica was—a stranger. I needed to keep reminding myself she'd chosen her side.

She crossed her arms under her breasts. "The conversations

we've had so far lead me to believe that you both want the same thing. You just have different opinions on what's best overall."

"We might have to agree to disagree, at least where the future of the business is concerned."

"Fair enough."

The group ahead of us stepped aside, and I gestured for Danica to go first. She might piss me off, but she was still a woman, and I'd been taught to be a gentleman.

"You were here first." Danica didn't budge.

If I'd been the eye-rolling type, I would have sent them spinning multiple times based on the way her jaw set tight and her arms clamped down over her stomach. She was one of the most stubborn women I'd ever met, and coming from a long line of Bishops who had no trouble speaking their mind, that was saying something.

I got to the counter and ordered two large coffees, black. The woman behind the counter had owned this place since it opened over twenty years ago. She made small talk while she filled the cups, asking about my mama and how business was going. Aware that Danica was probably soaking up every word, I kept my responses vague and neutral. She wasn't going to get any intel from me.

With coffee in hand, I stepped away from the counter and gave Danica a slight nod. "I'll see you around."

"Have a good day, Cole." She set her purse on the counter and rattled off a complicated order containing words like "non-fat" and "no whip" while I fled to the safety of the back room.

Vaughn had his laptop open, and I set his coffee down next to him.

"Thanks." He looked up from his screen and steepled his

fingers under his chin. I knew that look. It was his "I've got an idea, but I'm not sure how to bring it up" look.

"What?" I slumped into the chair across from him and let the scalding coffee burn my tongue.

"I was thinking…"

"Stop right there. I don't know where you're going, but my answer is no." I could sense his reluctance to share. It was probably a twin thing, but my gut knew I wasn't going to like whatever he was about to suggest.

"How can you say no when I haven't even asked yet?"

"I can feel it. Whatever it is, it's a bad idea." I pulled my own laptop out of the bag and flipped the lid open. We both had extremely busy schedules over the next couple of weeks with the Stewarts heading out of town. If we wanted to get started on some sort of plan to present to the board, we needed to lay the groundwork soon.

Vaughn continued to stare at me, the weight of his gaze feeling like a thousand-pound dumbbell sitting on my chest. "Aren't you the tiniest bit curious about what I was going to say?"

I shook my head. "Nope. We need an updated mission statement to set the tone for our vision for the distillery. Have you come up with anything?"

When he didn't respond, I glanced up. He had his arms crossed and was nodding to some internal tempo only he could hear.

"Well?" I asked.

"What if we could get a sneak peek at what the Stewarts are working on?" Vaughn asked.

As much as I wanted to know what tricks they had up their sleeves, I wouldn't sink to that level and neither would Vaughn. "We don't do corporate espionage, remember?"

"That's not what I mean." He leaned forward. "What if Danica happened to let something slip? Say in normal conversation?"

"Because she's planning on spending so much time with us?" A low laugh rumbled through my chest.

Vaughn didn't respond, just stared at me, a knowing look on his face, waiting for me to catch on.

"No, absolutely not." I could tell what he was suggesting, and it wouldn't work. There was no way I could put myself in a position to spend time with her on the off chance she might let a nugget of info slip.

"I guess I could invite her out to dinner and see what happens." Vaughn shrugged.

For half a heartbeat, all I could see was red. Like hell, I'd let my brother ask my one-night stand out on a real date. "No. She's practically a Stewart. Don't even go there."

"Consider it done." He lifted a shoulder. "Unless you'd rather take one for the team and see if she has plans one night this week."

I closed my eyes and took what should have been a calming breath. Instead, my pulse ramped up as I pictured Vaughn putting the moves on Danica, nudging his nose into her coconut-scented hair and planting his hand on her hip. Fuck. Knowing he'd have access to her was even worse than fighting my own attraction.

"Fine. I'll do it."

"Now's your chance." Vaughn looked past me into the main area of the coffee shop.

I followed his gaze, letting it land on Danica, who was trying to balance a tray of coffee in one hand and grab her keys from her bag at the same time.

"You're going to owe me for this." I glared at my brother while I pushed back from the table. The legs screeched across the linoleum floor, a satisfying summation of the silent scream ricocheting through my chest.

Vaughn grinned back, the kind of smile that told me he knew a lot more than he was letting on. Had he heard us in the empty office across the hall from his the other day? Or was it just a divine benefit from sharing exact DNA with another person? Sometimes I hated the twin connection.

"Hey, you need some help with that?" I reached for the fifth drink balancing precariously on top of the beverage carrier as I got close to Danica.

"Oh, thanks." She handed over the tray, almost spilling a full cup of coffee down the front of my shirt in the process.

"Careful there." I held the tray in one hand and the extra cup in the other.

"Sorry. I offered to pick up coffee on my way in this morning. This must be a popular place."

"It's the only place besides the gas station where you can grab a cup to go. Can I help you to your car?"

"You don't have to do that."

"Yeah, but for your sake, I'd feel better if I did." I wasn't kidding. Based on how she'd been managing on her own, she wouldn't make it out the door without losing at least one beverage.

"Okay, thanks." She moved toward the exit and held the door open for me to pass through. "I'm in the gray compact over here."

I set the carrier on the roof of the small two-door car, then reached down to pull the door open for her. "I wanted to apologize for the other day. Seeing you in Beaver Bluff caught me off guard."

"That's understandable. I think we were both surprised." As she took the cup of coffee from me, our fingers brushed.

Why did this woman make me feel like a bumbling

teenager again? I shook the feeling away and focused. What was that saying about keeping your friends close and your enemies even closer? Danica wasn't exactly my enemy, but since she'd aligned herself with a whole group of Stewarts who'd love to run my family off, she was enemy-adjacent.

"It sounds like we're going to be working together for the foreseeable future. I thought maybe we could start over. Maybe even as friends?"

She put her hand up to shade her eyes from the sun peeking out between the clouds. "I'd like that."

Relief bloomed in my chest. "Great. Let me know if you need anything once Davis and Harper leave town. I'd be happy to give you some additional history of the distillery or walk you through the process of how we do things around here."

"Thanks, Cole." Her eyes softened at the edges and her lips curved into a gorgeous smile that might have knocked me off balance if I hadn't been leaning on her car.

"I'll see you around." I backed away while she settled the coffee and got behind the wheel. Having her in town working with the Stewarts didn't have to be a bad thing. I'd play nice and hopefully get a really good idea of what kind of angle she wanted to pitch. That would give me the chance to use the Stewarts' plans against them.

I pressed my fist to my chest to dislodge the guilt that threatened to settle. I'd always thought of myself as a good guy, not someone who would double-cross a friend.

But Danica wasn't a friend. She was working with the Stewarts on a plan that might change the course of my family's business for generations to come. Sometimes a man had to put his personal feelings aside and make a move for the greater good.

I'd just need to keep my dick in my pants and forget how fucking amazing it felt to lose myself inside her. Unable to fight off the guilt, I tried to make peace with it as I turned to rejoin my brother.

CHAPTER 10
Danica

I SCOOTED my chair close to the desk in my temporary office at the distillery. Even though I'd gone back to Knoxville for the weekend, I kept thinking about Devil's Dance and how best to revamp their business. Davis and Harper had left for their two-week cruise, and I was on my own to pull together enough of a plan that we'd be able to review it when they returned. I'd made good use of the time we'd had together, but I still had so many questions.

While I waited for my laptop to boot up, I caught sight of Cole as he leaned through my open doorway.

"You came back for week two." He had on a snug T-shirt that molded to his pecs. I'd tried to forget how good looking he was, though it would take a lot longer than two days away to erase the way his smile made my entire body come online.

"Did you think you scared me off?" I joked.

"I wasn't sure. Should be quite a bit quieter around here for the next two weeks." His hand rested on the doorframe.

He had great hands. If I closed my eyes, I could still feel them roaming over the contours of my hips. Best not to go there. I'd spent the weekend flip-flopping between trying to remember how it felt to have his hands all over me and desperately trying to forget.

We'd decided to be friends. Not friends with benefits. Just friends.

"I'm checking in to see if you need anything. A tour of the distillery? Suggestions on where to grab a bite?"

An invitation to join him for a repeat performance of our time in the elevator? I squeezed my thighs together, chasing away the aching sensation that being around him always brought on. Why couldn't my body get the message that "just friends" meant no more tingles, and definitely no more aches?

"Harper took me through the distillery last week before she left. Thanks."

He nodded and a chunk of hair flopped into his face, accentuating his boyish charm. "This might be a weird question, but have you ever played softball?"

"That came out of left field." Sometimes I cracked myself up. Cole grinned back at me, evidently just as much of a sucker for cheesy comebacks as me. "Like on a baseball field?"

"More like on a softball field." His smile widened. "We're short a few players for our game tonight since the Stewarts are gone. We could use a center fielder or someone to play third base."

"Oh, I'm no good at third base."

Cole's brows lifted and heat flickered in the depths of his eyes. "I beg to differ."

The ache between my thighs deepened, and I pressed my palm into the desk, willing it to dissipate. Spending time outside of the office with him would be like setting a giant chocolate cupcake with fudge frosting two inches from my mouth and telling me I couldn't taste it.

"I wish I could, but I'm busy tonight. I've got loads of data to sift through."

"I bet. If you change your mind, the invitation's open. It might give you a chance to chat with some of our employees." He pushed off the doorway. "Davis mentioned you wanted to get to know some folks from the warehouse and bottling operation."

He had me there. I did want to chat with some of the employees who worked the front lines at the distillery to get their thoughts. Based on what I'd learned so far, many of them had deep ties to the business and had never worked anywhere else. "I'll think about it."

"Great. I hope to see you then." With a final flash of a smile, he turned and walked away.

I listened to his heavy footsteps travel all the way down the hall before I let out my breath. Maybe I preferred the grumpy version of Cole—the one I'd first encountered when I showed up last week. This friendly, charming, smiling side of him was much harder to resist.

I typed my password into my login screen and pulled up the reports I'd been sifting through. Davis had shared enough sales figures and forecasts to keep me wading through data for weeks. That was time I didn't necessarily have, not if I wanted to have something ready when he got back.

The issues facing Devil's Dance, beyond the feud everyone seemed to know about, but no one wanted to talk about, centered around their plans for growth. While Cole wanted to dive deeper into expanding their whiskey offerings, Davis wanted to take the business broader and diversify into distilling other spirits. Based on my initial research, it seemed like both were viable options. They just didn't have the resources to pursue both goals at the same time, which meant one of them was going to be disappointed.

Talking to some of the employees to get an idea of their thoughts would be a good way to get some intel. After staring at my screen for the better part of an hour, I grabbed my purse. Looked like I was headed to a softball game tonight.

I found Cole staring into a giant vat of what Harper had told me was sour mash. The smell reminded me of my grandmother's kitchen when she had a few loaves of bread baking in the oven. He motioned me over, and I stepped onto the metal catwalk that ran alongside the huge containers.

"Hey, I'd like to take you up on your offer to come to the game tonight." I had to shout over the noise generated by all the machinery in the warehouse.

Cole motioned to his ear, indicating he couldn't hear me. At the risk of sending my uterus up in flames, I leaned closer. His scent surrounded me, immediately making my knees go weak. I grabbed onto the steel railing and yelled into his ear.

"I said I'd love to come to the game tonight."

He nodded, his face so close I could see the individual whiskers that made up the dark shadow of scruff on his cheeks. "By 'come to the game,' I'm assuming you're willing to play?"

The last time I tried to do something athletic, I ended up on crutches for six weeks. But if this was a way in with the employees at the distillery, I was willing to stand in the outfield and dodge anything that came my way. "Sure. I'll play."

"Great. I've got an extra jersey, but do you have a glove?"

A glove? Why would I have a glove? I shook my head, barely avoiding brushing my nose against his when he turned to face me.

"Come with me." He covered the distance to the office door in long strides while I tried to keep up by taking two steps to every one of his.

Once the door to the warehouse closed behind us and

blocked out the loud background noise, he tucked his thumb through a belt loop and faced me.

"Where are we going?" I'd adopted the more casual dress of the management team and instead of a tailored suit, I had on a pair of black pants and a silky top.

"You need a glove. Probably a pair of shorts or sweats too?" Cole asked, his gaze drifting up from my lower half.

"I wasn't expecting to play softball while I was in town." Nothing like stating the obvious.

Cole shook his head. "It's okay. I'll drive you over to Martin's and we can get what you need."

"Martin's?"

"They sell tackle, athletic gear, and bath and body products."

"Together?" Visions of baseball-shaped soap and fish-scented body wash filled my mind—a marketing profession-al's nightmare.

Cole chuckled as he gestured for me to lead the way down the hall. "You'll see."

FORTY-FIVE MINUTES LATER, I followed him into one of the strangest stores I'd ever entered in my life. Deer gazed down at me from the walls, their glassy stares looking out over a mixture of outdoor equipment, fishing rods, yoga accessories, and flowery-scented bath bombs.

"Hey, Cole. What can I help you with today?" An older man came out from behind the counter as we entered.

The two men shook hands while I stood next to Cole, feeling very much like an out-of-place out-of-towner.

"Danica, meet Martin O'Hare." Cole put his hand on the small of my back, propelling me forward. "Danica's in town to work with Davis on a plan for the distillery."

"Is that right?" Martin didn't extend his hand. I got the impression his feet were firmly planted on the Bishop side of the feud by the way his eyes narrowed, even while his lips curved into a hint of a smile.

"It's nice to meet you." My mom always said a person could attract a lot more flies with honey than they could with vinegar, so I split my lips into a wide smile and thrust my hand at Mr. O'Hare.

His grip lacked both firmness and enthusiasm, but at least he took my hand. "What can I help you with today?"

"We're down a few players, so Danica's going to pitch in on our team tonight." Cole moved toward some shelves at the side of the room. "She'll need a glove, along with some shorts or sweats."

"Shoes too?" Martin directed the question to Cole.

Cole rubbed a hand over his chin and studied my favorite black sandals with the chunky heels. "Did you bring any sneakers?"

"Like I said before, I wasn't expecting to play softball while I'm here." I didn't mention that I wasn't expecting to do anything athletic at all. My idea of fun included things like spa days, wine tastings, and movie nights. I didn't understand the appeal of working up a sweat for the sake of exercise alone.

"Shoes too," Cole said.

I suppressed the urge to call the whole thing off and tried to distract myself by reaching for a handcrafted fish-shaped pillow. Someone had stitched a saying along the front that read "Size matters." I pulled my hand back, but not before Cole noticed.

"My grandma makes these, though I've never seen this particular saying on one of her creations before." He grabbed the pillow and held it out to me.

"Your grandma?" I didn't want to touch it, especially not

knowing his grandma was handcrafting items bearing a saying that would be more likely to apply to a man than a fish.

He set the pillow back on the shelf. "She's a character. You'll have to meet her someday."

I wasn't sure how to respond to that, so I gave the rest of the pillows a wide berth and made my way to where Martin knelt on the ground next to a stack of shoeboxes.

"What size are you?" He eyed me through narrowed lids.

"About a nine." My feet were big for my height. Or my height was short for my feet. Either way, I'd never felt more disproportionately built as I did standing in front of Martin O'Hare while he studied my ankles.

"Try these on." He pulled out a box from near the bottom of the stack.

I waited for the rest of the boxes to topple, but they swayed back and forth slightly before stilling. Taking the box from him, I turned to settle into one of the chairs so I could remove my sandal and try on the sneaker. It had been so long that I couldn't even remember the last time I'd laced a pair of tennis shoes.

"Let me help." Cole sat on the stool in front of me and pulled the shoe from my hands. He expertly loosened the laces, then wrapped his hand around my calf and steered my foot into the shoe.

Was this how Cinderella felt when the prince's footman held the glass slipper? Warmth snaked up my leg, twining around my calf and over my knee until it reached the same spot that had been humming with attraction since the moment I first laid eyes on Cole Bishop.

If only I'd been a size six with narrow feet and high arches. My foot jammed halfway into the shoe. I dug in and tried to push my toes all the way in.

"Want me to loosen it for you?" Cole slid his palm down to my ankle, then pulled at the laces again.

"I've got it." I pushed harder, determined to sink my foot into the shoe. It was like something was already there, though. I lifted my ass off the seat so I could put some weight behind my effort to stuff my foot inside the damn sneaker. My foot slipped.

The next bit happened in agonizing slow motion. Cole's head snapped back as the shoe connected with his nose. The shoe that was half-on, half-off my foot.

I gasped and scrambled to my feet. But with one foot in the air, instead of reaching out to make sure he was okay, I ended up in a heap on the floor in front of him. His large, capable hand cupped his nose while the other closed around my upper arm and he helped me to my feet.

It didn't take a genius to figure out this was bad.

CHAPTER 11

THE WOMAN WAS a walking disaster zone. My nose throbbed with pain and blood trickled through my fingers, plopping down the front of my T-shirt.

"I'm so sorry." Danica regained some semblance of composure. Her hands flitted around my face like she wanted to help, but had no idea what to do.

That made two of us. How was I supposed to handle an unintended assault by the consultant my nemesis had hired? My guess was that typical rules of engagement didn't necessarily apply in this situation.

"It's fine." I pinched my nose to try to stop the bleeding.

"Oh my God, you're bleeding. Do you need a tissue?" She hopped over to where her purse laid on the ground and pulled out a tiny packet of tissues.

"Thanks." I yanked all of them out of their plastic wrap and held the bunch to my nose. It wasn't broken. I'd been in enough fights with my brothers growing up that I could tell the difference between a well-placed shot to the nose and a full-on break. Even if it was, there wasn't anything anyone could do about it.

"Do you want some ice? I'll go get Martin and see if he has some—"

"I'll be fine." I tried to reassure her. "Too bad we're not playing soccer tonight. You've got a hell of a kick."

A deep crease furrowed her brow. "I don't know what happened. I'm so sorry."

"No big deal. There's a bathroom in the back. I'll just go clean up a bit, then we can get the rest of your equipment. How's that sound?"

"I'm not sure I should play tonight."

I wasn't sure she should either. Putting a bat in her hands seemed like a bad idea, since she couldn't even put on a shoe without giving me a bloody nose. We needed the bodies, though. If we didn't have the minimum number of players, we'd have to forfeit. When we started playing softball, it was more about blowing off some steam and grabbing a few beers after. Over the years, it had turned into a much bigger event. We hadn't canceled a game in over ten years, and the first one in a decade wouldn't happen on my watch.

Against my better judgment, I reassured her. "You absolutely should play tonight. Direct all of that energy toward taking down the opposition. We're playing a craft brewery team and they're undefeated."

"If you're sure…"

The only thing I was sure about was that I needed to get to a sink. "I'll be back in a few. Try not to damage anything while I'm gone, will you?"

She let out a soft laugh. "Sure."

Satisfied she wouldn't bail on me, I headed through the racks of clothes and fishing displays to the small bathroom in back. A quick glance in the mirror confirmed my nose still sat in the center of my face, mostly straight, definitely bruised.

Blood stained the front of my shirt. There was no way I'd be able to go back to the office without changing.

I grabbed a few paper towels from the dispenser and turned on the tap. Head injuries always bled the most. My brothers and I figured that out early on, especially me and Vaughn. I wiped away the blood and washed my hands.

"Hey, Cole. I brought you a clean shirt." Danica lightly knocked on the door.

I opened it to find her standing on the other side, an olive-green T-shirt in her hand. "You didn't have to do that."

"Yes, I did." She held it out to me. "I guessed at the size. Is extra-large okay?"

"It's fine." I held it up so I could see the design on the front. "You went for the fish, huh?"

"I can pick something else if you want."

"This works." The front of the shirt said, "I jerk it every chance I can," with two fishing poles crisscrossed underneath. The message seemed especially appropriate since Danica had been in town. "Thanks."

Her cheeks took on such a slight shade of pink that I might have imagined it. She was sweet when she wasn't working for the opposition.

Or drawing blood.

"I'll wait for you out front." She stuck out her thumb and gestured over her shoulder.

I nudged the door almost closed, then yanked my shirt over my head. Not even my mom's tried-and-true stain removal trick would work on this one. Then I pulled on the shirt Danica gave me and thrust my arms through the sleeves. The fabric was rougher than I liked, but nothing a run through the wash and a little fabric softener couldn't fix.

With a final glance in the mirror, I scowled at the light

purple and blue tones appearing under my eye. So help me, if she'd given me a shiner, I'd never hear the end of it.

I tossed my old shirt in the trash and exited the bathroom. For better or worse, I still had a reluctant center fielder to prep. After this morning, there was no way I'd put her on third base. That was way too close to the other players. She'd be better suited to standing in the outfield.

"I think we've got everything she needs." Martin stood at the checkout counter and squinted up at me through his bottle cap glasses. "How's your nose?"

"It's still there." I wiggled it to prove my point. Sonofabitch, that hurt. I was too manly to admit it, but Danica sure packed one hell of a kick. How could someone so small have so much power in her legs? "You got her a glove? Pants? Shoes?"

"Check, check, and check." Danica held up the brown paper shopping bag. "I bought your shirt, too, since I ruined the other one."

"You didn't need to do that."

"Actually, I think I did. I'd also like to buy you lunch to try to make up for my little, um, accident." She bit her lip like she was worried I might not accept.

Gut instinct told me to politely refuse. I wasn't used to a woman doing anything for me, especially treating me to a meal. But something about the way her eyes narrowed, almost like she was wincing, made the "no thanks" on my lips change to a "yes" on the way out of my mouth.

"Yes. That sounds good, thanks."

Her eyes went wide, confirming my suspicion that she hadn't expected me to agree.

"What are you in the mood for?"

Her eyes went even wider. "Maybe you can suggest something, since I don't know all the options around town?"

"It's a short list. You've been to Jackie Jay's, right?" Davis and Harper had taken her there on her first day. Beaver Bluff was small enough that word made it back to the office before they'd even ordered their drinks.

She nodded.

"We can hit up the diner, or there's a food truck that parks by city hall on Mondays if you like Thai." In the summer, our options multiplied. With so many tourists passing through, we had a different food truck parked outside city hall every day of the week. This time of year, we were lucky to have Taste of Thai show up on a consistent basis.

"I'm up for Thai if you are."

"Let's do it. Martin, tell Tess I said hi. I hope she brings her cowbell to the game tonight."

Martin straightened the pens in the holder by the register. "Wouldn't be a home game without it."

"Why does she bring a cowbell?" Danica walked ahead of me, her hips swaying from side to side, drawing my attention like a hungry, horny bee to a patch of wildflowers.

"For cheering. Martin's wife Tess is one of our biggest fans." I took a few steps ahead to push the door open. When we exited the dim interior of Martin's, the sun felt especially bright. "The whole town comes out to watch the games. There's not much else going on this time of year."

"Wait,"—she stopped in the middle of the sidewalk—"you mean people are going to come watch us play tonight?"

"Well, yeah. Is that a problem?"

Her eyes rolled and her lips corkscrewed. "You never said I'd be playing in front of people. I'm going to make a fool out of myself."

"Hey." I turned back and reached for her hands. "It's just friends and family. Gives everyone something to do." It was also a chance for the entire population of Beaver Bluff to put their differences aside and, for a few short hours, forget that we all operated on opposite sides of a gigantic rift. On Monday nights, there weren't any Bishops or Stewarts. We were all just Beaver Bluff Beaves.

"I don't know." Danica slid her hands out of mine.

I wanted to reassure her, but my phone rang. She stared down at her feet while I fished it out of my back pocket.

"Cole here."

Miller cleared his throat. "Hey, I told Charity she doesn't have to play tonight. Arlo's meeting in Nashville got canceled, so he won't need a sub after all."

"That's great." Charity didn't usually join in on the ballgames on Monday nights. I wasn't sure if it was because she took her job of remaining neutral so seriously, or if she just really hated softball. "What did you say to convince her to play in the first place?"

"Wasn't me. It was Vaughn," Davis said. "He can be pretty damn smooth when he wants to be."

No one knew that about my twin better than me. Especially when we were younger and people couldn't tell us apart. I used to have people come up to me all the time and ask about the shit he'd promised them or stuff he said.

"Did you find us a center fielder?"

"I did. Were you worried you weren't going to get to play tonight?" As a single dad with a kid at home, he didn't get out much. On Monday nights, our mom watched his son so he could join in.

"Nah. You always come through on the important stuff, Cole. See you at the field around six?"

He might not have meant it as a compliment, but his words coated my heart with a thick layer of sugary-sweet goodness. "I'll be there."

I shoved my phone back in my pocket. We hadn't stopped

walking while I talked and the Taste of Thai food truck sat about fifty feet in front of us. I could already smell the cilantro and cumin in the air.

"Sorry about that. It was Miller, letting me know that we're all set for tonight."

"Which area does he work in?"

"He actually works for a firm in town and handles the distillery's books part-time." We joined the short line in front of the order window. "You met him the first day you were in the office, remember?"

"That's right. I feel bad saying it, but there have been so many new faces over the past several days, I'm losing track of everyone. I used to have a trick on how to remember names, but I'm out of practice."

"I'm terrible with names." Names always seemed to elude me, though I never forgot a face. "What's your trick?"

She flipped her hair over her shoulder, sending a wave of coconut-scented air straight to my still throbbing nose. "I'm not sure I want to tell you. It's silly."

"Hey, if it works, who cares if it's silly?" I'd always been one to own my process, even if it didn't work for others. "How did you remember my name the first time we met?"

"I'm not telling." The person in front of her stepped aside, and it was Danica's turn at the window. "It's my treat. What can I get you?"

The sun made different shades of blonde show up in her hair. She glanced up at me, squinting to block out the brightness of the gorgeous early April day.

I leaned past her and put a hand on the windowsill. "The usual for me, please."

"And for you?" The guy working the window turned his attention to Danica. He'd started Taste of Thai a few years ago, and I'd been ordering the same thing since day one.

"What's 'the usual'?" she asked.

"Chicken Pad Thai with a four out of five pepper heat and an order of roti on the side," I said.

"That sounds good. Make it two." She slid her credit card over the counter to pay.

My stomach rolled around in my gut at the sight of her signing her name on the tablet and slipping her card back into her purse. I wasn't chauvinistic, but I preferred to pay when I asked a woman out. Though I kept having to remind myself that I hadn't asked Danica out. This was lunch, not a date. Just a friendly business relationship. Did that mean we were involved in a bizship? I wasn't sure what the ideal blend of business and friendship ought to be called.

"You want to pick a table while I wait for the food?" I offered.

"Sure." She moved to the table holding condiments and utensils while I stood near the pick-up window, letting my mind run through potential labels to define the shaky foundation of friendship we'd decided to build on.

I suppose I didn't need to define it as much as I needed to make sure I lived by the rules. They were there to benefit both of us. She'd be gone within a couple of weeks and I could get back to what I did best… making the best damn whiskey in the state and keeping to myself.

CHAPTER 12
Danica

I SLID my sunglasses over my eyes so I could study Cole's backside while he waited for our food. There had been a moment back at Martin's, in between me bloodying his nose and paying for my purchases, when I saw something I couldn't explain. Before I'd turned around to give him some privacy, I caught a glimpse of his reflection. His skin stretched over his shoulders, shiny and smooth and disfigured. Like he'd had some sort of horrible rash.

Or like he'd been burned.

"I hope you're ready for some spicy Pad Thai." Cole stepped over to the bench and set a tray down on the picnic table.

The skin on his arms and hands looked normal. As I thought back to the night we'd spent together, I'd never seen his bare back. My mind spun with the possibilities, trying to make sense of what I'd seen. Maybe he'd been in an accident when he was a kid.

Or was it something more horrific?

"Danica?" Cole handed me a bottle of water. "You okay?"

"Yes, just hungry." I clamped down on my curiosity. "This looks delicious."

"It is." He slid a bite into his mouth, closed his lips around the plastic fork, and slowly drew it back out again.

I pulled my shirt away from my body, trying to prevent myself from overheating. It was probably all of seventy degrees outside, but if he kept treating his fork like a long-lost lover, I might spontaneously combust. Trying to distract myself, I focused on the noodles on my plate.

"I still want to know how you remember names." He set down his fork and reached for his bottle of water.

"It's a trick one of my college professors taught us. I'm sure you've heard it before."

His forearms flexed as he unscrewed the tight cap of his spring water. "Try me."

"All I do when I meet someone new is repeat their name in my head three times, then associate the first letter of their name with something that will help me remember." I spun my fork around in my noodles and shoved the bite in my mouth before he could ask another question.

"So if I met Martin for the first time, I'd pick another word that starts with M?"

Nodding, I continued to chew the way-too-big bite I'd taken.

"Martin likes Mustangs. He has a 1967 convertible that he takes out for parades. Is it that easy?" He popped a piece of roti into his mouth and chewed. I'd never seen a man who could make the simple act of eating something from a food truck look like X-rated porn.

"Yep, that's right. Now that I know about Martin's love for Mustangs, I think I'll use that word for him, too."

He eyed me over his noodles. "What was your word before?"

I shifted my gaze off into the distance. The words I came up with were supposed to be just for me. Admitting how strangely my brain worked at times would be like letting him get a glimpse into the inner workings of my very messed-up mind. "I used menthol. It smelled like vapor rub when I got close to him."

Cole covered his mouth and laughed. "He does have a tendency to get carried away with the Vicks."

"I thought it was just me."

"Nope, it's Martin." He picked up his fork again and twirled it around in his noodles. They slid against each other, twisting and twining until he'd filled his fork. "What word did you pick to associate with me?"

Ever since he started asking about my trick for remembering names, I knew he was going to try to go there. I didn't want to admit the word I'd come up with for him.

I scrunched up my nose and shook my head. "It's not important."

"Why don't you want to tell me?" It was the look in his eyes that did it. He gazed over at me, curious, but with the tiniest bit of fear hidden underneath. It made him look vulnerable, like I could hurt his feelings with just one word.

"It's just something I do for myself. I don't usually share them." There was no way I'd admit the word that first came to mind when I'd met him.

"No?" The flash of vulnerability disappeared, leaving me to wonder if I'd ever seen it at all.

"Fine." I tried to come up with a word that start with a "c" on the fly. Then I blurted out the first non-sexy one I could think of. "It's coleslaw."

"Coleslaw? I make you think of coleslaw?" His brows drew down like he was trying to figure out how he reminded me of something made from cabbage.

Ugh. Cabbage could have been another option. Anything was better than what my depraved mind originally used.

"Damn, I can think of quite a few more flattering 'c' words you could have come up with."

I shrugged, fully committed to my little white lie. "Yes, coleslaw. Sorry."

"Coleslaw." He said the word like he was trying it out for the first time. "The green stuff you eat on a barbecue beef sandwich, right?"

"Can we talk about something else? Like what I'm supposed to do when I stand in centerfield? I'm assuming if the ball comes to me, I can just run the other way and let someone else catch it?"

"Have you never played baseball?"

I shook my head.

"Softball?"

I shook it a little harder.

"Ever throw the ball around with your brother or sister?"

"I don't have siblings." I'd always wanted a baby sister. I prayed for one, added it to my Christmas list every year, and even asked the Easter Bunny in case Santa got too busy and forgot. Looking back, it was probably a good thing I didn't have a younger brother or sister to worry about. Keeping my mom happy took up enough of my time.

"Maybe we can cut out a little early this afternoon, and I can give you some pointers."

"I'd like that." I hadn't figured out his angle yet, but I would. He was either being sweet because he was a genuinely nice person, or he wanted something. As much as I hoped the former was true, in my experience, most people were out for themselves. If he thought he could outsmart me, he'd find out the hard way that I'd been handling guys like him for most of my life. And if that hadn't prepared me, dealing with my mother had. She had a sweet, syrupy way about her until she got what she wanted.

I wouldn't be anyone's fool, especially Cole Bishop's.

CHAPTER 13

"ARE you sure you didn't get into a fight?" Miller squinted at me from his spot on the bench.

I'd been running through the batting order, trying to figure out our best strategy to tie the score. We were down by two and only had half an inning to go. Either he wasn't very observant or the bruising around my eye had gotten worse over the past couple of hours. "No, I caught a shoe to the nose earlier today."

"You're six-foot-three. How did someone reach your nose with their foot?" Miller cocked his head.

"Maybe he had his face somewhere it shouldn't have been when it happened." Vaughn clapped me on the shoulder.

I glanced to where Danica sat at the edge of the bench. She wouldn't make eye contact. I didn't blame her. She'd had a rough game so far, and I was surprised she hadn't called it quits. A wild pitch caught her on the arm her first time at bat, and she'd been striking out ever since.

"Can we focus on the game, guys?" I tried reining them in. "We've got one last chance to score a few runs. We need to focus or we'll never hear the end of it if these guys win."

Miller executed a neck roll and stretched his arms across his body one at a time. "We've got this."

"You're up first." I nudged my chin toward Vaughn. "Try to keep it on the ground."

Vaughn grabbed his bat and executed a few practice swings before taking his spot at the plate. We were a competitive bunch by nature, especially when going up against the craft brewery in the area.

The crowd cheered or booed, depending on which team they were there to support. Vaughn wiggled his hips and got ready for the first pitch. The ball sailed right over home plate. Vaughn swung, connected, and sent it sailing into left field, exactly where he'd sent it the past three times he'd been at bat.

I squinted, following the ball's descent, hoping the outfielder would lose sight of it in the glare from the lights. Vaughn rounded first base, heading toward second. The outfielder caught it, bobbled it, and dropped it. We had a runner on second.

"Way to go, Big V." Miller cupped his hands over his mouth and shouted out to our brother. He was up next and had gotten a hit every time he'd batted tonight. He nailed the first pitch, sending a grounder toward third. Vaughn stayed put and Miller made it to first base.

My little sister Ruby warmed up, testing her swing before stepping up to the plate. She didn't love playing, but loved the afterparty, so she joined us for most games. The pitcher threw three curveballs right in a row. Ruby could belt a fastball out of the park but had never been able to get a piece of a curveball.

Danica stood and walked over to where the batting order was posted on the fence. She ran her finger down the list, stopping when she reached her name.

Two outs, two runners, two scores down. It was my turn to bat. I needed a hit. If I struck out or got tagged out, the game would be over. If I got on base, the fate of the game would rest on Danica's shoulders.

"Good luck." She didn't even try to smile. I could feel the weight of everyone's expectations pressing down on her.

"Thanks, you too." I stepped up to the plate and stared down the pitcher. He'd only been pitching since the bottom of the seventh, so he was still fresh. He served me a change up, then a fastball that barely grazed the strike zone, and I was one strike away from cementing our loss. The ball flew from his hand, heading straight to the plate. My bat connected, and the ball sailed into right field, flirting with the foul line but landing just inside. Vaughn and Miller took off, and I ran toward first, giving it everything I had.

Bases loaded with two outs, Danica slowly made her way to the batter's box. She glanced up, her gaze connecting with mine.

"You've got this, Danica." I clapped my hands together, trying to get the crowd to give her some encouragement.

"Let's go, Beaves!" Tess rang her cowbell and, in solid Beaver Bluff tradition, the sound of dozens of fans stomping their feet on the metal bleachers thundered around us.

Danica tucked her head down like I'd shown her and stuck her ass out behind her. I wished I'd had my phone so I could snap a picture. It was the first time seeing someone about to swing a bat made my cock twitch in appreciation.

She swung at the first pitch. The ball landed with a loud thwack in the middle of the catcher's glove. The next pitch went wide, along with two others, putting the count at three balls. One strike.

"This is it, Danica. You've got it." I got ready to run, hoping like hell she'd catch a piece of the ball on her next swing.

The pitcher let it fly. She closed her eyes and swung. A sound like a blast from a shotgun rang out. The ball popped up and sailed over the fence into the crowd behind home plate.

"Full count." The umpire adjusted his mask.

My nerves were fried. The next thirty seconds would determine whether I'd be partying until the wee hours of the morning or heading home right after a consolatory beer.

Danica swung hard at the air, just like I'd shown her. Then she settled behind the plate again, ready for what would probably be the very last pitch of the game.

The pitcher did a wind up and sent the bail sailing straight to the plate. I watched in slo-mo as Danica's bat connected with the ball, sending it sailing. The centerfielder backed up. Farther, farther, even farther, as the ball soared over his head.

Danica stood at home plate, the bat held loosely by her side. I took off toward second, cupped my hands around my mouth and yelled at her. "Run!"

CHAPTER 14

AS SOON AS I crossed home base, the team picked me up. I wasn't exactly a teeny tiny thing, so it took about a half dozen guys, including Cole and his brothers, to hold me over everyone's heads. Someone's hand went under my ass and I hoped like hell it was his. Victory hadn't sunk in yet. I'd never done anything athletic in my life, but somehow, I'd managed to hit a softball and steal a win for the Beaver Bluff Beaves.

My cheeks hurt from smiling. How had I—a woman who didn't trust herself to even own a pair of sneakers because she was so uncoordinated—managed to survive a softball game?

"That's enough. We ought to go shake hands." Cole shooed the other guys toward home plate where the Harris Hoppers lined up to congratulate us on our win. He caught me in his arms as the hands supporting me disappeared. "That was a hell of a hit."

"Thanks. I didn't know I had it in me." We should have been lining up behind the rest of the team, but he held me there, one arm curled under my knees, the other behind my back.

"I think you can do anything you set your mind to." His eyes were clear, two pools of truth. He must really believe that.

"I think I got lucky." Reality started to sink in. We won the game. I must have had karma, luck, and the collective prayers of every Beaves fan in history on my side to be able to pull off that hit.

Cole shifted, sliding me from his arms to set my feet on the ground. "You don't give yourself enough credit, do you?"

That was a pretty serious question to lay on me in such a lighthearted moment. The idea that he might see through all of my self-deprecating humor and catch a glimpse of the real me caught me off guard. "What do you mean? That hit? It had to be some sort of divine intervention. You saw me practice earlier."

He held my gaze a few beats longer than necessary. "You're something special, Danica Watson."

Before I let myself get swept up in the warmth in his eyes and start to think there might be something else besides awe behind the compliment, I bumped his shoulder with mine. "Should we be good sports and go shake hands?"

I didn't wait for him to reply and headed toward the end of the line, where my teammates offered a mix of "good game" and "sorry, losers" to the opposing team. Cole was on my tail. I could feel his closeness, like the pull of a magnet. It would be easy to give into the draw. Whatever attraction buzzed between us had only intensified during the time I'd spent in Beaver Bluff.

"Are you joining us at Pappy's? The Hoppers are buying tonight." Miller fell into step next to me on the way back to the bench.

"Of course she is." Cole came up to flank my other side. "The losers provide a designated driver so we don't have to drive ourselves home."

I hesitated. Part of me wanted to join in the celebration. I'd never been on a winning team before unless I counted the debate team in high school. But Davis had warned me not to spend too much time around the Bishops while he was gone. He had a feeling Cole would do whatever it took to make sure his plan for the distillery was the only one that moved forward. I wasn't sure I wanted to subject myself to that.

"Come on, Danica. You won the game. You've got to come out with us, even if it's only for one beer." Miller didn't have the chiseled, more aloof good looks of his brothers. He was like an adorable overgrown puppy, full of enthusiasm and smiles. I found it hard to believe he did the books. Most other accounting types I'd worked with had been serious number crunchers who'd rather spend time with their spreadsheets than on a ball field.

"How can I say no when you put it that way?" I adjusted the baseball cap Cole had given me, wishing I had time to run back to the B&B and freshen up.

"That was a great hit." Charity had on a Beaves T-shirt and met me by the fence line. "Do you need a ride over to Pappy's?"

"That would be great." She'd given me an easy way to avoid spending time in the cozy confines of Cole's truck. I glanced up, catching a flash of something that might have been disappointment in his eyes before he looked away.

"See you there." Miller slung his bag over his shoulder and gave me a smile.

"Sounds like you're all set?" Cole asked.

"She's riding with me." Charity linked her arm with mine.

"If you bail and don't show, we'll send Miller after you," Vaughn threatened.

Charity laughed and tugged me toward the parking lot. "We'll be there."

I let her lead the way, still a bit stunned at the way the game ended. "Thanks for the ride."

"My pleasure. We haven't had the chance to spend much time together since you've been in town. I thought we could use the opportunity to connect."

"How do you get away with not having to play?" There had only been a few women on the team. Why had I been targeted when there were plenty of others who didn't step up?

"I'm the very last resort. They learned a long time ago that I make a better spectator than player." Charity stopped when she reached a no-nonsense four-door sedan. It reminded me of her… dependable, strong, practical. Based on what I'd learned about the distillery, she was the main reason the two families hadn't ripped the whole place and each other into pieces.

"I'm pretty sure I make a better fan as well."

"You were the MVP tonight. There's no way they'll let you stop playing now." She popped the trunk so I could set my bag in the back.

"I've only got another week or two of work. I should probably quit softball while I'm ahead… before they figure out I'm a one-hit wonder and kick me off the team."

"Are you getting everything you need from Cole?"

My cheeks heated at the question. I was definitely getting what I needed as far as the business went. My personal needs were a completely different story. "So far."

"Good. He can be a bit difficult at times. Let me know if he gives you any trouble."

Difficult was an interesting word choice. I wanted to ask her what she meant by that, but I didn't want to be too forward. Curiosity won out and as we pulled out of the gravel parking lot, I risked it. "Difficult how?"

Her gaze cut to mine while she steered around a corner, then she refocused on the road. "He doesn't like change."

I could see that about him. Nodding, I tried to put myself in Cole Bishop's shoes. Very large shoes. He'd made several comments about history and honoring the legacy of the men who'd come before the current leadership team at Devil's Dance.

"What about Vaughn? Does he feel the same?"

Charity let out a breathy sigh. "Vaughn's... well... Vaughn's just Vaughn."

There definitely seemed to be something hiding behind that comment, but I didn't know Charity well enough to press. I recognized the sigh, though. Jolene had made the same kind of noises when she had it bad for one of her college professors. It was the universal he'll-never-be-mine exhale.

I stared out the window while we drove by the one-story high school and headed toward the edge of town. My school had two-thousand students, over seven hundred in my graduating class alone. What would it be like to live in a place where everyone knew everything about me from the time I was born?

I shuddered. There wouldn't be room for secrets. I couldn't imagine growing up in a place where I hadn't been groomed to put on a front and pretend like everything was just fine.

"Are you enjoying your time in Beaver Bluff?" Charity asked.

"It's an interesting change of pace." The road twisted to the left, then switched back to the right. I'd probably never get used to the bends and curves that wound their way through the foothills.

Charity navigated with one hand loosely wrapped around the wheel while the other fiddled with the radio. "I probably ought to warn you about Pappy's before we get there. It's been around for generations. Some folks say they ran a speakeasy out of the cellar during Prohibition."

"Is there really a 'Pappy' at Pappy's Place?" I might not

ever get tired of hearing the colorful history of the area around Beaver Bluff.

"Of course." Charity flicked on her blinker and slowed. "Though they're not all related. When the current Pappy is ready to move on, he'll just pick someone else to become the next Pappy."

"How many Pappys have there been?"

"Who knows? This one's been in charge since well before I was born. The teams hang out there because he's got the cheapest beer and there's always enough room for everyone."

We turned into the gravel lot, and Charity parked close to the door. A variety of pickup trucks and SUVs filled most of the spots. I'd been hoping to fit in a few conversations with some of the distillery's warehouse employees at the game, but I'd been too nervous about making a fool out of myself on the field. Chatting over a beer might be my chance.

I flipped down the mirror on the visor, afraid of what I might look like.

"You look great," Charity assured me. "You'll be enough of a draw since you're from out of town that people won't care if you've got dirt smudged across your cheek or tangles in your hair."

I brushed my fingers over my cheek on the off chance she'd actually seen dirt on my face. "How long do people usually stay?"

"Last call's at two. This was a big win. I wouldn't be surprised if half the warehouse shows up late tomorrow morning."

"Can I ask you a question?" I unbuckled my seatbelt, trying to summon the courage to enter the bar.

"Sure." She tucked her keys into her purse and twisted slightly to face me across the front seat.

I paused, wondering how best to phrase what I wanted to

ask. "Cole said your family has always been in the middle, like a peacemaker between the Stewarts and the Bishops. Why?"

She relaxed against the back of her seat. "All I know is what's been passed down from generation to generation. When the distillery started, the three families were friends and neighbors. Each did an equal amount of work and shared in the profits. Something happened in the late 1800s or early 1900s that changed all that."

"What?"

Her eyes shone brightly in the dim interior of the car. "I wish I knew. A lot of the history was lost in a flood at the turn of the century. After that, they decided to divvy up important documents, so they didn't lose everything like that again. Each family got a stack and some of it was lost over the years, including any documentation about what started the original feud."

"I've never heard of anything like it—two families so torn up over something no one can even remember."

"Yeah, well, they might not remember, but generation after generation has sprinkled salt on those old wounds. It probably doesn't even matter who started it or what it was about. It's so ingrained in the distillery, in the town, that people wouldn't know what to do without it."

"How do you stay neutral when everyone else in town appears to have picked a side?" I couldn't explain my fascination with the history of the feud.

"The Devines have been in the middle since the whole thing started. My great-grandma used to tell me that someone had to keep the peace or they'd all lose everything. I hope someday they'll figure out how to mend the rift that's divided them for so long. But knowing Vaughn and Cole and how they butt heads with Davis at every decision, I'm not sure that day will come in my lifetime." She pulled a tube of lip gloss out of her bag and swiped it across her lips. "Are you ready?"

"I suppose." Would I ever be ready to be the object of so many strangers' stares? Probably not. But the sooner I walked in that door, the sooner I'd be able to start up some conversations and make progress on my to-do list.

"Let's go." Charity got out of her side of the car and I met her on the way into the dilapidated building.

I pasted on a smile and crossed my fingers. Hopefully, both the building and my plan would stay together tonight. I wasn't in the mood to lose, either.

Congratulations swirled around me, faster than the pats on the back that seemed to come at me from every direction as I passed through a gauntlet of bearded men holding full cups of beer in their hands.

"Great game."

"Good job."

"That was a hell of a run."

"There you are." Cole handed me a full plastic cup of beer before stepping behind me and providing a buffer against the crowd.

My eyes adjusted to the dim lighting, and I picked out faces I recognized from the distillery. Vaughn had his arm loosely wrapped around a tall woman with long, dark hair. Miller's booming laugh rang out over the crowd as he stood at the bar next to their other brother Evan, both hands wrapped around a cup holding a dark-colored beer, their sister Ruby at his other side.

Whatever rivalry and animosity that existed between the two teams must have been left on the field. Beaves sat next to Hoppers, sharing plates of cheese-covered nachos and buckets of popcorn. Several TVs showed the hockey game. I hadn't paid much attention before, but after meeting Cole at the hotel bar in Knoxville, I'd started watching a little hockey here and there and knew the Predators were in first place in their division.

"Do you want to sit down somewhere?" Cole asked. He used his body as a shield, protecting me from the crowd of softball players behind him.

"I'm fine for now." I took a sip of my beer, recognizing the sharp taste of hops. "Do you always draw such a big crowd?"

"You should have seen it the night we played the Mayfield Mad Dogs. It was standing room only."

"Did you win?" I asked.

"We didn't have you there to clinch it at the last minute, but yeah, somehow we pulled it off." He tapped the rim of his plastic cup against mine. "Cheers to you for securing the win. You don't know it yet, but you might have just become the most popular person in Beaver Bluff."

I'd never been popular at anything or anywhere. I was about to laugh in his face, but then the bartender leaned over the counter and pressed another cup of beer into my hands.

He had frizzy gray hair pulled back to a scraggly ponytail at the base of his neck. "That was some hit. I hope you'll be joining the team on a regular basis."

Not sure how to respond, I looked to Cole for some guidance. "Um, I—"

"Danica, meet Pappy, the owner of this illustrious establishment."

"Pappy, it's nice to meet you. I've heard so much about your place." It wasn't a lie. I had heard a lot. Mostly warnings about how likely it might be to fall down around us, but a lot was a lot. I didn't have to be specific.

"It's not much, but it's mine." He leaned forward like he was about to share a national secret. "Until I pass it on to the next lucky bastard."

Miller called Cole's name from across the bar. Cole glanced up and squinted across at his brother. "I ought to go see what he needs. Will you be okay for a few minutes?"

"I'll keep her company," Pappy said.

My heart lurched at the offer. Then I realized spending a few minutes with Pappy might be just what I needed. "Go ahead."

It's not like Cole was required to watch over me all the time. We might have played on the same team tonight, but technically, I was working against him, aligned with his biggest enemy. I needed to remember who was paying my outrageous hourly rate and stop letting myself get distracted by the way Cole Bishop filled out his baseball pants.

"So, Pappy,"—I turned the full force of my attention on the wiry bartender with the grizzled beard—"what's your take on the Devil's Dance Distillery?"

CHAPTER 15

I MOVED through the crowd toward my brother while keeping an eye on Danica. She huddled over the bar, leaning in toward Pappy like the two of them were old pals sharing war stories. I wasn't jealous. Not of Pappy. But the pang that sliced through my side sure felt like an attack from the green-eyed monster. It had been so long since I'd experienced anything remotely related to a jealous reaction that I might be confusing it with something else.

"What's so important?" I reached Miller, who'd surrounded himself with a few of the players from the opposite team.

My brother clapped a hand on my shoulder. "I was just telling them about the new release you've got coming out this summer. Small batch that's been sitting in a barrel for how long? Twelve years?"

"That's right." It had been years since we'd offered a product that had been aged that long. I was excited to start talking about it, though we hadn't exactly gone public with it yet. I still needed to get Harper on board before I started spreading the word. "We're still working out the details, so do me a favor and keep it to yourselves?"

One of the co-owners of the Hopper brewery cocked his head. "My granddad had a bottle of the Devil's Dance Distinct. That was some of the best whiskey I've ever had in my life. When are y'all going to re-release that one?"

My jaw tightened. Distinct was the original whiskey blend the founders of Devil's Dance used to make way back when they started. It was the blend the distillery was built on and the one everyone wanted. The one I'd been trying to recreate ever since my dad let me near the mash bills.

"It's a work in progress. If y'all will excuse me, I need to go check on our MVP." I ignored the pointed look from Miller and headed back to the bar. Danica wasn't on the stool where I'd left her. I scanned the room, trying to locate her in the sea of baseball caps. The guys around here were harmless. Most of the players on the team had married their high school sweethearts and had two or three kids already. Beaver Bluff was a family town built on small-town values, so I wasn't worried she'd been carted out of the bar or that someone was trying to take advantage of her.

What was I worried about, then? That one of the few single guys in town might catch her eye? The thought made my chest tighten. I rubbed a palm over my sternum, trying to wipe the irritating feeling away.

Vaughn stood near the edge of the bar with his on-again-off-again girlfriend.

"Hey, have you seen Danica?"

"Why?" He eyed me with curiosity. I could tell he knew there was something going on between me and the curvy consultant. It was a twin thing. Neither one of us had ever been able to lie to the other. Sometimes I appreciated the superpower, but now wasn't one of those times.

"She's new in town, and I want to make sure she's okay." I added a nonchalant shoulder shrug, hoping he'd let it go and tell me if he'd seen her without making this into a thing.

He nudged his chin toward the hall. "I saw her follow Pappy to the back room. No doubt he's trying to show her his special stash."

"Thanks." I took off down the hall. Pappy never missed an opportunity to show off his private collection of whiskey. It was a decent assortment. He had a couple of bottles I hadn't even been able to get my hands on. But he also knew a hell of a lot about the history of Devil's Dance. No telling what kind of crap he might be filling her head with if he got a few minutes alone with her.

Low voices filtering into the hall told me they were in the back room. I put my hand on the door to push it open, then paused. This might be one of those times I could get a little intel and try to figure out what kind of angle Davis might be working. Instead of pushing the door open, I leaned against the wall just outside and waited.

"So this is the Devil's Distinct I keep hearing so much about?" Danica asked.

"The last one I've got." The scratchy, low tone of Pappy's voice was unmistakable.

"I heard a few of the warehouse guys say that unless they make a bold move, the distillery might fade into oblivion. What do you think?"

My gust twisted. Were my guys really saying shit like that behind my back? I'd have to ask Evan about it. He oversaw the production and warehouse teams. I leaned closer to make sure I caught Pappy's response.

"I think it's too late. Those two families have been tearing each other down for over a hundred years. This new generation is the worst. I wouldn't be surprised if they ran it into the ground in the next ten years."

I clenched my fists, tempted to bust through the door.

"Cole seems to have a plan." Danica's voice came out soft. I could picture the look on her face as she came to my defense. The edges of her lips would be curled up in a slight smile while light danced in her eyes. Maybe she wasn't diametrically opposed to the plans I wanted to put in place.

Pappy snorted. "Unless Cole Bishop can talk to the dead and figure out how to get Devil's Dance Distinct back on the shelves, he's going to have a tough time of it."

That was the problem. My ancestors had built Devil's Dance on the backbone of that blend. I'd tried so many times over the years to figure out what it was about those barrels that made it so incredible. There were only so many ways I could change up the mash bill, especially considering the limited resources they would have had way back then. It's not like they were adding some unique grain or using some of the modern-day methods of creating complex flavor profiles. I was missing something, though. Maybe a unique strain of yeast that they used in fermenting. Whatever it was, Pappy was right. I needed to figure it out.

"I should get back to the others," Danica said. Footsteps shuffled toward the door.

Not wanting to get caught listening in on a conversation that clearly wasn't meant for my ears, I took long strides back to the bar area.

Vaughn caught my eye from the opposite side of the room and lifted his brows. I shook my head the slightest amount. We'd have to catch up later. He needed to know what I'd overheard. It was time for the Bishops to come together. Time to reclaim the Devil's Dance brand.

"There you are." Danica eased onto a stool next to where I stood at the bar.

"I'm not the one who ducked out. Everything okay?" I turned toward her, wondering if she'd admit to where she'd been.

"Yeah. Pappy offered to show me his stash of the good stuff. He's got quite a collection." A casual observer might not have noticed the way her cheeks flushed the slightest bit, but I did.

"Can I get you another beer?" I lifted my hand to signal to Pappy.

"No, that's okay. I think I'm going to head back. It's been a long day and I'm going to need a hot bubble bath to ease the aches and pains away. Nothing like playing softball for the first time to remind me how out of shape I am."

Visions of Danica lying in an antique clawfoot tub drifted into my head, with piles of bubbles covering her from the neck down. Blood rushed to my cock as I imagined what it would feel like to sink down into a tub of warm water and wrap my hands around her.

"I'll drive you." I'd been so distracted with keeping track of her that I'd barely choked down half a beer.

"Are you sure? I thought you said there was a designated driver?"

Pappy slapped a palm down on the bar. "I'm the designated driver tonight, sweetheart. I'd be happy to take you wherever you want to go."

Danica glanced from Pappy to me. "Thanks, but I don't want to drag you away from paying customers. If Cole's heading out, I'll catch a ride with him."

"Suit yourself, sunshine." Pappy clucked his tongue before turning back to the taps.

Sunshine... that was a fitting nickname for Danica. She

seemed to carry some sort of light with her that lit up everything around her.

"Are you sure you're okay to drive?" She took my arm and let me lead her through the crowd.

"Yeah. I only had half a beer. That's one thing my family doesn't mess around with. Sheriff Bayard would love to slap one of us with a DUI." Odds were, he'd probably be waiting just up the highway to try to catch someone heading home from Pappy's.

"Why's that? I thought everyone in Beaver Bluff got along?" Danica let her hand fall from my arm once we cleared the front door and stepped outside. "Or at least everyone besides your family and the Stewarts."

The night air had cooled since the sun went down. It was that time of year when the days started to warm up, but the nights still held a chill thanks to the elevation.

She shivered, rubbing her hands up and down her arms to chase away the cold.

"Hop in and I'll get some heat going." I held the passenger door open and waited for her to climb inside.

"So, what's the deal with the sheriff?" Danica asked.

We only had a few minutes before we reached the B&B. There was no way I could distill years of bad blood into a sentence or two. "The Brayards were supposed to be the fourth family when the distillery started. Before everything got set up, the other three families kicked them out."

"How come?" She turned to me, her eyes wide in the dim lighting of my truck cab.

"Rumor has it there was some sort of love triangle involving a Brayard, a Bishop, and a Stewart. I don't know the details, but whatever happened landed the Brayards on the outside of the group and they've been holding it against us ever since."

She shook her head and let out a soft laugh. "And I thought history was so boring back in high school."

The porch lights blazed as I pulled into the circle drive in front of the bed-and-breakfast. Danica reached for the door handle, but I hopped out and raced around the front of the truck to open it for her. I had an idea—one that wouldn't come without risks—but was probably worth it to help her get a clearer understanding of my family's position on the distillery.

"Thanks for the ride." She stopped at the front door of the house. If we were two regular people who'd been out on a date, this would be the moment when I'd wonder whether or not I should kiss her. The way she looked up at me, her guard down, her lips slightly parted, made me wish we'd met under different circumstances.

"Hey, I was wondering…"

"Yes?"

"Any chance you'll be around this weekend? The whole town is celebrating Maynard Days, and I thought you might want to check it out."

"I'm supposed to go home this weekend. My aunt eloped last month and they're finally having a reception to celebrate. You've got me curious, though. What's Maynard Days?"

What was the best way to explain an entire festival centering around mules? "It's an event that's been going on in Beaver Bluff for almost a hundred years. They've got vendors, lots of bluegrass music, maybe a mule or two."

"A mule? Like a donkey?"

I didn't want to get into the difference between mules and donkeys and horses, but I also didn't want her to embarrass herself if she wandered into Maynard Days without me. "Kind of. A mule is the offspring of a male donkey and a female horse. Folks around here used them for hauling and plowing long before trucks and tractors were invented."

She squinted and tilted her head. "Thanks for the lesson on animal husbandry."

"You know what? Never mind. I didn't think you'd be interested."

Her fingers touched my arm. "If it means an opportunity to learn more about the distillery and the town, I'd love to check it out."

My skin heated from her touch, even under the fabric of the long-sleeve t-shirt I'd pulled on. Somehow, I'd managed to keep my attraction for her in check since she'd showed up in town and rocked my carefully constructed world. I wasn't sure how much longer I could keep it under control. If I didn't try to get the intel, I was sure Vaughn wouldn't have any trouble inviting her out for coffee or, even worse, a cocktail. The thought that she might enjoy his company made my blood simmer, and not in a good way.

"If you won't be around this weekend, my folks are having the family over Thursday night for their annual pre-festival party. Maybe you can stop by then. Mom always makes a big batch of cornbread so we can try out her entry for the corn-bread cake contest, and Dad usually opens up a bottle of whiskey from his private collection. What do you think?" If Davis found out I'd invited her to the house, he'd be livid. My pulse ticked up while I waited for a response.

She considered it for a long beat, then nodded. "I'd love to meet the rest of your family and get their take on what they think the distillery needs."

"Great. Want me to pick you up?"

"That's okay. Why don't you just text me the address?" She'd moved her hand from my arm to tuck the hair that had escaped from her ponytail back behind her ear. "Thanks for making me play tonight. I had fun."

"Ouch." I squinted at her. "I hope you don't feel like I forced you to play."

"Well, you strongly encouraged me." Her nose crinkled, making her look much younger, especially with the baseball cap I'd given her pulled down low on her forehead. "Is that better?"

I lifted my head, gazing straight into those emerald eyes. "You should never let anyone make you do something you don't want to."

She blinked and glanced at the narrow floorboards of the porch. "You've got a way about you that makes me do things I probably shouldn't."

I chuckled, my mind wandering back to the night we shared. "I never said not to do things you shouldn't, just things you don't want to."

The implication weighed heavily between us, and my pulse ticked up while I waited to see what she'd do next.

"Goodnight, Cole." She gave me a final smile before she disappeared inside.

It might have been the way the porch light reflected in her eyes, but the heat rising in my belly made me think she might not be opposed to another night like the one we spent in Knoxville.

Giving in to that desire would leave me in a terrible position. I needed to keep my head on straight if I wanted to ensure the future I imagined for the distillery. No matter how much I ached to lose myself in her arms.

CHAPTER 16
Danica

THE NEXT FEW days flew by in a whirlwind of meetings, interviews, and so many hours staring at my computer screen that my vision went blurry. Though I'd promised to get on the road to head home for my aunt's wedding reception, Cole's invitation to stop by his parents' house tonight weighed on my mind. Davis and Harper would be back in the office on Monday, along with the rest of the Stewarts who'd been gone for the past two weeks.

The vibe would change. Taking Cole up on his offer might be the last chance I'd have to get his family's side of things before I got swept up in the Stewart tide.

His advice not to do anything I didn't want to kept playing through my head. I wished that were true. Always having to give into the demands of being an only child meant I'd never been able to stand up to my parents. Maybe now was the time to start.

I picked up my phone and dialed my mom's cell.

"Are you on your way home yet?" Typical Mom. She didn't even bother with a greeting. "I was hoping you'd be able to sneak away a day early. If you hurry, I might be able to get you in with my stylist to see if we can do something about your hair."

"About this weekend, Mom..." I paused, summoning the inner strength to hold my ground.

"It's going to be lovely. Your cousin is even flying in from New York to help us celebrate." Her tone left no room for negotiation, but I was determined to forge ahead.

"Something came up at work. I don't think—"

"You're not going to let a temporary position get in the way of celebrating a family milestone, are you?"

"I hardly think celebrating Aunt Angela's fifth marriage is a family milestone." Especially when none of us had been invited to the spur-of-the-moment wedding in Fiji last month. My mother never had been able to understand her sister, but after fifty some years, she was still trying to keep up with her.

"What's everyone going to think when my only daughter doesn't show? It'll be like a slap in the face to Angela and..." She fumbled, probably trying to remember my aunt's new husband's name.

"Thomas, Mom. Her new husband's name is Thomas." I'd found out the news when everyone else did—from a post on social media.

"I know his name."

"Of course you do. We must have a bad connection." The habit of making excuses for my mother was a hard one to crack. I'd been hoping a little distance would give me some perspective as well as a chance to get out from under her thumb. So far, that hadn't worked as well as I'd hoped.

"The party starts at seven on Saturday night. I'll expect to see you there."

"Mom, I—"

A click came through the phone. Did she just hang up on me? "Mom?"

It wasn't the first time she'd cut me off, and I'd be a fool to think it would be the last. But over the past week, something had started to become more important to me than risking my mother's wrath.

I wanted to find out more about Cole's side of the feud. Digging into the history of the distillery made me curious about his point of view. I was still Team Stewart—they were the ones signing my checks—but I'd begun to wonder if maybe there was something in the past we could use to our advantage when putting together a plan for the future.

Once Davis got back, my time would be spoken for. If I wanted to learn more about the Bishops, it had to be now.

I rounded the corner and caught sight of Cole sitting behind his desk. His elbows rested on the desktop and a pair of glasses sat on his nose. He looked strong and smart and sexy all at once—an intoxicating combination. His shoulders bunched, making the cotton T-shirt strain. His fingers tapped on the keyboard, and I could almost feel his strong hands gliding over my skin—a sensation I'd imagined more than I'd like to admit over the past two weeks.

He studied the screen in front of him, his brow furrowed in deep concentration. I leaned against the doorframe, content to watch him and wonder what had captured his attention.

Lost to my own daydreams about the two of us tangled up in hotel bedsheets, I didn't catch him looking up until he cleared his throat. "Hey, Danica. Can I help you with something?"

Startled, I flushed at being caught. "Sorry, you looked so deep in thought. I didn't want to disturb you."

He slid his glasses off and set them on the desk. "Just trying to figure something out. Come in."

"Thanks." I took a seat across from his desk. I liked Cole's office. It lacked the formality of the large corner office where

Davis operated. Black-and-white pictures of the distillery covered the walls, and built-in bookshelves filled the space behind his desk. His office was a nod to the past, which fit Cole to perfection.

"What's up?" He'd stood when I entered, and his chair creaked as he settled into it again.

"I was thinking about your invitation earlier this week."

"Oh yeah?" He leaned forward, resting his elbows on the desk again. "What were you thinking?"

My throat went dry as his warm, chocolate gaze met mine. I started to speak, but no words came out. Great, add awkward to my list of not-so-endearing personality traits. "Um, about tonight. The party at your parents' house?"

"You're welcome to stop by." His eyes held a trace of humor. Damn him for enjoying how uncomfortable I felt.

"What time should I come?"

"You're welcome to come anytime you want." His response sent heat straight to the spot between my legs, a reminder of what coming with Cole might mean. The humor in his eyes passed, and his irises darkened.

After our shaky truce, we'd kept things mostly professional around the office. I'd flirted a little here and there, but managed to avoid getting caught up in the kind of heat-inducing banter we were currently engaged in.

My hormones raged. Desperate to regain control, I changed the subject. "Can I bring anything?"

"Just yourself." His gaze raked over me, traveling a slow path from my eyes to my belly and back up again. "But make sure you come hungry."

"All right. See you later tonight." I got up and turned on shaky legs, eager to flee to safety. Or at least somewhere away from Cole, where I wouldn't continue to shove my foot in my mouth.

"I'm looking forward to it," he called out to my retreating back. His voice sent shivers racing up and down my spine.

The sooner I got done with this job, the sooner I could head back to Knoxville and start building my client base. A client base free from Cole Bishop and his not-so-thinly-veiled passes.

VEHICLES LINED the long dirt driveway leading to Cole's parents' house, mostly pickup trucks and SUVs, with an occasional four-door sedan. I parked behind a four-wheel-drive truck painted in camouflage with a license plate that read "SHOT4U."

With more than a little trepidation, I climbed out of my car. The mouthwatering smell of something cooking on a smoker teased my nose. Music drifted from the backyard, and I followed the path of ribbons strewn between poles to the open gate.

The Bishops had the perfect setup for entertaining a large crowd. A tall wooden fence lined the perimeter of their over-sized yard. Two enormous smokers sat at the edge of a large flagstone patio. Dozens of people sat around in lawn chairs or stood in small groups. This looked a lot more like a block party than a family get together. For a long moment, I thought about tucking tail and escaping to the safety of my car.

"I wasn't sure if you'd show." Cole walked toward where I stood at the edge of the yard, two longnecks in hand.

He had on the same snug T-shirt and jeans he'd worn to work. The only difference was the shades he'd slid over his eyes. It wouldn't be long before the sun went down and left a chill in the air.

"I told you I'd stop by." I took the beer he offered, grateful for something to do with my hands.

"I'm glad you did." He lifted his bottle and took a swallow.

Watching his Adam's apple bob up and down made me lick my lips. "Hey, if you're thirsty, you should try this. It's a local craft brew. Not as good as whiskey, but it hits the spot."

I glanced at the label. "Harris IPA? Are these the craft brewers we played the other night?"

"Yep. They brought over a case as a gesture of good sportsmanship. Come on, I want to introduce you to my folks."

My stomach doubled in on itself, flipping and twisting like it was trying to fold itself into some origami shape. Despite my reservations, I followed Cole into the gathering of Bishops, hoping they saw me as an ally, not an enemy.

Cole stopped by one of the smokers where a tall man with salt-and-pepper hair tended a rack of ribs. "Hey, Dad, I want you to meet Danica Watson. Danica, this is my father, Ronan Bishop."

Mr. Bishop turned toward me, his eyes filled with interest. "Ah, so you're the bulldog Davis hired."

I gulped. Bulldog? If I had to pick a dog to describe myself, it would probably be more like a Golden Retriever. I didn't like conflict, just wanted everyone to get along all the time. The only Golden Retriever I knew was my cousin's shy, timid female who peed herself every time she met a stranger. Okay, scratch Golden Retriever. Maybe I was more like a Yorkie. A curvy, introverted Yorkie.

"She's hardly a bulldog, Dad." Cole smirked and met my gaze. "Danica's interested in learning more about the history of the distillery and possibly working some of the past into the plans she's putting together for Davis to propose."

"Is that so?" Mr. Bishop studied me, tongs in one hand, a tumbler with two fingers of what I presumed was one of Devil's Dance's best whiskeys in the other.

"It's nice to meet you, Mr. Bishop. I'm looking forward to

finding a way to incorporate a little bit of both families' points of view in my presentation."

"Call me Ronan, and I'll drink to that." Mr. Bishop lifted his glass and clinked it against the neck of my beer before taking a sip.

Cole clapped a hand on his dad's shoulder. "I'm going to go introduce her to everyone else before the festivities start."

Mr. Bishop nodded and turned back to the smoker. Festivities? Cole didn't say anything about there being festivities.

"What kind of festivities are you talking about?" I matched his stride, taking two short steps for every one of his. After barely surviving meeting his dad, I wasn't sure how many more surprises I could take.

"Nothing to worry about. I told you my mom makes everyone sample her cornbread cake. Then we usually let Cletus out to say hi to everyone before we take him into town for the festival."

"Who's Cletus?"

A woman brushed by, holding a giant plastic bowl of salad in her hands. "Cletus is the oldest mule in Beaver Bluff. He'll be forty-nine this year."

"Hey, Mom. I want you to meet Danica Watson. She's the—"

"Consultant Davis Stewart hired to run the rest of us right out of the business." Mrs. Bishop delivered the barb with a smile that smacked of sass and sincerity... a confusing combination.

"Now, Ma." Cole took the bowl from her and moved to set it down on the table. "Danica's just doing her job."

I felt like a scout who'd been able to sneak behind enemy lines but got stuck. We were all trying to make the best out of things. Though I was pretty sure the Bishops weren't worried that their livelihood was at stake.

"I'm sorry." Mrs. Bishop cast an apologetic look toward Cole. "We know you're just a hired gun. It's not your fault Davis is out to ruin us."

I'd been called a lot of things throughout my life, but "hired gun" had never been one of them.

"Ma." Cole's voice came out even and calm, though the way his body tensed made me think he'd taken offense to his mother's comment.

"Well, it's true." Mrs. Bishop put an arm behind Cole and snuggled against his side. "I know you boys are doing your best to make sure your vision is the one that carries the company forward, but those Stewarts are like snakes lying in the grass. They bide their time, waiting for everyone else to do the hard work, then strike when the moment is right."

Cole leaned forward, his arm resting on his mom's shoulder. "Please excuse my mother. She's spent the past thirty-five years putting up with the Stewart BS."

I caught the exasperated look Mrs. Bishop gave Cole before pasting a smile on her face. "Forgive me for being rude. I hope you'll be able to come up with something that works for everyone." Her over-friendly smile shifted and a hint of hope seemed to shine in her eyes. "For all of our sakes."

For the umpteenth time since I'd arrived in Beaver Bluff, I felt overwhelmed and totally outside of my area of expertise. Before I had a chance to come up with an excuse that would buy me a little time to pull myself together, Cole's brother Miller joined us, a tow-headed boy in his arms.

"Uncle Cole, someone wants to go give the birthday mule a carrot. Since you're his favorite uncle and all, I thought I'd ask you first." Miller passed the wriggling boy into Cole's arms. "Hey, Danica, this is my son Jack."

"Hi Jack, it's nice to meet you." I smiled at the boy, who

couldn't be more than four or five. Miller had such a baby face, it was surprising to see him with a kiddo of his own.

"Jack, say hi to Miss Danica." Miller ruffled his son's hair.

"Hi, Miss Danica." The boy climbed up onto Cole's shoulders, using his uncle like a jungle gym.

"Favorite uncle, huh? I think his favorite is whoever's giving him the most raspberries." Cole flipped the boy so he could reach his belly and blew a loud raspberry onto Jack's tummy. Loud laughter erupted and the boy's knees drew up, knocking into Cole's chin.

Miller put a hand on each of his son's cheeks and pressed a kiss to his forehead. "I've got to load some stuff for the festival in the back of my truck. Do you mind keeping an eye on him for a few minutes?"

"Of course not." Cole hoisted Jack onto his shoulders. "Jack and I will introduce Danica to Cletus and try not to ruin his appetite before he gets his birthday cake."

"Thanks." Miller pushed Jack's boot back onto his foot before it fell to the ground. "See you in a bit."

"You ready to meet the oldest, most stubborn mule in Shellacky County?" Cole held tight to his nephew's legs while Jack kicked his boots against Cole's shoulders.

"You can carry one of the carrots, Miss Danica." Jack thrust a fresh-picked carrot toward me, the long leafy greens still attached.

"Let's do it." With a final wistful glance toward where I'd parked my car, I dismissed my reservations and turned toward Cole and his adorable nephew. I was off to meet a birthday mule.

CHAPTER 17

"HAPPY BIRTHDAY, dear Cletus! Happy birthday to you!" Danica softly sang along while Jack directed us in a rousing version of "Happy Birthday." Cletus wouldn't celebrate his birthday for a few more days, but I wasn't about to ruin Jack's fun by telling him.

"Now you scratch him behind the ears and give him the carrot," Jack said.

Danica reached a hand over the gate to the mule's pen and carefully touched her fingers to the coarse hair behind his ears. "Like this?"

Jack nodded. Like father, like son. Though he was even bossier than Miller at times.

Cletus's eyes closed and opened in a few slow, lazy blinks. His lips curled up in as much of a smile as a mule might be capable of, like he was rubbing it in that Danica had her hands all over him instead of me.

He must have caught a whiff of the carrot. Without warning, he shoved his head over the top of the gate and tried to sniff out the treat. He blew out a snort while his lips wiggled and pressed into Danica's chest. Suddenly, I found myself incredibly jealous of a forty-eight-year-old mule.

"Ooh, hello there." Danica backed up a few steps.

"You can give him the carrot," Jack said.

"Like this?" Danica held the narrow end of the carrot out to the greedy mule. Cletus nibbled on it up to the point where Danica's fingers rested. "Oh, that tickles."

"His nose is soft," Jack said.

Danica lifted her hand to run over the top of Cletus's nose. "I can feel that. Thanks, I've never fed a donkey before."

Jack looked at me, his disappointment obvious based on the deep furrow between his tiny brows. "Dad told me everybody knows how to tell a mule from a donkey."

Danica's eyes widened, and she bit down on her lip. "Mule. So sorry if I offended Cletus."

"Can I go help Nana now?" Jack bent over, trying to climb down my chest.

I grabbed his arm before he catapulted himself off my shoulder and set him down on the ground. "Sure. Take the dog with you."

"Come on, Titus. Wanna treat?"

The dog's ears perked up, and he ran ahead of Jack. I kept an eye on them all the way up the hill until my nephew ran into my mom's legs.

"They sure are a handful, aren't they?" I mumbled the question more to myself than out loud.

"They sure are." There was a wistfulness to Danica's voice that made me wonder what was behind it. Before I had a chance to ask, she turned to me and crossed her arms over her chest. "You're so good with your nephew. Do you ever think about having kids?"

"Oh, definitely. At least a dozen."

"A dozen?"

"Well, since I'm getting a late start, maybe a half dozen." I leaned against the wall of Cletus's stall and absentmindedly ran my hand over the mule's nose.

"What do you mean 'a late start'?"

"My folks had me and Vaughn when they were in their early twenties. Miller's got Jack already. Hell, I'm thirty years old and nowhere near to settling down." I gritted my teeth, frustrated at myself for sharing too much.

"Thirty years old, wow." Danica sized me up, her gaze running all the way from my toes to the brim of the Devil's Dance baseball cap I'd pulled on. "Yeah, you'd better get moving on that."

"Forget it." I gave Cletus a final pat, then turned, my way of shutting down the conversation. Nothing good would come out of discussing my future parenting plans with a woman I wasn't supposed to touch.

Her hand on my arm stopped me. "Hey, I'm just giving you a hard time. I think you've got plenty of time to start a family. Not that I would know anything about that."

I searched her gaze, trying to figure out if she was messing with me. Her eyes were clear… honest…kind. I shifted my attention lower, focusing on the curve of her lips. She had a tiny freckle just to the right of her upper lip. I wanted to lean down and kiss it. Knowing it would be a mistake if I did, I couldn't seem to stop myself.

Something drew me to her, pulled at me, made me want to press my lips to hers and lose track of time.

The loud clang of the dinner bell startled me back to reality. I jumped back a step, my heart beating like a hundred horse's hooves against the walls of my chest.

"What's that?" Danica asked, a wad of my shirt fisted in her hand.

I hadn't even noticed when she grabbed it. "Dinner's ready. You sure you want to meet the rest of my family?"

She must have realized she'd gripped my shirt. "Oh, look what I've done."

"It's okay." I smoothed my hand over hers as we both tried to rub the wrinkles away. "Come on, Mom will send someone after us if we don't get up there."

"Right." She pulled her hand back. "Sorry about that. I don't know what came over me."

I didn't confess I knew exactly what had come over her. It was the same damn thing that had captured me in its grip and held me tight. I didn't have a name for it yet, but that didn't stop me from cursing the attraction between us.

"Ready to head up to the house?" I swallowed the urge to confide in her about my growing feelings. It wouldn't do any good. I was a Bishop, and she was working for the Stewarts. The only thing that would come out of that was heartache and hurt. Because no matter what happened, one of us was going to walk away from this as a winner, and one of us would be holding the pieces of the aftermath.

In my heart, I knew I'd have to do whatever it would take to make sure my family got what they needed out of the distillery.

Even if it meant she'd take the fall.

I MADE sure I introduced Danica to all of my siblings and their significant others before I left her in my sister's capable hands. If anyone could set her at ease, it would be Ruby. My little sister had a warmth and easiness about her that the rest of us seemed to be missing. Maybe it was because she was the youngest. More likely it was because she was the only girl. Whatever it was, she had a gift for making people feel welcome and wanted, and I hoped her magic would work to turn Danica Watson's sympathies toward my family's plight.

"Is she having a good time?" Miller took a seat next to me at one of the picnic tables.

"Who?" I tried to pretend like I hadn't been staring at Danica for a solid five minutes.

He fake coughed and mumbled into his hand at the same time. "Bullshit alert."

I landed a halfhearted punch to his rock-hard gut. "Cut it out. There's nothing going on there."

"Because there's nothing going on or because you're too chickenshit to take a chance?" Miller might be the youngest brother, but he was the best at reading everyone.

"Pfft." I blew out a breath and reached for the butter dish. "She's a consultant hired by the Stewarts. I'd have to be an idiot to get mixed up in that kind of shit."

Miller cocked his head and picked up a rib. "No one ever accused you of being a genius, bro."

"Not going to go there." I shook my head.

"Why not? There's clearly something going on between you. Even a five-year-old can see it."

"What?" If my nephew could sense something was happening, then I wasn't hiding my feelings nearly well enough.

"He said you must like Miss Danica because you teased her. Dude, it's classic kindergarten behavior. What did you do when you liked a girl in Mrs. Solomon's first grade class?"

I tried to remember that far back.

"You chased her around the playground at recess." Miller took another bite of his rib while I processed that nugget of info.

"What does that have to do with anything? Did you put

Jack up to this to try to piss me off?" That was a more believable reason.

Miller shook his head. He needed a haircut. Bad. "The kid takes after me. He can see things other folks can't."

"Maybe you should tell him to put a lid on that special talent. It's liable to piss off the wrong person someday."

"I'm just saying, if you like her and she likes you, where's the harm in that?" Miller gave me a goofy grin. A smudge of barbecue sauce sat on the corner of his lips, making him look like a typical twenty-five-year-old guy, not a single dad of a five-year-old.

"The harm is letting my guard down. What if Davis put her up to this? What if she's just trying to gather info on us to use against us?"

Miller rolled his eyes. "You've been listening to way too many true crime podcasts. What if she just happens to really like you? Have you thought about that?"

I glanced over at where Danica sat, sandwiched between Ruby and a few of my cousins on my mom's side. She met my gaze and offered a lopsided smile.

My pulse quickened like it always did when Danica was around. Maybe it was time to test Miller's theory.

I got up from the bench and grabbed my paper plate. "I'll be back in a few minutes."

"Where ya going?" Miller nudged his chin up, clearly expecting a response.

"I'm going to see about a girl," I muttered. If Davis was right—and I wasn't prepared to admit it yet—I might be shutting down a chance at something bigger than myself before it even had the opportunity to start blooming.

If he was wrong—well, I hoped like hell he wasn't, but if he was—then I'd let my family down for the second time in my life. That was a mistake I couldn't afford to make twice.

CHAPTER 18

COLE WALKED me to the spot where I'd left my car along the gravel drive. The sun had gone down, leaving the sky a gorgeous blend of purples and pinks. I'd enjoyed myself tonight. Much more than I thought I would, and a whole lot more than I should. The more I got to know the Bishop family, the more I liked them. The more I liked them, the less I wanted to come up with the kind of plan Davis Stewart was counting on.

We stopped at my car and Cole leaned up against the front while I fumbled with my keys.

"You locked your door?" he asked.

"Yeah, don't you always lock your car door?" My finger slipped as I pressed on the unlock button. Instead of the lock clicking open, the alarm pierced through the quietness of the night. Would I ever stop making a fool out of myself around this man?

"I can't remember the last time I locked a door, except for the door to the distillery." Cole cleared his throat. "Hey, I was wondering if you're planning on sticking around this weekend? If so, would you be up for going on a drive with me? There's something I'd love to show you."

"What do you have in mind?" I tilted my head, studying his features. The Roman nose, the sculpted jaw, the eyes that pulled at something deep down inside my soul.

"Something that will hopefully give you an idea of why the history of Devil's Dance is so important. Not just to me, but to everyone at the distillery, whether they realize it or not."

Could he be any more vague? Despite the lack of details, I was intrigued. "How long do you think it would take? Maybe we could go tomorrow afternoon and I could leave for home on Saturday morning instead."

"Shouldn't take more than a couple of hours." Cole steepled his fingers under his chin. "Though it's supposed to rain tomorrow. Might make it a little tricky getting to where we're going and back."

"You mean to tell me a guy who drives a truck like yours is afraid to put it into four-wheel drive?" I wasn't sure where that comment came from. Maybe it was the fear that this might be my last chance to spend a little time with him before the Stewarts crashed back onto the scene. Or maybe it was my need to find the heart of his story. The more I learned about the distillery, the more I recognized that the history was an integral part. Incorporating pieces of that into the plan I was creating for Davis would only make it better.

"I suppose we can go for it if you're sure you don't mind getting a little wet." The way he said it, I knew it was a call back to the time we'd spent together in the past. A shiver raced down my arms, pebbling my skin at the implication.

"I don't mind getting wet as long as you don't think it will be too hard." Two could play at the dangerous game he'd started.

One edge of his mouth quirked up. "Let's go for it then. I'll leave the office around three and swing by Jessie Jay's to pick up something we can take with us for dinner. I can stop back by the office to get you on the way out of town. Sound good?"

That sounded absolutely delightful, but I'd be damned before I told him that. "Sure, I think I can tolerate you for a few hours."

Cole tapped his fist on the roof of my car. "Oh, one more thing. Make sure you dress warm."

My body temperature had already heated a few degrees at the thought of going somewhere with him alone. "Sounds like a plan."

He started walking away, but turned after he'd crossed the driveway. "Oh, and Danica?"

My heart dove into my stomach. "Yes?"

"Plan on getting very wet."

THE NEXT DAY, I rode shotgun as Cole drove us out of Beaver Bluff. Rain pelted the windshield, making it difficult to see the road ahead. Thankfully, he'd been navigating these winding mountain roads his entire life, so I wasn't too worried.

"Where are we headed?" I wasn't a huge fan of surprises.

"I figured it would be good to show you where it all started, so you can get a better appreciation of what the families went through." He shifted his gaze from the road to briefly meet mine.

"I thought the building where the distillery sits was the original." That's what Davis told me during his quick overview of the history. He spent a whole lot more time describing his vision for the future than he did talking about how they'd gotten where they were.

"It is. But before they built the distillery, the families were neighbors. They started by running stills in the woods between their cabins." He reached out to adjust the defrost setting. "Are you warm enough?"

I nodded, snug as a bug in the oversized sweatshirt he'd given me to put on over the long-sleeved T-shirt I'd changed into. The clothes I'd brought with me consisted mainly of business casual attire, except for a few pairs of jeans and one or two long-sleeved shirts. I had a lightweight jacket, but Cole had laughed at that and tossed me a Devil's Dance hoodie instead. I tucked my hands into the pouch in front and breathed in the smoky scent that clung to the sweatshirt. It smelled just like him—a mixture of campfire smoke, whiskey, and musky earth.

"So we're going to a cabin in the woods?"

He turned off the highway onto a narrow, paved side road. "That's right. Assuming we make it up the mountain in the rain."

My muscles tensed. "A mountain?"

The grade of the road shifted, and the truck began to climb. "Don't worry. It's more like a big hill, but folks around here call almost everything that sticks up out of the ground a mountain. I haven't been up here in over a year, so hopefully we can find the trail."

"What kind of trail?"

"The truck will only get us so close. We'll have to hike in the last two miles on foot."

He was joking. Had to be trying to get a rise out of me. I wouldn't let him get to me, though. Deciding to play along, I let out a soft laugh. "Gotta love a good hike in the rain. Are you sure it's only two miles? I'd love to get in three or four, especially on a day like today."

"I can park farther down the hill if you'd rather take a longer walk." He sized me up, sliding his eyes over my face, searching for a crack in my facade.

"Let's play it by ear and see how we feel when we get there. By the way, when do you think that might be?" He'd never said how far we were going or how long it would take. I'd assumed it couldn't be too far away, but I'd learned that distance didn't mean much around here when I had to take the lay of the land into consideration. Traveling a dozen miles could take an hour or more, depending on how many switchbacks the road followed.

"We should be there before dark." Cole pointed to a small sign on the side of the road. "If you want to do something fun while you're in town, check out the wildlife rehabilitation site down there. They don't get many visitors, but they'll take you on a tour if you want. They specialize in beavers and my sister volunteers there in her free time."

I gazed out the window at the tree-lined, one-lane road leading off into the woods. "How does one rehabilitate a beaver?"

Cole bit back a grin. "It depends. Some of them are orphaned, so they just need a place to live until it's safe for them to strike out on their own. Others are injured by cars or boats or people knocking down their dams."

I'd never heard of such a thing. "Do they rehab many beavers? How many a year are we talking about?"

"They're a small group that's run by volunteers. Might only get a dozen or two during the course of a year."

I faced forward again. "Is that where Beaver Bluff got its name? Because there are so many beavers around here?"

Cole laughed, a deep, booming chuckle that made goosebumps pop up on my arms. "No. It used to be a trading post.

Beaver pelts were one of the most sought-after products back then."

"Huh. I guess you learn something new every day."

"The beaver population has actually been on the decline for the past fifty years. That's why the rehab facility started. Losing the beavers would change the environment. Plus, it wouldn't look good for Beaver Bluff to be beaverless, would it?"

"I suppose not."

"Are you ready for Davis and Harper to get back in town?" Cole asked, thankfully changing the subject from talking about beavers.

"Sure. It'll be nice to be able to share what I've done so far and make sure I'm on the right track." That was true, but I wasn't sharing all of my thoughts about their return. Once they got back, I wouldn't be able to arrange casual bump-ins with Cole in the hallways or linger over coffee when he was in the break room. I'd taken for granted all the spare moments that built up between us. I kept trying to remind myself it was for the best.

If we'd met under alternate circumstances, maybe things would be different. As it was, he'd always see me as a representation of the opposition, a reminder of his family's biggest rival.

Unless... a thought popped into my head, so ridiculous that I almost dismissed it outright. I stared out the window and tried to nudge it away, but it persisted.

What if I could somehow get them to reconcile their differences? Build a plan that would align the two sides and give them each the wiggle room they wanted to pursue their goals while still building the distillery together?

Wisps of an idea began to take shape in my mind. If I could

pull this off, maybe Cole and I could take the one-night stand we'd started with and see where it might lead.

He cleared his throat, drawing my attention back to the cozy interior of the truck cab. "We've gone as far as we can with the truck. Are you ready to take it the rest of the way on foot?"

CHAPTER 19
Cole

SHE THOUGHT I'd been joking about hiking the final distance to the cabin. I wished I was, especially with the light rain continuing to fall down on us. I'd handed her a water-proof poncho to pull on over her clothes when we got out of the truck. At least she'd stay dry, even if her shoes filled with mud.

"How's it going?" I called over my shoulder.

"Hanging in there. How much farther?"

It was hard to say since the dark clouds prevented me from seeing the landmarks I always looked for when I came out here. We'd been walking for a solid twenty minutes. It couldn't be that much farther up the hill. "Ten minutes, maybe?"

"Okay." Danica huffed out a breath. She was giving it her all and trying to keep up.

"Here." I reached back and grabbed her hand. "The last bit gets a little steep."

"Steep? What's this considered, level ground?" She laughed, but let me wrap my hand around hers.

"It's worth it, I promise." I glanced ahead, up the steep trail that led to the original Bishop cabin. This time of year, the trees had started budding and bright green leaves in every shape and size provided a canopy overhead. Pine trees mixed with the more common birch and beech. Even the air smelled different up here: fresher, cleaner, lighter.

The rain stopped falling, and I tilted my head back, trying to see if we'd reached a denser section of trees or if the rain was giving us a bit of a break.

"Did it stop raining?" Danica pushed the hood of the poncho back.

"I think so." I didn't want to let go of her hand, so I tried to shake the hood off my head. "You might get a peek at the view if the rain quits."

"What view?"

As the question entered the space between us, we reached the edge of the clearing where the cabin sat. It had been built into the hillside with a front porch that wrapped around to the side. Everything was just as I'd left it the last time I'd been up here. Warmth spread through my chest at the sight, and I rubbed my palm over my heart. This was where it all started… where my ancestors ran their first batch of whiskey through a homemade still and paved the way for generations to follow.

"Come here and I'll show you." I held her hand as we closed the distance between us and the cabin. A leaning fence sat off to the right, failing to protect a garden that had bolted decades ago. Life was resilient up here in the mountains, and even now I could see the first signs of asparagus peeking out of the ground.

Danica followed me up the stone steps carved into the hillside and onto the wide porch. "This is where your family settled when they first came here? How did they ever find this place?"

"The mines. A lot of folks worked the gem mines that were dug into these hills. That's where the families met." I remembered that much from the stories my great-grandad used to tell me while he sat out on this porch, smoked his pipe, and carved pieces of scrap wood with his pocket knife.

"How did they get supplies up here?"

"They rode to town on mules or horses if they were lucky enough to have them. It's been years since anyone's lived up here. My granddad was the last, and he moved down the mountain when he was just a kid." I set down the soft-sided cooler I'd lugged up the hill with us. "Here's what I wanted to show you."

Danica followed me around to the side of the cabin where a break in the treetops left the valley below exposed. She sucked in a breath. "Oh."

"Beautiful, isn't it?" I turned my gaze from the valley to study her reaction. Her eyes were wide, her lips curved up in a smile.

"It's stunning."

I wanted to tell her that looking at her put the view of the valley to shame, but I was above cheesy lines. Not so far above that I didn't think about it, though. Seeing her reaction—the same mixture of wonder and awe that always washed over me every time I came up here—made me wish things were different between us. That she wasn't an agent of change for my most bitter rival.

If I were looking for a woman in my life—which I wasn't—Danica would check off every box on the list. She was smart, had a wicked sense of humor, and was incredibly down to earth, especially when talking to some of the folks who'd lived in Beaver Bluff their entire lives.

I wanted to get to know her better, but it would be a worthless cause. What was the point when she'd be leaving soon? It's not like I would ever move away from Beaver Bluff, and as kind as she'd been to the locals, she didn't strike me as a woman who wanted to live the rest of her life in a one-stop-light town.

"Thanks for bringing me up here." She squeezed my hand before letting it go. "I can see why this place is so special to you."

"Can you?" I looked out over the trees, imagining how it felt for my grandad to take in this view every morning when he got out of bed, before he trekked down the mountain to attend school.

"Yes." She turned her head, taking in the full panoramic view. "This is part of your history."

"It's part of the distillery's history." This was my chance to get her to see how important the history was. "This is where our people came from. They worked the fields in the holler right over there,"—I pointed to the left of the trail we'd just come up—"and hid their stills in the woods while they perfected their mash bills."

"I get it, and I see what you're trying to do. The history of Devil's Dance is important, but so is the future."

She thought she understood, but she was missing a very important point. "Don't you see? There is no future if we don't honor the past. Davis wants to make a quick buck on some trends. I want to build on what's brought us this far. Every time someone takes a sip of a Devil's Dance whiskey, they connect with history. The corn in our mash bill was grown within fifty miles of the distillery. The oak trees the barrels are made from were cut down right here in Tennessee. The yeast we use in the fermentation process has been passed down from generation to generation."

"So when people take a sip of Devil's Dance, they're liter-ally drinking history." She cocked her head to the side. "That could make a pretty compelling marketing narrative."

The tightness I'd been carrying around in my chest since

the day Davis introduced her in the conference room eased. "Yes. That's what I've been trying to tell you."

Danica lifted her head and met my gaze. "I think I'm finally starting to listen."

The urge to sweep her up in my arms and swing her around almost got the best of me. Instead, I gestured to the steps. "How about something to eat before we head back?"

"Don't I get to see the inside of the cabin?" She got to her tiptoes and tried peering in through the glass.

"I don't have the key. We keep it locked to prevent squatters from setting up, especially since nobody gets up here much." I reached for the cooler. "There are pictures of the inside at the office. I'd be more than happy to share them with you when you come back next week."

"I suppose that will have to do, then." She lowered herself to sit on the porch and let her legs hang over the edge.

"Here, I got smoked brisket sandwiches with all the fixings." I unzipped the cooler to start setting out the food.

Danica reached in to help, and her fingers brushed against mine. That same heat I always felt around her sparked in my belly. What was it about her that made me want to ravage her mouth with mine? I tamped it down and focused on setting out containers of potato salad and coleslaw.

"This looks delicious." She unwrapped a sandwich.

"Even the coleslaw?" I joked.

"You're never going to let me live that down, are you?" She clucked her tongue against her teeth as she shook her head. "Especially the coleslaw."

I let out a laugh, then sat down next to her, letting the cooler act as a buffer between us. We ate in silence, enjoying the sounds of nature surrounding us. The tat-a-tat-tat of a woodpecker drifted down from the trees over-head. Wind rustled through the leaves and the plop-plop-

plop of raindrops splashed to the ground. Coming up here always relaxed me. No matter what was going on at the bottom of the mountain, once I left the car and trekked through the woods, I seemed to shed it like a too-warm winter coat.

A quick glance at Danica made me think she felt the same. She had a lightness about her. I could tell by the carefree way she let her feet swing off the edge of the porch, and I could see it in the ease of her shoulders.

"It's so peaceful." She balled up the wrapper from her sandwich and tossed it back in the cooler. "I'm surprised you don't come up here more often."

"I would if I had the time." I slid a forkful of potato salad into my mouth, finishing off the last of it.

"You've got to make time to do the things that are impor-tant." Danica got to her feet and walked to the opposite edge of the porch.

"Are you giving me advice you follow yourself?" I'd seen how hard she worked. Over the past two weeks, she was often the last one leaving the office.

She shed the poncho and hung it on a nail sticking out of a porch post. "I'm going to start following that advice."

"Oh yeah, when?" I zipped up the cooler, then walked over to where she stood.

"It's complicated. You know how it is. If I want to build up my business, I've got to put in the hours. I'm investing time and energy now so I can get to a point where I can take it easier later down the road."

"Sounds like a plan." I set my hand on the post a few inches above hers. "What made you decide to start your own business?"

The lightness in her eyes faded, and I cursed myself for unintentionally bringing up what might be a sore subject.

"I had some issues at my last job." One shoulder lifted, like she wanted to shrug it off.

"What kind of issues?"

She gazed out at the trees surrounding us while she took in a deep breath. "Let's just say my boss—ex-boss—and I had a difference in opinion on what my job description entailed."

The back of my neck prickled. I sure as hell hoped I was wrong about the thoughts crowding into my head. "What do you mean?"

"We traveled to meet with a client together and he got pissed when I wasn't willing to share more than a cab with him."

"He fired you for not sleeping with him?" My vision clouded at the edges.

"Basically." She turned toward me, regret in her eyes. "I can't believe I just told you that. You can't tell anyone. Promise?"

My hands clenched into fists. I wanted to hit something. Make that someone.

"Cole?" Danica's hand landed on my arm. "Please?"

"Did you go to HR? Report him to the cops?" I hated that there were assholes out there like her ex-boss who got away with shit like that.

"It was my word against his. We didn't get the job, so he made up some story about how I'd botched the presentation. He said it would cause me more damage to fight it than to let it go." She tilted her chin up, a look of resignation clouding her gorgeous face. "I thought about it and realized he was right. Unless I was willing to risk my entire reputation, it was easier to walk away."

"That's not fair." I reached for her shoulder, then thought better of it in light of what she'd just revealed. My hand hung in the air between us, awkward as fuck.

"Who said things were always fair?" She offered a sad smile.

I vowed in that moment that I'd find the douchebag who'd dimmed the light in her eyes and make him pay for his actions. "For the record, you shouldn't have to put up with crap like that."

"For the record, thanks for saying that. I wish more guys were like you." Her eyelashes fluttered against her cheeks as she glanced up at me and looked away.

I basked in the warmth of the compliment for a few moments before doubt leached in. She wouldn't feel that way if she knew Vaughn wanted me to try to get info from her.

Even though the days were growing longer, the sun had started its descent. "We probably ought to head back before we lose the light."

Danica put her hand on my forearm. "Thanks for bringing me here."

"You're welcome." I meant it. Sharing this piece of the distillery history—my history—might change the way she viewed things. I could tell by the look in her eyes the trip had been worthwhile. "Hey, there's something else I'd love to show you before we head back if you're up for it?"

"My muscles are screaming at me, and I'm already covered in mud. Why not?" She shrugged as she hopped off the steps onto the grass below.

"Great." I glanced at the sliver of blue sky I could see through a break in the treetops. We should still have enough time to make it there and back to the truck before it got too dark. "Right this way."

CHAPTER 20

Danica

"ARE WE THERE YET?" I teased. I'd been following Cole's lead through the woods for the past ten minutes. I'd never get tired of the view. Watching him ease through the woods, his jeans cupping the curve of his ass, his shirt straining over his broad shoulders, was a sight I could gaze at for days.

"Just up ahead." He pushed forward, holding branches back so I could pass behind him without getting slapped in the face.

The sound of running water played over the crunch of twigs underneath our feet. Cole stopped in front of me, and I bumped into his backside.

"Careful there." He turned back and took my hand to pull me next to him. "This is what I wanted to show you."

Water flowed over the rocks, bubbling up in a narrow stream that ran through the woods.

"It's the cleanest, clearest spring water you'll ever find." He knelt next to the bank, scooped up a handful of water, then tilted it into his mouth. "Want to try it?"

I squinted at the crystal-clear water. "How do you know it's not full of bacteria?"

"We have it tested every so often. The source is just a few feet away. If you were drinking from the bottom of the mountain, you'd be right to be worried, but not all the way up here." He drank another handful.

"Sure, I'm game." I squatted next to him and reached toward the water.

Cole's hand landed on my shoulder, preventing me from tumbling into the stream. "Can I help you with that?"

"Please." I sat back on my heels while he touched the edge of his palm to my lips. He was right. The water was ice-cold and more refreshing than any bottled spring water I'd ever tried.

"What do you think?"

"I think you should bottle this and sell it. Wouldn't it be easier than waiting four years on a barrel of whiskey?"

His warm laugh sent heat coursing through my veins. "Don't think Vaughn hasn't thought about it. There's not enough here to justify any kind of commercial operation. Besides, it would ruin the ambience of this place if we set a bunch of machinery up here, don't you think?"

He was right. I'd been finding he usually was right about most things. The realization was unnerving, and stirred up a lot of respect for the man in front of me.

"Want some more?"

I nodded. "Yes, please."

He bent toward the stream again and scooped up more water. "I should have brought our water bottles over to fill them up for the drive back."

"That's okay. Maybe we can do that next time." I gulped down the water he offered, surprised at myself for making that suggestion. There wouldn't be a next time for me. "What I meant was maybe you can do that next time you come up."

He held my gaze for a long beat. "I like your idea better."

Before I had a chance to come up with an appropriate response, the skies opened above us. Fat, angry raindrops pelted my head, furiously falling from the dark clouds, making me wish I'd thought to grab my poncho.

"Let's get back to the cabin." Cole had to shout over the rumble of thunder. He held out his hand, and I grabbed hold.

The narrow trail we'd followed on the way to the stream disappeared thanks to the wind and rain coming at us from every direction. Cole practically pulled me through the woods until we finally reached the cabin clearing. He led me onto the porch, where we could catch a break from the rain.

"What now?" I couldn't see anything beyond the edge of the clearing and wasn't eager to trek the distance back to the truck in the cold downpour. "How long do you think this is going to last?"

Cole gazed out at the storm. "The radar made it look like the worst of it was going to be north of us and not hit hard until later on tonight."

"Do you have service?" I'd pulled out my phone but didn't have a single bar.

"It's worthless up here." He put his hands to his eyes and peered in the window of the cabin.

I wrapped my arms around my middle to prevent myself from shivering. The temperature was already cooler this high up and thanks to the rain and being sopping wet, my teeth started to chatter.

"Looks like our options are fairly limited under the circumstances." Cole faced me, his mouth set in a serious line.

"We have options? That's good, right?" My attempt at humor fell flat.

"I'm not sure you're going to like either one."

"Tell me what you've got." I filled my lungs and tried to put on a brave face while I waited for his response.

He paced the length of the porch while the rain beat a rapid staccato on the tin roof over our heads. "Option one is we head for the truck as fast as we can and try to get the hell out of here. The only problem is that the trail gets pretty muddy with a hard rain, so we might end up getting stuck farther down the hill."

I shook my head, not liking the sound of that at all. "Or?"

"Or we hunker down here and ride out the storm." He turned toward the door of the cabin.

My heart skipped a few beats, then picked up the pace, sending blood whooshing through my ears. Ride out the storm? The two of us? Together? Here? "How long do you think that might be?"

He wrapped his hand around the doorknob and jiggled it. "Hard to say, but it might be overnight. I don't know about you, but it's probably not the wisest decision to go traipsing down the side of a mountain in the rain and,"—he lifted his head and his eyes drilled into mine—"in the dark."

Shivers zipped up and down my limbs. This situation sounded like the start of a horror movie plot I'd seen a dozen times. The one where a couple gets trapped in the woods at some abandoned cabin. When the hero goes outside to investigate a strange sound, some axe-wielding psychopath offs him, then stalks the heroine through the woods until she meets with an untimely gruesome death of her own.

"You okay?" Cole asked.

No, I wasn't okay. How could I be okay when both of us were going to be dead before morning? I bit the inside of my cheek and tried to force myself to calm down.

"Sure."

"That doesn't sound too convincing." Cole stepped away from the door and closer to where I stood by the edge of the porch. "What would you rather do, head for the truck or hunker?"

I shivered, more due to the scenes from every horror movie I'd ever seen racing through my head than from the cold. "Neither option sounds appealing to me. You pick."

Cole braced a hand on the wooden post where I'd hung my poncho. "I'd rather be stuck here where we can get out of the rain and dry off than be trapped in the truck on the side of the mountain."

Logically, that made sense. But the thought of spending another night with him had me on edge and not in a bad way. "Okay, then. Are we going to spend the night on the porch?"

"Stay here. I'm going to walk around and see if there's a way to get inside." He stepped off the porch and immediately disappeared around the corner of the cabin.

I counted to ten, then twenty, telling myself if he wasn't back by the time I got to one hundred, I'd go after him. Darkness had settled around the cabin, and I huddled against the outside wall, trying to shield myself from the blowing rain.

Something rattled the door, and I glanced over to see Cole pull it wide.

"Come on in. Let's get you out of the cold."

I grabbed the handle of the cooler and rushed through the open doorway. A musty smell hit me as soon as I stepped inside. My grandmother's attic smelled the same way—like a time capsule that had been undisturbed for too long to count. It was too dark to make out my surroundings, but I could feel the heat rolling off Cole's body behind me.

A narrow beam of light cut through the darkness and focused on the floor in front of me. "Here, my phone's got a little battery left."

I handed over the cooler, and he moved ahead of me to set

it down. Cole lit a match, then held it to a lantern sitting in the middle of a bare wooden table.

The light from the lantern allowed me to take a better look at the space. The cabin consisted of one room. A bed sat up against the corner farthest from the door and a huge pot-bellied stove took up the corner across from it. Lightning flashed outside, and the rapid beat of raindrops on the roof intensified. The window across the room was missing a pane of glass. That must have been how he'd gotten inside.

"I'm going to see if there's any dry wood over by the stove so we can start a fire." Cole took the lantern with him and I watched it sway back and forth until he set it down on top of the stove.

I peeled the sopping wet sweatshirt over my head and hung it over the back of a chair. I'd give just about anything to get out of these wet clothes. Twigs snapped and the hinges on the stove creaked as Cole got to work building a base for a fire. With no idea of how to help, I pulled a chair away from the table and took a seat. At least we had a roof over our heads. I needed to focus on the good in the situation instead of expecting the worst to happen.

"You okay over there?" Cole asked. He'd managed to get a small fire going in the belly of the stove and the flames cast a warm glow across his face.

"Yeah. Can I do anything to help?"

"If you want to move over here, it should be warmer." He brought the lantern closer so I could find my way over to the stove.

I rubbed my hands together, chasing the chill from my fingertips. "It's too bad we don't have a blanket or something. You've got to be freezing, too."

"Actually…" Cole fumbled with the lid of a trunk before flipping it open. "I've been meaning to clean out the rest of the stuff my granddad left up here. He redid the inside of the cabin before he died. I think he expected to come up here in the summers for a week or two at a time. He left some quilts my grandmother made in the cedar chest here at the foot of the bed."

I grabbed the soft quilt Cole handed me. "Thank you."

"You're welcome. I don't want to sound too forward, but if you want to take off your wet things, we could set them in front of the fire and give them a chance to dry."

Warmth traveled the length of my body, pooling at my core. "Are you suggesting we both get naked?"

He answered by pulling his shirt over his head and draping it over the chair. "You're welcome to do what you want, but I'm going to see if I can warm myself up by the fire."

I tried to focus my attention on the flickering flames licking at the open door of the stove, but the sound of Cole's zipper sliding down his jeans provided too much of a distraction. Huddled under the quilt, I hoped he couldn't see me. If he could, he might notice the way my gaze traced the path of his hands as he moved his jeans over his hips. He had his backside to me and the light from the fire danced along the curves of his ass. The same ass I'd gripped with both hands a few weeks ago while I begged him to pound into me harder and harder.

Heat pulsed through my veins, making my blood whoosh through my ears. The sound drowned out the staccato beat from the rain.

Cole had kicked off his muddy shoes and left them on the porch. Now he lifted a leg, pulling it free from his jeans. His cock hung down long enough that I could catch a glimpse of it between his legs from behind.

My breath hooked in my chest. Just because we were stuck here overnight, just the two of us alone with nothing to do but to wait out the storm, didn't mean we had a pass to repeat our night at the hotel.

He stepped out of the other pant leg, hopping around on one foot. His cock bobbed up and down as he tried to free his leg. He looked like a one-legged kangaroo. A very well-hung, one-legged kangaroo. I held onto the hope that trying to inject some humor into the situation might chill the heat pooling between my legs.

"You need some help?" I asked, desperately hoping he'd say no, so I didn't have to tempt myself by touching him. Even as I sat there doing nothing, his cock hardened. I bit my lip and fought off memories of how it felt to slide my hands up and down his shaft... how his cock had thickened in my palm... how it had filled me so completely when he...

"I've got it."

Thank goodness. I closed my eyes for a moment to try to regain my composure.

He must not have "got it" because he toppled over.

Onto me.

Naked.

CHAPTER 21

Cole

SHIT. I knew I wasn't going to make it to the edge of the table before falling over, but I hadn't planned on taking Danica down with me.

"I'm sorry." My fingers fumbled to release my foot from the jeans holding it captive. Finally, the wet denim gave up its grip, and I kicked them away. "Are you okay?"

She'd fallen sideways when I plowed into her. I reached out and pulled her upright, putting her at eye level to my raging hard-on. Double shit. I turned away and reached for another quilt, trying to wrap it around my hips before she got a face full of my cock.

Her laughter rang through the cabin and she wheezed in a breath. "I'm sorry, that was priceless."

"Which part? The bit where I tripped over myself trying to take my pants off or the part where I fell onto you buck naked?" I squatted down next to her. At least she was laughing about it instead of grabbing the fire poker and threatening to rip a new hole in my anatomy.

"All of it. Your face when you fell…" She continued to gasp for air.

"I'm glad you find me so amusing."

"I'm sorry." She reached over, smoothing her hand along my cheek. "I'm not laughing at you."

I turned into her touch. It had been too long since I'd felt it.

She slid her hand along my jaw. "I was laughing with you, Cole."

"Let's see you try to pull off your wet jeans on one leg," I challenged.

"Is that another poor attempt at trying to get me to take off my clothes?" Her voice dipped low, taking on a rough, sexy tone that filled my head with visions of the last time we'd been naked together.

My cock grew harder and thicker as I remembered what it felt like to run my tongue over her sweet skin and taste her lips. "Will it work?"

She shifted closer, cupping both of my cheeks with her palms. "When we hooked up before, I didn't know who you were."

"Does that change things now that you know?" I put my hands on hers and drew them to my lips. I kissed one, then the other while the quilt I'd wrapped around my waist fell loose.

"I don't know. Should it?" The growing fire reflected in her eyes. She was unsure. I could tell by the way her chest rose and fell in uneven breaths.

Wanting to offer reassurance, I pressed a kiss to her palm. "I didn't know who you were, either."

"Does it change things now that you know?" Her voice went soft, like a whisper.

"Now that I've gotten to know you, it's only made me want you more." It was true. The words came out raw and honest. I'd tried to fight it, tried to tell myself that I couldn't have feelings for a woman who had the power to ruin me.

It didn't matter.

My heart didn't give a flying fuck that she was aligned with Davis or that she'd been tasked with taking the business in the wrong direction.

All that mattered was the way she made me feel inside. When I was with her, I felt like a better man. Like I could transcend the box I'd stuffed myself in and be the kind of man she needed me to be. I'd spent most of my adult life trying to make up for the sins of my past. With Danica, I didn't feel like I was starting from less than zero. I didn't know how to put all of those feelings into words, so I didn't even try.

"The way I see it, we've got two options on how we can spend the next twelve or so hours."

"You and your options again… I can't wait to hear my choices." The sass in her eyes issued a challenge. "Please, continue."

I bit back a smirk. "Option one is you get out of those wet clothes and wrapped in a few quilts on the bed so you can get warm. I'll make up a spot on the floor by the fire and we both try to get some sleep until the rain stops and it's light enough to get down the mountain."

"What's option two?" She nestled her cheek against my palm.

The scent of coconut invaded my senses, making me hope like hell that she'd choose option two. "Option two is we get you out of those wet clothes, and I warm you up myself."

"You sure you're up for that?" Her eyes widened with mock concern.

"If you want to find out exactly how up for that I am, just keep moving your hand lower, sweetheart." I wasn't going to get a chance like this again. This might be the last time Danica and I would be alone before she moved back to Knoxville for good. I didn't want to let it go by without one last opportunity to hold her in my arms.

Fate had stranded us on the side of the mountain. It was up to me to find out whether there was more between us than the night we'd already shared.

Danica's finger traced a line down my jaw. She paused at the pulse point on my neck. "Your heart's beating so fast."

"Is yours?" I wanted to know, to see if she was as affected as I was by being so close together.

She let the quilt fall loose around her shoulders. "Find out for yourself."

Heat raced through me, making a beeline to my cock. "Are you sure?"

I needed to know she was all in. The first time we hooked up, we weren't aware of the consequences. Now that we knew each other and where we fit into the future of the distillery, the stakes were so much higher. If Davis found out about this, he'd assume her loyalty had been compromised and fire her on the spot. I didn't want to be responsible for ruining her chance to strike out on her own.

Selfishly, I also didn't want to have to bring a new marketing consultant up to speed and educate him or her about the history of the distillery. Danica seemed like she was finally willing to listen to me. I could tell she understood the importance of tradition, of history. If we got caught, she'd be gone, and I'd lose all the ground I'd covered by having to start over with a new adversary.

"Are you sure?" Her finger trailed over my shoulder and down my biceps.

I couldn't keep my hands off her. Not when she was this close. Not when she skimmed her finger over my skin. Not when she looked at me with a heat in her eyes that rivaled my own.

"I'm sure I want you, but I'm not sure what that means for tomorrow." If she told me to stop now, I still could. It would be hard as hell, and I'd probably have blue balls for days, but I still possessed a shred of control.

"Do we have to think about tomorrow right now?" Her hand reached my chest, and she smoothed her palm over my pecs.

The idea of not thinking about what would happen beyond tonight was tempting enough to make me slide my hands down her arms and brush the sides of her breasts with my thumbs. Her nipples hardened and my cock throbbed. I ached to taste her, to take one of those pebbled buds in my mouth until she ground her thick hips against me.

"What do you say, Danica? Should I grab you another quilt and tuck you into bed?" I waited, my hands still. The pads of my thumbs settled on the curves of her breasts.

"Only if you're coming with me." Her hand closed around my cock.

I hissed in a breath at her touch and let it out slowly as she ran her thumb over my tip. "I'll come."

"Good. I'm counting on it." She leaned into me, pressing her lips to mine.

I pulled her closer, settling her on my lap while I swept my tongue into her mouth. She was hot and needy, arching into me and pushing her tits into my chest while her tongue slid against mine.

Her hand went to my shoulder. I tensed as her palm skimmed over the skin on my back. I rarely took my shirt off unless I was alone. Danica hadn't seen my scars. The physical pain had faded years ago, but they were a constant reminder of my failure. Her hand paused, and I could sense the questions forming in her mind.

I should have left my shirt on, soaked and all. It would have been better than getting cock blocked by the evidence of a bad decision that had haunted me most of my life. I was about to pull away, about to put a stop to what was happening between us, when her hand settled on my scarred skin and she deepened the kiss.

Any hesitation I'd been harboring vanished.

I was in.

All in.

Tomorrow was a whole day away. I didn't have the bandwidth to spare a thought for something that far in the future when everything I wanted, everything I needed, was right here, right now.

The first time we'd been together, we didn't know anything about each other. It was hot. A night of phenomenal sex that left me fully sated with no expectations.

But now that I'd gotten to know her—beyond the heart-shaped face and hourglass curves—everything between us took on meaning. She wasn't just some hot chick from the bar. She was the woman who'd been brave enough to join my softball team, daring enough to follow me up the side of a mountain, trusting enough to open herself up to me.

She climbed off my lap and peeled her wet clothes away from her skin. I held back while she draped them over the back of the chair by the stove. Then she climbed back onto my lap and straightened her legs, sandwiching my waist between her thighs. I put one hand under her ass, kneading her butt cheek while she wrapped her arms around my neck.

The little moans coming from the back of her throat spurred me on. Did she have any idea how fucking sexy she was? Firelight bathed her skin, casting shadows on the wall of the two of us joined together. As we moved against each other, the shadows merged, and I couldn't tell where my body ended and hers began.

"You feel so good, Cole." She slid her mouth away from

mine, kissing a trail across the scruff on my cheeks until she nipped at my earlobe with her teeth.

"Not as good as I'm going to make you feel, baby." I slipped my other hand underneath her, propping her up on my legs so I could stroke through her heat.

"Mmm. There. Right there." Her hips tilted. "Just like that."

Her teeth scraped my ear as she dug her nails into my shoulders. If she wanted rough, I'd give it to her. I'd give her whatever she needed. With the glow from the fire dancing over her skin, she moved, grinding against my hand.

"What do you want, gorgeous girl? Tell me and I'll do it."

"You. I want you inside me."

She was ready. Hot and slick and wet for me. My cock throbbed with need as I notched the tip at her entrance. Fuck. No condom.

Her tits bounced against my chest as she settled on my lap. "It's okay. I'm on the pill and haven't been with anyone in over a year."

I didn't want to admit how long it had been since I'd let a woman get this close. "You're sure?"

"Are you safe?" She whispered against my ear.

Figuring by "safe" she meant clean, I growled out, "Yes."

She nodded. "I trust you, Cole."

My heart ripped in two as I thrust inside her. I didn't deserve her trust, but I couldn't hold back. Sinking into her slick heat, I cursed myself for not being able to resist. I'd always thought of myself as having strong willpower.

With Danica, I was defenseless.

CHAPTER 22

THE FIRST TIME had been hot and sexy and full of fun. The way Cole handled my body now was rougher, more raw, utterly primal.

And I loved it.

He rutted into me like a man possessed, his big hands clamped down on either side of my waist, lifting me up then bringing me down hard onto his cock. The walls of my sex stretched around him. I clenched my muscles together as he pulled out, wanting to make him feel good.

"That's it, baby," he mumbled against my mouth in between kisses.

My senses overloaded as my lungs filled with his musky scent. He tasted like whiskey even though he hadn't had a drop. His touch made my whole body tense, like a tree blowing in the wind that could only bend so far before it snapped. I ran my fingers through the short hair at the nape of his neck, pulling him closer, wanting to swallow him whole.

He lowered his head to my neck, scraping the scruff on his cheeks over my skin. I urged him on, pressing my chest into his. He licked along the curve of my breast. I arched my back, pushing my boobs up. My sole purpose in life zeroed in on wanting to feel his hot mouth on my nipple.

His tongue swirled around it, teasing my nipple into a hard, aching bundle of nerves. When I didn't think I could take another second, he nipped at it, scraping his teeth lightly over my puckered skin. I almost came undone around him, but he pulled back right before I reached the edge.

"Not yet, gorgeous." He moved to my other breast, lavishing the same level of attention.

I didn't recognize the needy, desperate woman I'd become. My body burned for him, ached for him. I would do anything to feel his lips on my skin and his cock driving deep inside me.

Cole dipped his head lower, tracing a path with his tongue along the cleft between my breasts. "You taste so sweet. I can't get enough of you."

The combination of his voice, his words, his scent, and his touch drove me to the edge. I clenched around him, trying so hard to get there on my own. It was right there… I could feel it building. Squeezing my eyes closed, I tried to push myself closer. I was on the verge of a cliff and wanted to hurl myself over the edge. So close, so ready, so needy.

"Come for me, Danica," Cole growled the words. The woman inside, the one he'd summoned, took over.

I let go, stopped trying to force it. My body took command, hurtling me so far over the edge I went spiraling into a freefall. I held onto Cole's big, broad shoulders like my life depended on it.

In a way, it did.

Just when I thought I'd crash, I stopped falling and began to soar as liquid heat flowed through my limbs. Every nerve ending I possessed came online. My orgasm started as a faint spark, so small that I wasn't sure it was even there, like the first strike of metal against flint before it caught fire. Cole coaxed the spark into a flame when he shifted me onto his lap. The new angle stroked something deep inside. The flame burned into a legitimate fire.

"That's it, doll. Just like that." Cole thrust, harder each time, driving deeper, connecting with my core.

I wanted more. Leaning back, I put one hand behind me, giving me more leverage. Cole moved his hand to my back and lowered me down to the bed. He hovered over me, his gaze snapped to mine. I spread my legs, shamelessly offering him everything I had.

He drilled into me, his forehead creased with concentration. My hips shifted up, meeting his thrusts with my own until I couldn't feel my legs, couldn't feel my breath, couldn't feel my own heartbeat.

The only thing I could feel radiated out from the spot where we connected.

My orgasm rolled over me like a freight train. All I could do was grab his shoulders and hold on, hoping it didn't rip me to pieces. Deep pulses thrummed through me as my entire body tightened. Cole's arm went under my back, holding me against his chest. I wasn't sure who came first. My release rocketed through me at the same time he slowed, groaning out his release, his hips continuing to thrust as he spilled into me.

We held eye contact, the fire in his gaze lighting up my soul as I watched him give in. The smoldering darkness gave way to something softer—a raw vulnerability I hadn't seen in him before. I wanted to look away at the same time I wanted to drown in his gaze. Seeing him so open, so exposed, scared me. I wasn't sure I wanted that kind of power over him.

I told myself to not be such a scaredy cat. That look in Cole's eyes was what I'd been missing in my life. It spoke of trust, promised a kind of happiness I'd never known. It also scared the crap out of me. This man was everything I'd ever wanted, everything I'd dreamed about, everything I never thought existed.

Now he was here, hovering over me, handling me like a fragile porcelain doll, lowering my hips to the bed gently, and gazing at me with a look in his eyes that spoke of happily ever afters.

I didn't want to overthink things, didn't want to hold back, didn't want to turn away because I was afraid.

I gazed up at him, letting go of the worries that had been holding me back.

"You look so beautiful right now." He lowered himself next to me, pulling me onto his chest, his cock still nestled inside me. "You okay?"

Okay didn't begin to describe how I felt. I racked what part of my mind hadn't been blown in the past few minutes for the right words to describe the mixture of emotions and sensations that swirled around inside.

"Yeah, I'm okay…um…better than okay. You?"

He grazed the small of my back with his fingers. "I'm better than okay, too."

My heart warmed at the reassurance. Seemed both of us had been caught off guard by the intensity of what had just happened between us. We laid there, lost to our own thoughts for what felt like hours, but couldn't have been more than a few minutes. I didn't want to move, didn't want to lose the connection.

"I should probably toss another log on the fire before it goes out." Cole's fingers stilled on my back. "Do you need anything?"

Besides wrapping myself up in his arms and never having to leave this magical place we'd carved out for ourselves? I shook my head against his chest. "I'm good."

"I hate to have to do this,"—he gently rolled me to the side and pulled back—"but I don't think I can carry you over to the stove with me."

Immediately, I missed the feel of his chest underneath me, the weight of his cock buried between my legs. I hated feeling needy, hated having to rely on someone else for anything, so I tried to shake off the intense craving I had for his return.

The fire had died down to an orange glow, but I could still make out the curve of his ass as he covered the short distance to the pot-bellied stove. I propped my head on my hand and rolled onto my side to enjoy the view.

He came back to the bed, stopping to grab his discarded shirt on the way. "Roll over and I'll clean you up a little."

I didn't mind the evidence of his release that covered my inner thighs, but I was eager for his touch, so I rolled onto my back and reached for him.

He used the hem of his shirt like a washcloth, gently wiping my legs clean. "I didn't realize what I mess I made."

"It's okay."

"Next time I'll be better prepared." He held my gaze as the words left his mouth, like he wanted to gauge my reaction to the mention of a possible future.

I swallowed the bait, hook, line, and sinker. "Next time?"

Satisfied he'd done his best on me, he ran the shirt over himself. "I'm going to be honest with you, Danica. That was pretty fucking awesome. I don't care if I have to drive to Knoxville several times a month. I want to see you again."

I was a talker who wasn't rendered speechless very often, but the look in Cole's eyes, the determined set of his mouth, the unapologetic way he told me what he wanted... The combination made my heart stutter to an awkward stop. He wanted to see me... again.

"What about Davis?" My voice came out soft and timid, like I was afraid if I reminded him of what was at stake, he'd suddenly remember there were bigger issues at play. That he'd snap out of the post-coital haze we'd both fallen into and realize that there was no chance of a future for us.

At least not where we both ended up with everything we needed.

"Fuck Davis." He let the shirt fall out of his hand before climbing back onto the bed. His heavy body created an indentation in the mattress, and I unintentionally rolled toward him.

"You don't really mean that…"

"Don't I?" He bent his elbow and rested his head on his arm. Then he slid his other hand under me, encouraging me to resume my cheek to chest position and nestle against him. "Come here."

Draping myself over Cole—the heat radiating off his body keeping me warm—was quickly becoming my favorite position. But still, I couldn't take any of this for granted. We'd carved out a sliver of time to be together. We couldn't expect to keep this up once we got back to real life. Could we?

I didn't want to let thoughts of real life burst the bubble where we existed. Not yet. Not while we still had all night to spend in each other's arms.

I was curious about the scars I'd felt on Cole's back and wanted to ask about them. Now, while we were both still feeling lazy and sated, might be the best time for him to open up. I didn't want to push, though. If he wanted to tell me about them, he would. "Will you tell me about the scars I felt on your back?"

His chest rose and fell under my cheek as he filled his lungs with a long, slow breath. I'd gone too far, maybe even broken the spell wrapped around us. I was about to tell him to forget it when he brushed his hand over my hair and pressed a kiss to my temple.

"They're from a fire."

My stomach dropped. I'd figured as much, but hearing the pain in his voice made me ache for him. "I'm sorry you went through that."

"It was my fault." His big hand continued to smooth over my hair. "I was out in the woods with my great-granddad. Not far from here, actually."

"What happened?"

He didn't say anything for so long that I thought he wasn't going to answer. Then he cleared his throat. "My great-grandpa came across a bunch of old pictures here at the cabin when they were cleaning it out. He knew how much I loved history, so he offered to show them to me. He'd never given up on the old ways, even though no one had lived up here for years. So we were sitting out in the woods where he'd set up an old-style still."

"Like the ones in the pictures in the conference room?" I'd glanced over the black-and-white framed photos, amazed that Cole's family had ever made a living making whiskey out of the metal contraptions they'd hidden out in the woods.

"Yeah, just like those." He tugged the quilt up higher. "He had to run back to the cabin to grab something, so he left me there looking through the pictures."

"How old were you?"

"Eight. It was three days before our ninth birthday."

I tried to imagine being left in the woods all alone at eight years old. A shiver rolled over my skin. Cole chased the goose-bumps from my arm by pulling me closer.

"We were up here all the time back then. Vaughn and I spent every moment we could out in the woods, fishing in the stream, and enjoying the freedom. I was supposed to be watching the still instead of poring over pictures. It caught fire."

I tensed, afraid if I interrupted, he wouldn't continue.

"I tried to put it out, but I panicked. Instead of using the fire extinguisher he always had lying around, I tried to smother it with a blanket. The blanket caught fire and it spread. By the time I realized it was out of control, it was too late. The whole still blew up right in front of me."

"Oh my gosh." My heart broke for the boy he'd been—alone and afraid.

"I paid attention in school so I knew to stop, drop, and roll." His chest bounced with a wry laugh. "I was lucky to get out of there with just third-degree burns on my back."

Snuggling closer to him, I ran my hand over the dark hair on his chest. "That doesn't sound lucky at all."

"We lost the pictures." He let out a loud sigh.

"That seems a small price to pay. I can't imagine how scared you must have been."

He shifted, pulling back to look down at me. I'd never seen the kind of hurt and shame reflected in his eyes.

"It wasn't just the pictures that I lost that day."

CHAPTER 23

Cole

SHE DIDN'T GET IT. I could tell by the slight furrow that creased her brow.

"What else did you lose? An illegal still? A few gallons of whiskey?"

I wished. The guilt washed over me just like it did every time I thought about that day. Shaking my head, I made myself break eye contact. I didn't want to see the disappointment in her eyes when I told her how I'd failed my family.

"I lost the most important piece of my family's history—of the distillery's history—that day. My great-granddad knew how much I loved Devil's Dance. Even at eight years old, I was fascinated with the process and would spend hours following the guys around the distillery. He knew I'd end up taking over as master distiller someday."

Danica shifted her cheek on my chest. Confessing what I'd done could change her opinion about me, but I had to tell her. There was no way we could move forward without her knowing the whole truth about me, especially if I wanted her to incorporate some of my ideas into the plan she presented to the board.

Bracing myself, I continued. "The original mash bill was in the documents I let burn that day."

She didn't say anything.

"The bottles of Devil's Dance Distinct that everyone raves about were made with that bill."

"That was the only copy anyone had of what went into that whiskey?" she asked.

"It was the only one written down. They were so afraid of someone stealing it, they never put it in writing. The mash bill was passed down from generation to generation, from one master distiller to the next by word of mouth."

"If your great-granddad knew the recipe, why didn't he write it down as soon as that one was lost in the fire?" Danica rested her chin on her fist. The weight of her gaze pulled at me, but I still couldn't meet her eyes.

"Because he wasn't as lucky as I was. The reason I got out of there with just the burns on my back is because he saved me." I couldn't stop myself from looking at her. I deserved to see the horror in her eyes. "I'm the reason he died in that fire."

Her eyes widened. The shock I knew she must be feeling was evident in the way her jaw dropped. "I'm so sorry, Cole."

I held her gaze until I couldn't look at her for another second. The sympathy in her eyes was too much to bear.

"It wasn't your fault. You were just a kid." She sat up and scooted to the head of the bed. "Come here."

She tried unsuccessfully to tug me up the bed.

I wouldn't let myself seek comfort in her arms. Even though it had been well over twenty years, the pain was still as fresh as if it had happened yesterday. I could still smell the smoke in the air, still hear my great-grandma's shrieks and wails.

"You can't keep punishing yourself for something that happened back then." Her words landed on deaf ears. I'd heard it before. No one had the balls to come right out and blame me for what happened, but I sensed it in the way Vaughn tensed every time someone mentioned Devil's Distinct. My heart wrenched in two when I saw the few pictures that remained of my great-granddad.

Wanting to move past the moment, I splayed my hand over her stomach. "Are you sorry you asked?"

She shook her head. "I'm just sorry you blame yourself. I can understand why the history of Devil's Dance is so important to you. It's your way of honoring your great-granddad."

"I need to make sure he's not forgotten." I shifted, resting my head on her stomach, just under the curve of her breasts. "I've been trying to recreate that recipe for almost a decade. I've come close, but there's something missing. I don't know if it's in the mash bill itself or if I'm not using the right strain of yeast. Hell, for all I know I'm not storing the barrels at the right spot in the rick house."

She ran her fingers through my hair. I relaxed into her touch, letting the feel of her nails on my scalp distract me from the darkness swirling around in my chest.

"I never knew how much goes into making a bottle of whiskey." Her heart beat a steady rhythm under my cheek. "It's a science."

"It's more than a science. It's a craft." A craft that Devil's Dance had mastered long ago. We'd lost sight of that through the years. And if Davis Stewart had things his way, we'd leave that mastery in the past.

"You're right. A craft." She opened her mouth, letting a huge yawn escape.

She had to be exhausted. She'd put in a full day of work, then I'd dragged her up a mountain in the rain and worn her out in bed.

"You need to sleep." Even though I could have laid there

for days with my cheek resting on the smooth, soft skin of her belly, she needed to get some rest.

"I'm surprised we both haven't passed out by now." She covered another yawn with her hand. "Sorry, I can't keep from yawning."

I lifted my head and nudged my chin toward her. "Get comfortable. I'll be your big spoon."

"How can I refuse an offer like that?" She snuggled down under the covers, stretching out before curling onto her side.

Wrapping my body around hers like a shell, I pulled her into me. My dick nestled in the spot between her legs, already primed for another round.

"Are you going to be able to fall asleep?" She held my hands in hers, pressing them into her chest.

My nose nudged into her hair, and I breathed in the scent of coconut and the aftermath of sex on her skin. This woman had no idea she held my giant rock of a heart in her slim, soft hands.

I knew better than to think sleep would come easy, but I didn't want her to worry about me. "Yeah, I'm exhausted."

"Good. You probably need to sleep more than I do. Goodnight, Cole."

"Goodnight, baby," I whispered. Then I held her in my arms while her breathing evened out. Within minutes, she was sound asleep.

I laid there as long as I could, holding her against me, molding my hard planes around her soft curves. When the fire had almost burned out, I carefully extricated myself from the tangle of limbs and quilts to add another log. The rain had stopped, so I wrapped a quilt around my shoulders and went out onto the front porch.

I'd forgotten how quiet it could get up here. The darkness of night swallowed me up as I lowered myself to sit on the edge of the porch. Crickets chirped and a light breeze blew through the treetops. Leaves rustled and the smell of wood smoke from the stove inside drifted through the air.

I closed my eyes, letting the memories wash over me. Talking about times gone by with Danica had brought the pain to the surface again. More than anything, I wished things had happened differently that day. I hadn't intended to share the most painful secret of my past with her, but I wanted her to know the bad along with the good. I'd never told another woman about my failure, never cared enough about anyone else to let them see that deepest, darkest part of me.

The door creaked open behind me. "Cole? Are you out here?" Her voice came out soft, barely audible over the sound of the breeze rustling through the trees.

"Over here, sweetheart." My eyes had already adjusted to the dark so I could make out her shape as she slowly moved across the porch.

"Where?"

I stood and reached for her hand. "Right here."

She shivered, and I opened up the quilt to take her into my arms. "I woke up, and you weren't there."

"I didn't mean to worry you." Pressing a kiss to her forehead, I pulled the quilt tight around us.

"It's cold out here. Do you want to come back inside?"

There wasn't anything I wanted more than to hide out here in the woods with her, but our time was limited. "Yeah, let's get you warmed up again."

Together, we walked toward the door. I steered her toward the bed, eager to chase the chill away.

"Thanks for sharing your story with me earlier." She pulled me down next to her to sit on the bed.

"You're welcome." It felt odd to say that, like I'd done her a favor instead of saddling her with my deepest, darkest failure.

"I understand better now about why you want to honor the history of the distillery." Her hands traced the outline of my pecs.

"I didn't tell you that to try to change your mind about working with the Stewarts." The need to make that clear stood out to me. I didn't want her to think I'd only shared with her just so she wouldn't try to obliterate the importance of the distillery in her plan.

Tentatively, she moved her hand just over my shoulder, edging her fingers to touch the point on my back where the smooth skin gave way to my scars. "I didn't think that at all. I want to get to know you... All of you."

My heart thudded to a stop, pausing in my chest while I waited to find out what she'd do next.

Her hand moved down, smoothing over the puckered skin that covered my shoulder blades. I couldn't remember the last time someone had touched me like that. I closed my eyes, relishing her touch. She got to her knees and moved behind me. For a moment, I figured she'd crawled to the middle of the bed to lie down. I shifted, ready to join her.

"Stay there." The warmth of her breath brushed across my spine. Then the mattress creaked as she leaned down. Her lips touched the spot right between my shoulders. My nerve endings had been dulled by scar tissue, but I could feel the gentle way she kissed my skin.

While I sat there, afraid to move, scared that if I did it would ruin the moment, she pressed kisses down my spine, touching her lips to each bone in my vertebrae. Her tenderness cracked the shell around my heart wide open. I wasn't an emotional man, but the acceptance she gave me in that moment wrecked me.

Her fingers traced the ridges of my scars while her kisses acted like a soothing balm to the pain I'd carried with me for most of my life. She couldn't erase the hurt, the guilt, and the shame. But knowing she accepted me dulled the ache.

"I think you're beautiful." Her whisper drifted over my skin.

Even with skin grafts they'd taken from my inner thighs, the doctors had been unable to repair my back. I'd always sport hideous scars—the kind that ought to make a woman wince. Danica didn't shy away. When she was done covering every inch of my back with kisses, she slid her legs to either side of my hips and slipped her arms underneath mine. Clasping her hands together around my chest, she embraced me. Her breasts pressed against my back, her cheek nestled between my shoulders.

My cock hardened at her touch. I didn't know what I'd done to deserve this woman, but I wasn't going to take her for granted. Every moment we shared between us was a gift. I lifted her hands to my lips, my heart full of emotion. Was this what love felt like?

With the darkness of night slowly shifting into a hazy gray, I got up, lifted her in my arms, and gently laid her down in the middle of the bed. Then I crawled on top of her, ready to show her with my body just how much her acceptance meant to me.

CHAPTER 24
Danica

COLE NUDGED my thighs apart with his knee, then settled between my legs, the tip of his cock notched at my entrance. I was more than ready for him again. All he had to do was look at me to make heat pool between my legs.

I dug my fingertips into his back, pulling him closer, needing to feel his weight. His scars didn't bother me. I thought they were beautiful, a part of him that showed the pain he'd suffered and the ordeals he'd overcome. I'd never met anyone like him. He had a tender heart and wasn't afraid to show his emotion now that I'd breached the tall walls he'd constructed to protect himself.

Eagerly, I spread my legs for him, wanting to show him the acceptance he deserved. He eased into me, filling me inch by inch until he'd seated himself deep inside.

He'd taken such good care of me last night, making sure I had what I needed before he let himself go. This was for him. I wanted him to know I was here for him, that I was willing to give him whatever he needed.

"What do you want, Cole? Tell me and I'll make it happen."

He threaded his fingers with mine and pressed my hands over my head. "I just want you."

His hips rolled, sending a pulse of need through me. He was good at this, exceptionally gifted at making me desperate for him.

"You've got me. All of me." I lifted my hips, thrusting toward him as he drove into me.

He pulled out almost all the way, his forehead creased with concentration. "I want to make you feel so good."

I shook my head. "Don't worry about me this time. This one's for you."

He shook his head. "Fine. Get on your knees."

I flipped onto my stomach and stuck my ass in the air. "Come on, Cole. Give it to me."

His hand splayed over my butt cheek. I glanced over my shoulder and saw him stroke himself. It had to be the sexiest thing I'd ever seen in my life... his huge hand wrapped around his giant cock, pumping himself into his fist.

I pushed back, bumping his hand with my ass, desperately needing him to fill me.

He leaned over, spreading my folds with his fingers. Then he licked me, flicking his tongue against my swollen clit before sliding it inside.

My hips bucked, and the scruff on his cheeks scraped across my inner thighs. He reached around, fingering me while he continued to thrust his tongue in and out. I didn't have a chance for my orgasm to build. I shattered around him—the combination of his fingers and his tongue sending me into orbit. My release came in waves, one right after the other. I didn't have time to catch my breath in between.

He switched his hand to slide his fingers inside me while he sucked my clit. I didn't think my body could feel anything else. I was wrong. Another release built, this one slamming into me so hard that I pitched forward on the bed, knocking my head into the iron headboard as my knees gave way underneath me.

Cole caught me around the waist and propped me up, his mouth wringing the last bits of pleasure from me until I whimpered against him. I was empty, wrung out in the most incredible way. How had he taken my offering and turned it around to satisfy me?

While I laid there, still spinning out of control, he lowered himself, kissing a path from my thighs, over my ass, and up the small of my back. His lips tickled, but I didn't have the strength to offer any kind of response.

"You weren't supposed to do that," I finally managed.

He paused between kisses. "I wasn't supposed to make you feel good?"

"No. I mean...yes...but I wanted you to feel good." My mouth pressed against the quilt, making my voice come out in a slurred, punch drunk way.

"Making you feel good is what makes me feel good." He ran his finger along my side, stopping when he reached the curve of my breast.

"You're like a unicorn."

"A what?" His laugh rumbled along my skin.

"A unicorn. A man who lives to satisfy his partner in bed? I can't believe I found you. I didn't think men like you existed."

"I thought you were calling me a unicorn because of my big, long—"

"No, that makes you a well-endowed unicorn." I somehow got my knees underneath me and lifted myself onto all fours.

His cock nestled between the cheeks of my ass. I slid up and down, encouraging him to take me from behind, even going so far as to bend down and line up the tip with the entrance to my sex.

He put a hand on either side of my hips, clamping down. Then he shoved inside me. From this angle, he filled me completely, buried himself all the way in my heat. I clenched around him, relaxed, and clenched around him again.

"Fuck, that feels good." He dragged himself out, tightened his grip on my hips, and thrust back inside.

This was what I wanted. I needed him to lose himself to me the same way I'd lost myself to him. He had to know I wanted him, all of him—the good and the bad.

Over and over he pulled out and thrust back inside, increasing the speed until he paused, his entire body straining. That's when I clenched around him, milking his release from his thick cock. Warmth spilled into me and he let out a low groan.

My pulse whooshed through my ears as he came. I pushed my ass back against him, sending him even deeper inside. His fingertips dug into my hips. Feeling him get off sent another quake through me. I couldn't get enough of this man. He'd turned me inside out and upside down, making me feel things I never knew were possible.

"Dammit, Danica." He grunted as he slid out of me. "You've fucking ruined me."

I leaned forward, warmed by the knowledge that he'd enjoyed himself.

He gently wiped me from front to back with his button-down shirt. "We'd better cut this out or I'm going to run out of clothes."

"Do we have to go back?" Even now, the fuzzy gray light of early morning was being chased away by the rising sun. Every moment I got to stay here with him was a gift... a reprieve from the obligations we'd both face when we headed down the mountain.

"You want to spend the rest of the weekend up here?" He

rolled me over on my back and hovered over me on his hands and knees.

"Yes, please." I wrapped my arms around his neck, gazing up into his eyes. The darkness that clouded them the night before had disappeared.

"What are we going to eat?"

"I'll feast on you." I nibbled his neck, willing to try to survive on the taste of his skin.

He lowered to his elbows. "How long do you think that will work?"

"A week? Maybe two?" Smiling against his skin, I licked the spot where his pulse beat. He tasted like whiskey with a hint of salt. I could swear the man bathed in it.

"You have to go home today, don't you?" He rolled off of me and got to his feet.

I marveled again at the perfection of his naked body. With the light filtering in through the thick panes of glass, I could see him clearly. He turned to reach for his jeans, and I got my first glimpse of the scars I'd explored with my fingers and my lips in the dark.

They crisscrossed his back, angry lines of skin that looked like they'd been melted. I shuddered, not at the sight, but at the pain he must have felt back then.

"What is it you're going to? A baby shower or something?" He stepped into his jeans while I propped myself up on an elbow.

"A wedding reception. I've got a ton of work to do before I meet with Davis and Harper on Monday. I can't believe I let my mom talk me into going back now."

"Can't you skip out?" He picked my shirt up off the back of the chair and held it to his cheek. "Here, I think it's mostly dry."

It landed on the bed next to me. Putting it on would mean

admitting that our time together had come to an end. "I already promised."

"Does she know how much you need to get done?" He tossed my jeans over next.

Resigned to the fact that I had to get dressed, I pulled my shirt on over my head, skipping the bra. "It doesn't matter. Mom only cares about her plans. The fact that I have a life away from her doesn't really register."

"Ouch."

"Yeah, harsh but true. It's easier to give in and not make a scene." I'd learned that the hard way.

"It's too bad someone can't drive you back so you could get your work done on the way."

My head jerked up. "What?"

"It was just a thought." He squatted down in front of the stove. "I ought to stay here, though. With Harper gone, there's no one else to watch over the run we're doing this weekend."

"I like that thought, though." The more I mulled it over, the more I liked it. "We could drive to Knoxville and spend the night at my place. Isn't there anyone else who can watch over things for you?"

He tilted his head. "We've been training a new guy. He's probably ready to handle it."

I grinned, sensing victory within my grasp. If Cole came to Knoxville with me, I could duck out of the party early and we could go on a real date. We wouldn't have to sneak around and worry about someone finding out there was something going on between us. "You wouldn't happen to know someone who might be interested in playing chauffeur, do you?"

A smile spread across his face. "I happen to know a very good driver. He's got a pretty clean record. No major offenses."

"Is that so?" I couldn't wait for him to spend the night at

my place, hopefully engaging in a repeat performance of last night…and this morning.

"It is."

"Does that mean he has some minor offenses?"

"Define minor." Cole poked at the remains of the fire.

"Speeding tickets?"

"Not on the record."

"Arrests?"

He didn't answer right away. "Just once, but technically, my buddy was the arresting officer, and it didn't really count."

"You, rebel. What did you do?" I picked up one of the quilts and matched up the corners while I pictured what a mug shot of Cole would look like.

He came closer and grabbed the other end of the quilt to help. "Indecent exposure."

I bit back a laugh. "Did you flash someone?"

"No. Not on purpose, anyway. Vaughn and I were fishing down at the stream, and I had to relieve myself. So did what guys always do in that type of situation."

"And Vaughn reported you?"

"No. I stepped into the woods a few feet and dropped trou. I didn't realize Mrs. Stewart was on a field trip with her gardening club."

A laugh bubbled up inside while I pictured Cole standing with his jeans around his ankles in front of the matriarch of the Stewart family. "How old were you at the time?"

He took a step forward, matching his corners of the quilt to mine. "Twenty-seven. It just happened a few years ago."

I doubled over, laughing.

"Hey, it's not that funny. She made me stand there while she called the sheriff's department."

"Did she at least let you pull your pants up?"

"Yeah." He set the quilt on the edge of the bed and picked up another.

"What did your brother do while this was going on?"

Cole held two corners of the blanket and tossed the other side to me. "The asshole packed up and left. He didn't want to get caught defending me to the Beaver Bluff Gardening Club."

"I always thought it would be fun to have a twin." I took his edges this time, folding the quilt to the same size as the first one, then stacking it on top.

"Sometimes it's fun. Other times it's a pain in the ass."

"I'll have to take your word for it. I don't have any brothers or sisters." The last quilt was the one Cole used to clean us up. I folded that one over a few times and decided to take it home to run through the wash.

"I got even with him for leaving me. When my buddy Hurley showed up, I told him my name was Vaughn."

"You didn't."

"I sure as hell did. We played football together in high school, and he's always been able to tell us apart. Mrs. Stewart thinks Vaughn was the culprit and Hurley dropped me off at home on his way back to the station."

"Cole, you're a such bad boy," I teased.

He tucked the folded quilts back into the chest at the foot of the bed. "Aw, come on. I'm not all bad. Sometimes I can be very, very good."

My toes curled at the heat burning in his eyes. I was playing with fire in the form of Cole Bishop. Even knowing that, I couldn't stop myself.

"That's it. I'll check in with the new guy and make sure he knows what to do." He took a few steps toward me, a cocky grin spread across lips that looked much too kissable in the light of day. "What do you say, Danica? Can I drive you home?"

CHAPTER 25

Cole

HEADING down the mountain was a hell of a lot easier than going up. We made it back to the truck with minor issues. Danica lost her footing once and ended up sliding down a section of the hill on her ass. I still thought she looked cute, even with a backside full of mud.

I'd planned on getting back to town and dropping her off at the bed-and-breakfast early enough that no one would notice. Even though we were both consenting adults, if anyone caught sight of her getting out of my truck and walking through the door that early on a Saturday morning, they'd make assumptions about how we'd spent the night before.

In this case, their assumptions would probably be true, but I didn't want Danica to get caught up in the Beaver Bluff gossip mill. My brothers and I spent enough time dodging rumors—mostly based on facts—that I knew what kind of toll it could take on a person.

"Hey, I'm going to do a drive-by of the bed-and-breakfast. Duck down so no one sees you."

"Are you kidding?"

"Unfortunately, I'm not. If someone sees you getting out of my truck, especially with a backside full of mud and the same clothes you had on yesterday, they're going to talk."

She gritted her teeth but sank down low enough in her seat that anyone looking in would assume I was alone.

I slowed my truck to a crawl as I turned onto the side street where the Beaver Bluff B&B was located. A group of women stood clustered around the base of the huge oak tree in the front yard. Mrs. Stewart shielded her eyes from the rising sun and stared right at me.

"Oh, shit. We've got a problem." I mumbled out of the side of my mouth so Mrs. Stewart didn't think I was talking to myself. Then I stretched the wadded-up quilt over Danica, trying to hide her blonde hair as Mrs. Stewart put up her hand, signaling for me to stop. "Stay down, okay?"

"Get us out of here," Danica whispered.

"Doing my best." I pressed the button, and the window lowered. "Good morning, Mrs. Stewart. Is everything okay?"

It was barely six-thirty in the morning on a Saturday and she looked like she'd been made up for hours. She had on a pink and teal running suit, though I doubt the woman had broken a sweat in over a decade, maybe two.

"Cole, is that you?" She put a hand to her heart.

"Yes, ma'am." I leaned one arm on the window, trying to block her view of the interior of the cab.

"Oh, good. I was hoping it was you and not that crude brother of yours."

Danica let out a soft snort, and the quilt moved. I cleared my throat in an attempt to cover up the sound. "What can I help you with this morning?"

"Well…" She stepped closer to my truck, close enough to rest her fingertips on the window ledge. "I just got back late last night from that cruise my mother-in-law insisted we take. I bet I gained ten pounds. Our speed-walking club was out for our morning walk and came across Mitzy Ballinger standing here because your brother's dog chased her poor cat up into the tree."

I glanced up at the huge tree, barely able to make out the orange tabby sitting on one of the upper branches. "How do you know it was my brother's dog?"

She clamped a hand on her hip. "How many other coon hounds run around here with a flask of whiskey dangling from their collar?"

Fair point. I kept telling Miller to get his damn dog neutered. Every night, Titus hopped the short fence and went on a joy run. One of these nights, he was going to meet with the wrong end of something bigger than him and not show up for morning chow.

"I'll call Miller and have him come get his dog. Where is he?"

"He's long gone. Probably off terrorizing some other poor, unsuspecting cat. What are you going to do about getting Clarabelle out of the tree?"

"Me?" I blinked.

"Yes, you. I suppose if you'd rather, you can give me a ride down to the firehouse, and I can get them to send for the hook and ladder truck." She huffed out a breath and started to walk around the front of my truck.

"Wait." I called out the window, causing her to stop at the corner of my bumper. "Why can't you just call the fire department?"

She stared through the window. "It's not even seven. I don't want them to sound the alarm and wake up half the on-call department for something as simple as a cat in a tree."

I didn't know what the hell to do in that moment, but I did know that I couldn't let Mrs. Stewart get anywhere near the front seat of my truck. "I'll do it. Give me a minute, and I'll climb up to get Clarawhatever down."

"That's more like it." Mrs. Stewart brushed off her sleeves and headed back to the yard. "It's okay, ladies. Cole's going to rescue Clarabelle."

"Is she gone?" Danica's whisper came from under the quilt.

"Barely. I've half a mind to peel out of here and let her handle things on her own." I pulled the truck to the curb and killed the engine.

Danica lifted the edge of the quilt and peered up at me. "You brought this on yourself, you know."

My jaw dropped. "What are you talking about?"

"Bad karma, Cole." She shook her head, making the blanket move. "You ratted out your brother and it's finally catching up with you."

"Don't be ridiculous." I fumbled around in the backseat, trying to find a shirt that I hadn't used to wipe up bodily fluids.

"I'm not the one who lied and is about to climb a tree to make up for it." Danica clucked her tongue like a mama hen chastising a misbehaving chick.

"I'll be back in a minute."

"You'd better be."

I opened the door, hoping no one would ask what the dried spots on my shirt were. Danica's hand closed around my ankle.

Pausing, I leaned down. "What?"

She lifted the edge of the blanket. "Be careful."

"Thanks." I stepped onto the asphalt and shut the truck door behind me. The urge to wrap my hands around my brother's neck and squeeze rushed through me. He should be the one standing at the base of the giant oak, about to risk life and limb to save Clarawhatever.

"Thank you so much, Cole." Mitzy pressed a hand to my shoulder, inches away from the evidence that I'd used my shirt as a washcloth the night before. I turned away just enough that her hand fell from my side.

"My pleasure." I stepped to the base of the tree, looking for the best path up. My brothers and I spent half of our summers scaling the treetops of the tall oaks around Beaver Bluff. Though it had been years since I'd scrambled up a tree, I hoped it was like riding a bike.

"Here." Mitzy pressed a fabric mouse into my palm. "It's one of her favorite toys. When you get close, wave it in the air. It's stuffed with catnip and should make her come running."

"Thanks." I stuffed the mouse into my back pocket, wishing I had on sneakers instead of muddy hiking boots. Here goes nothing. Grabbing hold of the lowest branch, I started to hoist myself up onto the limb. As I moved up the tree, several hands palmed my ass. I glanced down to see half of Mrs. Stewart's speed-walking club clustered together with their hands raised. "I've got this, ladies."

"We just wanted to help," Mrs. Stewart said.

Nothing like getting fondled by my nemesis's mom and a half dozen of her friends first thing in the morning. I hadn't even had any coffee yet. I climbed onto the next branch, leaving the women and their "helpful" hands behind. Clarawhatever paced the limb about twenty feet above. So far, so good.

"Oh, move to the left, Cole," one of the ladies advised. "That branch there looks like it can hold you."

Maybe if I were still in high school. I shook off the suggestion and looked for another option.

"Why's he going so slow?" another woman asked. "Does it look like he's stopped moving?"

I tried to block out their comments and suggestions. This was between me and the damn cat. If they wanted to figure out the best way up the tree, they could tackle it themselves.

The cat eyed me and let out a nervous *meowwwwwwwwwwwww*.

"It's okay, kitty. I'm coming." I continued to move up the tree, being careful to check my footing. Twigs snapped and branches creaked, but the tree held me.

Finally, I stood about two feet below the cat. I reached into my pocket for the stuffed mouse, thinking maybe I could entice her to come toward me if she got a whiff of catnip. Instead of being drawn to the stuffed toy, the cat took one look at it and bolted another few feet up the trunk.

Dammit. I glanced down at the women gathered around the tree's base.

"You scared her," Mitzy called up. "She's got high anxiety. You probably shouldn't make any sudden moves."

Instead of yelling down that it would have been nice if she'd told me that before I started up the damn tree, I squinted and tried to find where the cat went. Danica was probably laughing her ass off right now.

The alternative to coming down without the cat made me press on.

"Come on, kitty. Let's head back to the ground together. I've got you." I continued to talk to the cat in a slow, deep tone. "Don't you want to get back home?"

She gazed down at me, blinking her giant, round cat eyes, her body tensed like she was ready to either pounce on my head or rocket herself even farther up the tree. We were running out of tree, though. If she climbed any higher, there'd be no way the branches would support my weight.

"Hold up the mouse," Mrs. Stewart yelled.

Slower than a glob of barbecue sauce rolling off of perfectly seasoned rib, I moved my hand, trying to show Clarabelle the mouse without scaring her again.

The cat lifted her nose in the air and inhaled, like the skunk in one of those classic cartoons. Her eyes took on a wild shine, and she edged closer to the trunk of the tree. A couple more feet and I'd be able to reach her. I moved up to the next branch. The cat let out a soft mewl.

I stretched, brushing the fur on her side with a finger. I just needed a couple more inches. The "that's what she said" joke died on my tongue. Rising to my tiptoes, I got my palm under her stomach and scooped her up, tasting my first hint of success.

Applause erupted down below.

Mrs. Stewart called up. "Way to go, Cole. You got her. I knew you could do it all along."

Yeah, right. She'd probably organized a betting pool and had the odds stacked against me. Didn't matter. All that mattered was getting the damn cat, and myself, safely back onto the ground. With her in my hand, I realized something. There was no way I could climb down the tree while holding onto a cat. Especially a cat that didn't want to have anything to do with me.

I glanced over at the truck. Was that the top of Danica's head I caught a glimpse of? It damn well better not be. Waiting for a spark of inspiration wasn't working. I leaned a shoulder against the trunk of the tree and tucked in my T-shirt. Satisfied the cat wouldn't be able to escape through the bottom, I shoved her through the neck hole. Her claws scratched the hell out of my chest and stomach as she settled around my gut.

All I needed was for my shirt to stay tucked in. For a guy

who couldn't remember the last time he'd tucked in a T-shirt, that was a pretty tall order.

"You ready for this, cat?" I plotted out where to put my food on my descent. Then I stepped down, hoping like hell that I hadn't made a horrible mistake.

CHAPTER 26

Danica

I DUCKED back down under the blanket as soon as I'd made sure Cole's feet touched the ground. My heart still beat like crazy in my chest. It started the second he disappeared into the tree and wouldn't let up until he slid into the truck next to me.

The man had no fear. He had to have been fifty feet up in the air.

For a cat.

His voice floated in through the open window, over the excited chatter of the speed-walking club. "You're welcome. Yes, I'll tell Miller that he'd better keep Titus in the yard or you'll call animal control next time."

His heavy footsteps thumped across the road, then the door opened and the truck shifted as he slid inside. "Let's get the hell out of here."

I waited until he'd driven down the road and turned a few corners before I peeked out from under the quilt. "Is the coast clear?"

Cole reached out to pull the quilt back. "Yeah. Buckle up. I guess I'll take you back to my place so we can get cleaned up."

I clicked the seatbelt back in place and looked over at him. My chest squeezed tight. "What happened to you?"

Scratch marks covered his neck, several clusters of three puffy red lines.

"Turns out Clarabelle didn't get her anxiety meds this morning before she decided to dart up the tree." He winced at his reflection in the mirror. "I can't wait to see what my chest looks like."

I swallowed hard. "I'm sorry. Maybe you should have left the cat up there."

"And let Mrs. Stewart hop in the truck for a ride to the fire house?" He held my gaze for a long moment. "You don't think she'd wonder why you and I were out toodling around at dawn?"

The realization of why he'd actually risked his life for a cat walloped me upside the head like someone had just hit me with a cast-iron skillet. He hadn't actually done that just for a cat.

He'd done it for us—to keep everyone in Beaver Bluff from finding out we were slinking around in his truck at six-thirty in the morning.

"Do you have a first aid kit at home, or should we stop somewhere on the way?" I put a hand on his shoulder and studied the red welts. "I think we need to clean these."

He reached for my hand and set it on his thigh. "I'll be fine. We'll head back to my place to get cleaned up, then I'll figure out a way to sneak you into the B&B so you can pack your stuff to head home for the weekend."

"Are you sure you don't mind going with me?" I wondered if things had changed. Maybe the magic between us had faded as we walked down the mountain and made our awkward re-entry into normal life.

"Have you changed your mind?" He stopped at the one

light in town and turned the full force of his gaze on me. I looked past the extra scruff on his cheeks and beyond the cat scratches that seemed to be growing angrier by the moment.

"No. Of course not." The idea of him sharing my small one-bedroom apartment with me overnight might make my heart race, but I wanted him to come with me. I wanted to see how things could be between us away from the prying eyes in Beaver Bluff.

"Then let's get to it." He lifted our hands to his lips and pressed a kiss to my knuckles.

I was so engrossed with watching his lips touch my skin, so enamored by the hint of heat in his eyes, that I didn't notice the car next to us until a horn sounded. Loud and long, the beep jerked me out of my haze.

"Oh, shit." Cole looked past me, and I followed his gaze.

His brother, Miller, sat behind the wheel of a truck just as tall as Cole's. While my heart deflated, he rolled down the window and gestured for me to do the same.

I glanced at Cole, hoping for some direction. He squeezed my hand and pressed on the button to lower my window. "What are you doing up so early?"

Miller leaned out the window, his eyebrows raised so high it caused rows of wrinkles to crease his brow. "I left Jack with Mom so I can head into the office and get some work done. Then I got a call that Titus was on the loose. Looks like I should be asking you the same question."

Cole didn't skip a beat. He nudged his chin toward me while he directed his words at his brother. "I took Danica up to the old cabin yesterday to show her around. We got stuck in the storm and finally made it down the hill this morning."

Miller rested his wrists on the top of his steering wheel and eyed us both with doubt clouding his eyes. "You took her up to the cabin?"

The light turned green. I wished Cole would step on the gas and get us away from his brother and his questions.

"I thought it might help for her to see the history I keep talking about up close."

"And did she?" Miller smirked like he knew he wasn't getting the whole truth.

"Yes. Then I tried to drop her off and got cornered by Mrs. Stewart, who said your dog chased a cat up a tree. How about you don't mention this to anyone and I don't kick your ass for having to climb up a tree and bring down a cat?" Cole's voice rose as he talked. As his voice rose, Miller's eyes widened even more.

"So you hiked down the mountain, climbed up a tree, and rescued a cat already this morning?" he asked.

"And got groped by the over-seventy speed-walkers club," Cole added.

"Damn, bro. It's barely after seven."

Cole blinked—a long, tired, weary blink. Then he turned toward the other truck. "Do you think you can keep this between us for a change?"

"Yeah, sure." Miller looked like I felt inside… a little apprehensive about Cole's mental state at the moment.

"Thanks. Oh, do me a favor? Tell Mom I won't be there for Sunday supper tomorrow."

Miller shook his head. "No way. You're not dumping that on me. You want to back out of that, you'll have to tell her yourself."

Cole stepped on the gas, propelling us away from the stoplight and leaving his brother behind. "The number of times I've saved his ass, you'd think he could do me one favor."

"I don't want you to miss Sunday supper with your family. Maybe I should just head to Knoxville on my own." Disappointment lodged in my throat. I knew what it was like to put family first and let other obligations and commitments take precedence over the things I wanted. I'd been living by that creed my entire adult life.

"I'm coming with you." Cole stated it so matter-of-factly that I didn't dare disagree. "If you want me there, if you'll have me, I'm coming."

I did want him with me. Not only to shift some of the attention away from myself, but also to have the chance to get to know him away from Beaver Bluff. "Okay then, it's settled."

THREE HOURS later we'd both showered, changed, packed, and were barreling down the four-lane highway with fifty miles under our belts. Cole had dropped me off a few blocks from the bed-and-breakfast, then ran errands while I got ready. By the time he came back to get me, I'd changed clothes three times and unpacked my overnight bag and repacked it twice. I didn't want to let on how much of a big deal it was for me to be bringing someone home with me.

Not just someone, either.

Cole was a man. I'd never introduced my parents to a single guy I'd dated except for the boy who asked me to the Homecoming dance our sophomore year of high school. The only reason they got to meet him was because neither of us had a driver's license, so my dad had to take us to the dance and his mom drove us home. I'd never been as embarrassed as I was to have my mom and dad grill him for the entire fifteen minutes it took to get from his house to the Italian restaurant he'd picked out.

I wasn't eager to repeat the inquisition, but Cole could probably hold his own better than the trombone player with a unibrow.

"So, where's the party tonight?" Cole asked.

"At my aunt's new husband's country club." I wasn't looking forward to it. Just another family function where everyone would ask when I'd be the one getting engaged. I didn't think I could handle everyone's puppy dog eyes when they did the math and realized that Aunt Angela had been married five times and I hadn't even been proposed to once.

"If it's like my family get-togethers, nobody will notice if you skip out early. Especially after they've had a few drinks."

"That's what I'm counting on." My phone rang, and my mother's picture flashed on my screen. I wasn't eager to chat with her while I was driving with Cole, but if I didn't answer, she'd just keep calling back. "Hi, Mom."

"Are you close? I was hoping you'd be here in time to visit Ricard's studio with me."

Cole glanced over. I tried to turn the volume down on my phone so he wouldn't overhear. It was bad enough I had to listen to my overly critical mother.

"We're on the way now." I cringed. Hopefully, she wouldn't pick up on the "we."

"We're?" Her voice hit a new high. "Don't tell me you're bringing someone home with you?"

Now wasn't the time to engage in a discussion with my mother about my dating life. Truthfully, there would never be a time I'd want to fill her in, but especially not now with Cole not even two feet away.

"Sorry, I caught a ride back to Knoxville."

"With who? Is it someone you know? You can't be too careful nowadays."

"I'm fine, Mom. I won't be there in time to visit Ricard's with you." I peeked at Cole, who immediately started fiddling with his playlist. "I'll do my own hair tonight."

"Don't be ridiculous, darling. I'll have Ricard stop by your place on his way home. We're doing family pictures since we'll all be there."

I hated how dismissive she was. "Really, Mom. I've got it."

"I'll have to tip him extra for driving out of his way, but it will be worth it." She let out a dramatic sigh. "Your father and I will expect you at ten to seven. That will give us a few minutes to say hello before we enter."

She made it sound like we were going to a royal ball where they'd announce our presence before we walked through the door.

"I'll see you then, and I don't need Ricard to stop by."

"Goodbye, dear." She ended the call—her way of making sure she always had the last word.

I let out a frustrated breath.

"Everything okay?" Cole asked.

"It was my mother."

"I kind of gathered that. Is she a little uptight about the reception tonight?"

"More like uptight about life." I propped my elbow up on the door and massaged my temple with my fingers. "My mother is used to getting her way."

"Has it always been like that?" His forehead creased with concern.

I reached over and squeezed his hand. "It's just her way. She was an only child, and her parents catered to her every need. When they passed away, my dad took over. It's easier to go along with her than make a fuss."

"What about what you want?" He squeezed back. It was a small gesture, but the show of support did more to bolster my mood than anything else had lately. "Don't you get a say in things?"

"I do." Sometimes. Okay, rarely, but I didn't want him to think I was a total doormat.

Cole shook his head. "You're worth the fight, Danica."

"What do you mean?" My stomach tightened as I waited for him to respond.

"With your ex-boss. With your mom." He took his eyes off the road long enough to meet my gaze. "Standing up for yourself isn't being rude. It's your right."

I thought about that for a few long moments. "It's not that I don't stand up for myself. I try, but I don't want people to think I'm being too assertive."

"It's okay to step away or pause a conversation if it's not working for you."

"Maybe you should be the one to talk to my mother." I laughed, but the idea wasn't as outrageous as I thought. "Actually, about tonight…"

"What about it?" He flicked the blinker and got in the left lane to pass a semi that was driving a few miles under the speed limit.

I wasn't sure how to broach the topic, but it seemed silly to have him drive all this way and be stuck in my apartment all night. "How would you feel about going to the reception with me?"

"As your date?"

"Well, I guess. I mean, it wouldn't have to be a real date. We'd just be going together. Not together, together, just at the same time. Casual. As friends even." Why didn't I ever know when to shut up? I didn't want to force it on him, though. He'd said he wanted to get to know me better, but did he really?

"What if I want to take you out on a real date?" He offered me a stick of red licorice from the bag he'd picked up when we stopped for gas. "Taking you to your aunt's wedding reception wouldn't be my top pick for a first date, but since we're already heading there…"

I shook my head. "No. I can't have our real first date ruined by being at a family function."

"How do you know it would be ruined?"

"It's a foregone conclusion. This is my aunt's fifth marriage. You'd think if she were going to be successful at it, she might have found her stride by now."

"For some people, it takes more than a time or two to get it right."

He probably didn't mean to sound like he was defending a perfect stranger, but those rules didn't necessarily apply when it came to Aunt Angela. "Her last wedding reception was at the zoo."

"Like a petting zoo?"

"No, that might have been fun. This was at the big zoo. They have a primate enclosure there that people can rent out for events. Or at least they used to be able to rent it out before Aunt Angela's reception."

"Do I want to know what happened?"

"No, no you don't. At least not until tomorrow when the party is over and it's too late for you to not go with me." Though I loved my family, so far what I'd seen from Cole's siblings had nothing on the kind of stunts my aunts, uncles, and cousins had pulled over the years.

"Now you've got me curious. I think I'd better go with you tonight."

"I should have said something earlier. It's pretty formal. I'm sure you didn't bring anything to wear."

He got a bit of a gleam in his eyes when he turned toward me and offered a lopsided smile. "I was hoping you might extend an invitation, so I went ahead and packed something, just in case."

"Are you kidding me?" I landed a playful swat on his arm while my heart did cartwheels and backflips inside my chest.

For the first time in a long time, I was looking forward to attending a family function. I wouldn't be alone. I'd enter on Cole's arm—a man who looked like he could have walked right out of a centerfold in Men's Fitness—and prove to my family once and for all that I wasn't the hopeless, mousy intro-vert they all thought I was.

An air of excitement filled my lungs. There was something else there too... something hidden behind the bravado... something I hadn't held in my heart in a long, long time.

Something that felt an awful lot like hope.

CHAPTER 27

THOUGH MY VISIT to Knoxville had been an impromptu decision, now that I'd committed, I couldn't wait to see where Danica came from. She directed me off the highway and into a large complex of newer apartment buildings. They all looked exactly the same. I navigated through the lot until she pointed to a spot right by the curb.

"You can pull into the visitor spot here."

Was it just me or had some nervous energy built up the closer we got to Knoxville? She practically bounced out of the cab and onto the sidewalk. I grabbed our bags from the backseat and joined her in front of a door on the ground floor.

"This is me." She pulled her keys out of her purse and fumbled while trying to slip the key into the lock.

I eyed the front door, wondering how hard it would be for someone to jimmy the lock or kick it open. Maybe I didn't have the right to feel that way, but I didn't like that she lived on the first floor or that an overgrown bush shielded her front door from view of the parking lot. Someone could easily wait for her behind the branches and she wouldn't be able to tell until it was too late.

"You hate it already." Her hand stilled on the doorknob.

"I don't hate it. Someone needs to trim the bushes, though, so you can see your door from the lot."

Her eyes softened at the edges. "Look at you getting all worried about me."

"It sounds like someone needs to keep an eye out for you." I said it with a smile, but I was only partly joking. Even then, I wondered what kind of tools I had in the back of my truck. There had to be something I could use to give the damn bushes a trim.

"If I decide to take applications for the position, I'll let you know." She pushed the door open with a flourish. "Home sweet home. Come on in."

I had ideas of what the inside of her space might look like, but none of them looked anything like the contemporary set up she revealed when she opened the door. It was like stepping inside of an Ikea catalog. Everything was shiny and white with chrome accents—the exact opposite of how I had my space set up at home with a mix of antiques that had been passed down over the years and stuff made by local artisans.

"Make yourself at home." She set her purse down on a thick glass table with chrome legs. "Do you want something to drink right away?"

A light fixture with long, spiky arms hung from the ceiling over an oversized white leather couch. I was afraid to touch anything... afraid of leaving a set of smudgy fingerprints on any of the glossy surfaces.

"How long do we have until we have to leave for the reception?" I draped the bag holding my dress pants and shirt over the back of a chair, still awed by the furnishings of Danica's apartment.

She checked her watch and let out a groan. "If we leave in forty-five minutes, we'll be there when my mother told me to.

Any later than that and we'll officially enter the red zone when it comes to meeting her expectations."

"I don't want to start off in the red zone. Is there somewhere I can change?"

"You can put your stuff in my room if you want." Danica spun around, her teeth worrying at her lower lip. "Unless you'd rather sleep on the couch? I don't want to assume."

"Assume, please." I wrapped my arms around her and nuzzled my nose into her hair. She'd tied it up during the last hour of the drive, so I took advantage of the unfettered access I had to her neck. "I came here to be with you."

"I know." Her arms went around my waist and she pulled me tighter against her. "I guess I'm finding it hard to believe that you're willing to come all this way just for a few petit fours and an open bar."

"We both know that's not what brought me here."

"Want to admit what did bring you here? I hope it wasn't the promise of good home cooking."

I shifted a hand to her hip. "It's the stimulating conversation."

The feel of my palm against her hip made me wish we didn't have to walk out the door in forty-five—better make it forty-four minutes.

"Can we save the stimulating for later?" she joked.

I kissed the spot on her forehead, right between her brows. "You get to decide when the stimulating starts, okay?"

"Do we have to go to the party?" Her bottom lip stuck out in a pouty grin as she rose onto her toes to press her mouth to mine. The kiss immediately sent blood toward my dick and made me weigh the consequences of my actions against the benefit of starting the stimulation right then and there.

"You'd better cut that out if you don't want me to make you late and get you into trouble with your mama." I loosened my grip on her backside, full of all kinds of regret that we didn't have more time.

She let out a sigh. "Do you ever get tired of doing the right thing?"

I could have done a TED Talk on the pitfalls associated with that kind of decision. Not to mention that "the right thing" was often a very subjective opinion. But now wasn't the time or the place to launch into my personal opinions that had been thirty years in the making.

"Go get dressed." I patted her gorgeous backside. "I'll change out here so you can have the bathroom and the bedroom."

She pressed one more kiss to my lips before heading into her bedroom.

I only needed a few minutes to change. With sounds of water running and drawers opening and closing, I ducked out of the front door to take care of something that had been bothering me since we pulled into the lot.

TWENTY MINUTES LATER, Danica emerged from the bedroom. She had on a pink dress with tiny white flowers printed all over it. The top tied behind her neck and gave me a hard-on inducing view of her tits. Her hair piled on top of her head in a mass of curls and she'd painted her lips in a matching shade of pink.

I wanted to tell her to forget the party so I could lift the hem of her skirt and find out what she had on underneath.

Before I had the chance, someone knocked at the door. I stood closest, so I turned and put my hand on the knob.

"Want me to answer it for you?"

"Sure." She moved to my side while I pulled the door open.

A man stood on the other side. He had on a teal suit that looked uncomfortably tight but seemed to work on him. The smile on his face faded, then deepened as his gaze drifted over me.

"Ricard, what are you doing here? I told my mother not to waste your time." Danica reached for the man.

"What your mama wants, your mama gets. I'm sorry I'm running late. She couldn't decide whether to go sleek and sophisticated or let me back comb a little bit of her bob for some volume." He gave her a light embrace and peered up at me over the rim of his designer glasses. "Who's the man candy, Dani girl?"

Danica blinked hard. "Sorry, Ricard, this is Cole Bishop. He's one of the owners of the Devil's Dance Distillery I've been working at in Beaver Bluff. Cole, this is Ricard, my mother's personal stylist."

"Nice to meet you." I thrust my hand at the man.

Instead of shaking it, he gently lifted it to his lips and kissed the back of my hand. "The pleasure is definitely all mine."

"Ricard's a terrible flirt," Danica said.

"Guilty as charged." He dropped my hand and eyed Danica. "Well, you shouldn't have started without me, but I can probably fix it."

"Actually, I think I'm good. I'm sorry you came all this way, but I told my mom I could handle getting myself ready for tonight. After all, it's Angela's event. Nobody cares what I look like."

Ricard's dark eyes flashed. "Stop that nonsense, Dani girl. You look lovely and will outshine them all."

She rolled her eyes while her cheeks colored. "I know why my mother likes you so much."

"If you're sure you don't need anything,"—Ricard fluttered

his eyelashes—"I suppose I should tell you to have fun at the party tonight." He waved at us his over his shoulder as he turned to go.

"Bye, Ricard." Danica closed the door behind him and turned to me. "I told my mom I didn't need his help. Do I? How do I look?"

Uncertainty clouded her eyes. That wouldn't do, not for this woman. She needed to know how gorgeous she was, how absolutely stunning she looked.

"You look amazing. Good enough to eat."

Her lips curved up. I loved knowing I was the one to put a smile on her face.

"I mean it. If we didn't have to get out the door, I'd spread you out on the couch right there and gobble you up like my favorite dessert." Even thinking about it had my dick standing at the ready.

"That might be the nicest thing anyone's ever said to me." She blushed, the color on her cheeks almost matched the shade of her dress.

"You deserve to hear nice things. All the time." Cautiously, I pulled her into my arms. I didn't want to mess up her hair or wrinkle her dress. At least not until we got back later tonight.

"I'm glad you came with me." She kissed my cheek, then immediately wiped at it with her thumb. "Shoot, I got lipstick on you."

"It's all right. Maybe I'll leave it there so everyone knows I'm yours." I was only half joking. More than anything, I wanted to be hers, and I wanted her to be mine.

"You don't need to be marked. I'll make sure they know you're with me." She went to the kitchen and brought back a damp paper towel. Too soon she'd removed her lipstick mark, though it felt as if it had been imprinted on me permanently.

"Shall we?" I held out my arm, and she wrapped her hand around the sleeve of my button down.

"You clean up well."

"Thanks." I held the door open for her and used her key to lock up behind us.

"What the hell?" She stopped just outside her apartment. "Cole, what did you do?"

I swept my gaze over the freshly shorn bush that no longer blocked the view of her front door. "Just looking out for my girl. I'll feel better if I know your apartment door isn't hidden."

She shook her head, but the grin that tickled the edges of her mouth made me think she wasn't mad I'd taken it upon myself to give her bush a trim. "I'd better not get in trouble with the management for that."

"Anyone gives you grief, just send them my way."

"Oh, don't worry, I will. Are you ready to meet my family? This is your last chance to get away while you still can."

I pulled open the door to the passenger side of my truck. "You'd better get in then. Because I'm not going anywhere without you."

The ride to the country club didn't take as long as I'd hoped. Too soon I was handing over my keys to the valet and sliding my palm along the small of Danica's back. She hadn't been kidding when she said the location was a bit pretentious. White marble columns flanked the entrance, making me think we were entering a Roman coliseum instead of a place where regular people played golf and tennis.

We headed inside but were stopped by a man in tails at the door. "I'm sorry, sir. This is a formal affair. We can't let you in without a tie or a jacket."

Danica frowned. "He's wearing dress pants and a button-down shirt. The invitation didn't say anything about a required dress code."

"I'm sorry, miss. We base our rules on the desires of the wedding party."

"That's ridiculous."

"It's okay. I'll head back to your place. Just call me when you're done and I'll come back to get you." I didn't want to cause a scene or draw any attention to Danica.

"If you'd like to borrow a tie, we can accommodate you, sir," he offered.

"Sure." I didn't have anything to lose by wearing a borrowed tie, but had everything to gain.

"You don't have to do this," she said.

I leaned close and kissed her cheek. "It's okay. I want to."

The attendant returned with a necktie draped over his arm. "I'm sorry, sir. Usually we have several to choose from, but this is the only one left."

"You can't wear that, Cole." Danica looped her arm through mine and tugged me toward the door.

"I've worn worse." I took the tie from the attendant and flipped my collar up. As I stepped toward the mirror hanging by the door, I executed a perfect Windsor knot. Upon examining my reflection, maybe I'd underestimated the ugly factor of this particular necktie. It was designed to look like a fish, most likely a salmon. The tip of the tie was supposed to be its mouth and the body of the fish stretched from my belly button to my throat.

Danica grimaced, but to her credit, she quickly recovered. "You look stunning. Should we get this over with so we can get out of here and have some fun?"

"You're in charge, Ms. Watson."

We entered the main room where servers in tails passed champagne and artfully arranged small bites on silver trays.

Thousands of candles provided soft light, complemented by the dimmed crystal chandeliers overhead.

"What does your aunt do for a living?" I muttered against Danica's ear.

"Marries well." Her shoulders tensed as an older couple approached from the other side of the room. "Incoming. Last chance to abort your mission."

Too late. The woman reached out to take Danica's hands. "Darling, I'm so glad you could make it tonight, though I wish you'd been here when I asked."

"Hi, Mom." Danica followed her mother's lead, pressing air kisses to her cheeks.

"Who's this?" Her mother's brow arched while she slid an appraising gaze over me. It felt like I was being sized up by an opponent. An opponent trying to figure out if I was worth the effort it would take to defeat me or not.

"Mom, Dad, I'd like you to meet Cole Bishop. He's part-owner of the whiskey distillery where I've been working for the past couple of weeks. Cole, these are my parents, Coco and Charlie Watson."

Coco? Her mom's name was Coco? I took Mrs. Watson's outstretched hand in my grip. "It's nice to meet you."

"Master distiller?" Coco's nose turned down a bit. "Making whiskey is a rather crude profession, isn't it?"

"Mom!" Danica's eyes flashed with annoyance.

"Sorry, darling, but it's true. I don't know why you insisted on taking that position. If you wanted to promote some sort of alcohol, you should have moved to Napa."

"I enjoy a whiskey now and then." Danica's dad gave me a friendly smile. "What's the name of your operation?"

I shook his hand with more enthusiasm than I'd shown Danica's mother. "Devil's Dance, sir."

"I shared a bottle of Devil's Dance Distinct with a colleague once. You make some mighty fine whiskey, son."

Danica put her hand on my shoulder. "Cole's the master distiller. He's the one who makes all the decisions about mash bills and blends and—"

"What on earth are you wearing around your neck?" Mrs. Watson's features pinched, making it look like she was experiencing severe pain. "It hurts my eyes to even look at it." She squinted as if her eyes were literally burning out of her head.

To Danica's credit, she came to my defense. "Mother. Don't be rude. Cole didn't know about the dress code, so he had to get a tie from the front desk."

"Darling,"—Mrs. Watson ignored her daughter and reached out to her husband—"is that the MacPhains? I think it is. They haven't shown their face in public since the scandal about that Ponzi scheme they were in blew up. What did she do to her hair?"

"Excuse us, please?" Mr. Watson nodded to both of us, then took his wife's arm and propelled her to the opposite side of the room.

"So, those are your parents?" I asked.

Danica summoned a smile—one that seemed a little too bright given the brush-off we'd just received from her mom. "Yeah, that's Coco and Charlie."

I put my arm around her shoulder and kissed the top of her head, being careful not to mess up her complicated hairdo. "What do you say to grabbing a couple glasses of champagne and a tray full of those tiny snacks and finding a place on the patio where we can sit down?"

Her smile grew wider. "I'd say you're on."

The Danica I'd gotten to know in Beaver Bluff returned. She shed the look of disappointment and grabbed my hand.

"Come on, I know where we can get some big plates and our own bottle of champagne."

That was my girl.

The fact I'd started thinking of her as my girl wasn't lost on me. How had that happened so quickly? With one hand securely wrapped around hers, I rubbed my palm over my heart. We'd have to find a way to make this work. I wasn't sure I could handle the alternative.

CHAPTER 28

DESPITE THE LESS-THAN-WARM welcome my mother extended to Cole, he seemed to have a good time. We even danced a few slow dances once the band began to play. I welcomed any excuse to have his arms wrapped tight around me. Even in a salmon tie, he was the most gorgeous man I'd ever seen.

We lasted longer than I thought we would. Even shut down the reception with a few of my cousins out on the dance floor. After we sent the bride and groom on their way with a shower of expensive, custom-perfumed bubbles, I turned toward Cole.

"You ready to head back to my place?"

He tightened his grip, pulling me up against him. "I thought you'd never ask. I can't wait to get my hands on you and find out what you've got on underneath that dress."

The insecurities I'd felt earlier in the evening vanished. He made me feel sexy, desirable, wanted.

"Should I leave this here for the next poor bastard who underestimates the dress code?" His fingers lingered on the knot at his neck.

"I think you ought to keep it. Maybe it will bring you luck if you wear it during your presentation to the board." I gave him a big smile when I said it, my lips stretching wide.

He pulled the tie from around his neck, then coiled it into a roll that he shoved in his pocket. "Let's go, gorgeous."

I felt like I was sitting on pins and needles the entire way home. Anticipation slowly unfurled through my body until every nerve ending was on high alert. A quick brush of his thumb over the back of my hand nearly sent me into orbit. My body was attuned to his, ready and eager for what the night held in store.

We barely made it through the doorway before he eased his hands down my thighs and slid the hem of my skirt up to my waist. I pushed into him, not caring what he might think. The need to feel his hard length fill me completely pushed every other thought out of my head.

"I've got something for you." He pulled back enough that his words weren't muffled against my mouth. "Something I want you to try."

"What is it?" My cheeks tingled from rubbing against the scruff on his chin. I ran a palm over my skin, relishing the sensation.

"Whiskey." He dipped down and nibbled my earlobe. "A special bottle I wanted to give you to celebrate our first official date."

During the short time I'd spent in Beaver Bluff, I'd noticed the people associated with the distillery commemorated special occasions with bottles of whiskey. They paid attention to the date a barrel was stored in the rick house or the date a bottle was filled. Knowing Cole thought our date was whiskey-worthy sent warmth flowing through my veins, like I'd just taken a sip of Devil's Dance. But instead of the burn being limited to my belly, it spread through my limbs.

"Do I get to try it?" I didn't want to let go of him, not even long enough for him to retrieve a bottle from the kitchen.

"I have a better idea." He led me into the bedroom and slowly stripped off my dress.

I shivered as he guided me to lie down on the bed. Within moments, he'd shed his shirt and picked up something from the nightstand.

"Is that my whiskey?" I propped myself up on my elbows, trying to make out the shadowy form he held in his hands.

"It is." He gently pushed me backward until my back met the mattress.

"What are you planning?" Anticipation made my nipples tighten. Need pulsed between my legs.

"Hold still, baby." Liquid dribbled onto my stomach, pooling in my belly button and running between my breasts.

I gasped. "You'd better not be wasting good whiskey."

"Who says it's going to waste?" He bent over me, licking the liquid from my skin. "I'm going to lap up every drop. Then I'm going to turn you over onto your stomach and do it again."

Pleasure coursed through me. Every touch of his tongue to my skin made me moan until I couldn't take it anymore.

When he felt like we'd both had enough, he finally gave me what I'd been craving the most. I fell asleep nestled in his arms, his cock still buried deep inside me.

I STARTLED AWAKE, the blare of Cole's ringtone putting an abrupt end to the erotic dreams I'd been having. Were they dreams? I ran my hand over my stomach. The phone rang again. I pressed a kiss to Cole's cheek.

"Hey, someone's trying to get a hold of you."

He fumbled for his phone on the nightstand, finally grabbing it and pressing it to his ear. "Yeah?"

I'd seen the name pop up on his screen. His brother Miller's voice came through the phone. "Where the fuck are you, bro?"

Cole rubbed a palm over his face. "I'm in Knoxville tonight. What's going on?"

Something was wrong. Cole's expression went from an irritated scowl when he answered the phone to one of total shock.

"Hey, are you okay?" I nudged him with my elbow.

He seemed to snap to it, barked some orders into the phone, then kicked the sheets off his legs. "I've got to head back. There's a fire at the distillery."

"What?" My throat tightened, choking out the air.

"That was Miller. There was an explosion in the distilling area. I've got to head back now."

"Of course." I flung the sheet back and climbed out of bed. "I'll come with you."

He put his hands on my arms and lowered his chin, meeting my gaze. "You don't have to come back with me."

"I want to." Whatever was happening between us was new, but I wanted to be there for him. Especially after he'd told me about the fire he'd been through when he was a kid. He needed someone there for support.

I wanted to be that someone, even if it meant risking the wrath and disappointment of my mother for not showing up for the gift opening the next day.

"If you're coming, we've got to go now." He nodded, more to himself than to me. "We need to head straight to the distillery. I can't lose it, Danica."

The way he said my name, like a desperate prayer, made my heart ache for him. "Of course. Give me two minutes to pull on some clothes and grab my things."

He spun back and planted a firm kiss on my lips. "Thank you."

I squeezed his hand, then watched him take long, smooth strides from the room. Within minutes, I'd pulled myself together enough to throw a few things into a bag and yank on a pair of yoga pants and a sweatshirt.

He waited for me in the truck, his hands wrapped around the wheel, his grip so tight that his knuckles were white.

"Are you sure you want to go with me?" he asked.

I pulled the door closed, narrowly missing catching my own foot in the door. "Yes. I want to be there for you."

"Okay, buckle up."

I snapped my seatbelt in place as he pressed on the gas, peeling away from the bright lights of my complex's parking lot. He spent most of the drive on the phone, trying to get updates on the situation at the distillery. I'd never felt so utterly helpless. There wasn't anything I could do except sit next to him with my hand on his thigh, trying to let him know he didn't have to go through this alone.

The drive from Knoxville to Beaver Bluff usually took three hours, but we made it in just under two. Cole tried to get close to the distillery, but the police had put up caution tape and a crowd of people blocked the drive. He pulled over on the grass and had barely stopped the truck before his hand was on the door handle.

"Go. I'll catch up to you." I'd slow him down, so I watched while he disappeared into the crowd. Please let everything be okay. I slid my feet into my sneakers and made my way through the people to the front of the crowd.

Smoke rose into the air from the section of the building where the distilling equipment was housed. Cole stood beyond the barrier, surrounded by his brothers and sister. I glanced around, expecting to see Davis or Harper or someone from the Stewart side.

"It's a damn shame, don't you think?" A gruff voice came from over my shoulder. I turned back to see Pappy standing there, arms crossed over his chest.

"Has anyone said what happened?" All I'd been able to gather from Cole's conversations was that someone had mishandled a piece of the equipment.

"Musta had someone new running point on one of the stills. The damn thing blew up. It's a miracle nobody was hurt." Pappy nodded toward where an ambulance parked. "So far, the only thing anyone's been treated for is a few scratches and scrapes."

The tightness around my heart squeezed even harder. Cole would never forgive himself if someone got hurt. Even though he'd been two hundred miles away and had nothing to do with what happened tonight, he'd probably wonder if things would have been different if he'd been around. I wanted to go to him, to wrap my arms around him and try to tell him everything would be okay.

"I suppose this will change their plans about how they move forward," Pappy said. "I've half a mind to wonder if one of the Stewarts had something to do with this."

"Why would they want to damage the distillery?" Maybe it was time for this Pappy to pass the name onto the next guy. He sounded like he might have fallen prey to some wild conspiracy theories.

"It'll be a hell of a lot cheaper to buy a new still that can churn out that fancy kind of vodka Davis has his heart set on than to replace the one that got damaged. That dinosaur's so old they'd have to have someone come out and make custom parts." Pappy shook his head. "It's a damn shame."

I shifted my gaze to the front of the building. The firefighters had put out the flames, but smoke still drifted out of the shattered windows, filling the air with the scent of burning wood and strong alcohol. Davis might be desperate to move the business in a new direction, but he wouldn't resort to sabotage. I'd met the man. He wasn't on my list of favorite people, but he had scruples.

Didn't he?

Cole saw me standing behind the yellow tape and motioned me over. "Hey, I'm going to be here for a few hours. Do you want to take my truck back to the bed-and-breakfast? I can stop by and get it in the morning. Just leave the keys under the front seat."

"Is there anything I can do?" Despite the heat radiating off the building, the night air held a bit of a chill. "Do you want me to go grab coffee for everyone?"

"I'll be fine." He didn't make a move to embrace me or brush a kiss against my cheek. I told myself he was still in shock, that it didn't have anything to do with not wanting people to know we were together.

"Okay. Call me if you need anything."

"I will." He leaned over, giving me something that might have passed for a half-hug. It was the kind of embrace I might give someone I hadn't seen in a long time just to get them off my back. Unsettled, but sympathetic to the emotions that must be rolling through his system, I nodded.

"I'll talk to you soon?"

"Yeah." He lifted a hand to wave, but he'd already turned to head back to his family.

It wouldn't do me any good to wait here. With a heaviness in my heart, I jiggled the keys Cole had given me in my hand.

"I'm heading back to the bar and brewing up a fresh pot of coffee so people can gather there and wait for more news about the fire," Pappy offered. "I can save you a stool at the bar if you want."

I'd rather sit at Pappy's with a bunch of relative strangers than head back to the bed-and-breakfast with nothing but my own thoughts to keep me company. "I'd like that."

"I'll see you there." He lifted a gnarled hand to his forehead and gave me a pseudo salute.

THOUGH IT WAS after three o'clock in the morning, a crowd had gathered at Pappy's. Unlike the party atmosphere the last time I'd visited, the crowd tonight was very subdued. Clusters of people gathered around the bar-height tables or stuffed themselves into narrow booths. The only noise came from the live coverage on the giant TV screens scattered throughout the interior.

Pappy had been true to his word and saved me a seat at the edge of the bar. As I slid onto the stool, he stopped and placed a large plastic cup full of ice water in front of me.

"Thanks, Pappy. Have you heard anything else about the fire?" I took a big sip of my water, trying to remember the last time I'd had anything to eat. I might have to risk the deep fryer and get an order of French fries or something else to tide me over until morning.

"I guess Davis showed up and caused a scene. Now everyone's pointing fingers, trying to decide whose fault it is that the still blew up." Pappy adjusted the ball cap on his head. "Seems to me they ought to be more worried about how they're going to keep production going than casting blame. But then again, nobody asks for my opinion."

My stomach clenched as I imagined the face-off between Davis and Cole. Pappy didn't strike me as the sharpest pencil in the bunch, but right now his theory sounded like the most credible. I checked my phone for the hundredth time in the last ten minutes to make sure I hadn't missed a call or text from Cole.

With nothing else to do, I slid my phone back into my purse and pulled out my laptop. The plan might change based on the fallout from tonight's fire, but I'd promised to provide suggestions in time for the meeting I had with Davis on Monday, and I wasn't about to miss a commitment.

While Pappy served coffee and the conversation around me flowed, I opened up my document and dove in. I'd learned a lot from Cole about the importance of the distillery's history over the past two weeks. Though I couldn't change Davis's plans completely, there was definitely room to weave in a little more of the narrative Cole had shared.

As an outside consultant, I was supposed to be an impartial party. Davis had given me pretty clear direction at our first meeting. He wanted to slingshot the distillery into the twenty-first century and lay down a foundation that would carry them through the next hundred and fifty years and beyond. He didn't care so much about keeping things the same as he did about getting on the front end of new trends.

Cole was the exact opposite. He wanted to honor the history and tradition that had been established by the founders. Based on the research I'd done on the market, whiskey had a solid hold and was predicted to grow over the foreseeable future. My heart ached to lean in the direction Cole wanted to go. I could picture the short video pieces we could create in my head. Descendants of Devil's Dance would talk about how sipping one of their whiskeys was like stepping back in time.

It had to be possible to work in the best of both worlds, and I had some ideas on exactly how they could do it. My fingers flew across the keyboard as I reworked the plan Davis had originally asked for into something that would honor the past and the future.

I was so engrossed in the project, I jumped when my phone rang. Cole. I pressed it to my ear, straining to hear him over the noise inside the bar. "Just a sec. I need to step outside."

I pulled the phone away. "Hey, Pappy. Will you watch my stuff for a minute?"

He nodded, so I hit the button to save what I'd done so far and practically ran to the door.

"Hey, what's going on? Is everything okay?"

"Yeah. We lost one of our stills, but nobody was seriously injured. In the grand scheme of things, that's what matters." He sounded tired. Not just tired, totally exhausted.

"Do you need anything? I've still got your truck. I'm at Pappy's, but I can come pick you up—"

"Miller's going to drop me at home so I can change. I'm beat. I think I'll hit the sack to try to get some sleep and catch up with you in the morning. How's that sound?"

I squashed the disappointment to prevent it from coming through in my voice. "Of course. If you need anything, just call."

"I will. I'll talk to you in the morning. Oh, and Danica?"

"Yes?"

"I think it's going to get pretty ugly between me and Davis. I'm not saying it's going to come to it, but you might want to prepare yourself to have to pick a side. I know he's the one who hired you, but…"

"I'm with you, Cole." If it came down to it, the choice would be easy. I'd put business above my heart in the past and it hadn't turned out well.

"If you change your mind, I'll understand. I've got to go. Miller's heading out. Sweet dreams."

He hung up before I could reassure him that I'd always put

him first. What did he mean that if I changed my mind he'd understand? That didn't sound like the man I'd spent the better part of the past twenty-four hours with. Or the kind of man I wanted to spend the rest of my life with.

With doubt creeping into my mind, I faced the door of Pappy's. I'd let Cole get a good night's sleep tonight. But tomorrow he was going to hear exactly how "with him" I intended to be.

CHAPTER 29
Cole

I WOKE to the sound of someone banging on my front door. "Cole, you in there?"

Events of the night before flooded my head. Seeing Danica dressed in pink, the drive back to Beaver Bluff, the fire... dammit, the fire. I flung the covers off and stumbled out of bed.

"Cole?" The knocking continued.

I peered through a crack in the shades, not sure whether I was more surprised to see Pappy awake before eight a.m. or to see him standing on my front porch.

"Hey, what's up?" I pulled the door open, not even caring that I stood there in nothing but my underwear. I'd been so tired the night before that I barely stumbled out of the shower before collapsing into bed. Pappy was lucky I'd had enough awareness to put on my boxers.

"I did you a solid, my friend." He held something between his fingers.

I squinted, finding it hard to open my eyes with only a couple of hours of sleep. "What is it?"

"The key to your future." Pappy juggled it from one hand

to the other. "You're going to want to kiss me for this one."

Highly doubting that, I staggered toward the kitchen. "Let me put a pot of coffee on."

Pappy followed. "I know I'm not supposed to take sides, but when the opportunity popped up for me to give fate a little nudge in your direction, I just couldn't help myself."

"What are you talking about?" My fingers fumbled with the paper coffee filter. I'd thought about getting one of those machines that took the little pods, but I liked my coffee extra-extra strong. More interested in separating one flimsy filter from the stack than listening to whatever nonsense Pappy was spouting about, I blinked away the need for sleep.

"That consultant the Stewarts hired. She was at the bar last night with her computer."

"Danica?" I needed to call her this morning. After I caffeinated and got rid of Pappy. The fire last night had made me see things crystal clear.

"Yep. Had her fancy laptop sitting up on the bar. I didn't think anything of it until she stepped outside. Didn't want anybody to spill on it, so I flipped it around to close it for her. That's when I saw what she'd been working on." Pappy grinned through his scraggly gray beard.

"You spied on Danica?" My fingers twitched—the need to protect her rising.

"Hell yes, I did, and you'll be kissing my wrinkled old ass when you see what I brought you." He held out his hand, giving me a look at what he'd been tossing around. A black USB drive sat in the center of his palm. "Go on, load it up. You need to see what she's planning on presenting to the board before she buries you with it."

My pulse pounded through my ears as I squinted at the drive. "You stole a file from her computer?"

Pappy shifted, scuffing his boots across the wooden planks

of my kitchen floor. "I didn't steal it. She left it right there in front of me, like she wanted me to see it. All's I did was make a copy. It's not like I stole it from her. She's still got it."

The air felt too dense to breathe, and I coughed as I tried to suck in a breath. "Doesn't matter if she still has the original. You made a copy and stole it. I can't use this. It wouldn't be right."

"What do you mean, you can't use it? Davis Stewart's been gunning for you. I heard people talk last night that he might have even set the fire. Did you think about that?"

I'd heard the same thing and clenched my fists, determined to get to the bottom of the rumors no matter how long it would take.

"I know your heart's in the right place, but I can't look at the file. It wouldn't be right." I wouldn't do that to her. Despite my hatred for Davis and his plans, Danica deserved a shot at striking out on her own. As much as I wanted the future of the distillery to honor the past, if the board felt like her ideas were better, I'd have to be okay with that. She was the business guru. I was just a guy who loved making the best whiskey I could and sharing it with others, hopefully at a profit.

"Damn you, Cole Bishop." Pappy tossed the drive on the counter. "Your pride's going to be your downfall."

"I'm not proud. I just know the difference between right and wrong, and using information you acquired through less than honest means wouldn't be right." At this point, my morals might be all I had left. I didn't say that part out loud, just braced my palms against the counter while I waited for the coffee to drip into the glass carafe.

"Well, I hope you're proud of yourself when you run that business into the ground." He shook his head, then stomped through the living room, showing himself out.

Yeah, it was tempting. The black plastic drive mocked me

from where it landed next to the sugar bowl. It would be too easy to pop it into my laptop and find out what Danica had been working on all this time.

I wouldn't do it, though.

Before I could change my mind, I pulled open the cabinet door and tossed it into the trashcan. She was already going to be hurt by what I had to tell her. I wasn't about to rub salt in her wounds and add insult to injury by spying on her as well.

The coffee pot belched out the last of the dark brew. I filled a mug and burned my tongue on the first sip. The longer I put it off, the worse it would be. With my fingers wrapped around the handle of my Save the Beavers mug, I forced my feet to carry me back to the bedroom so I could put on some clothes.

"I WAS STARTING to get worried. I'm so glad you called." Danica slipped down from behind the wheel of my truck. She looked so cute sitting in the driver's seat. For a moment, I was struck speechless by the way her jeans molded to her hips and the way the sun sparkled in her eyes when she slid her sunglasses on top of her head.

"Sorry, there's been a lot going on." I took the keys she handed me. "I thought maybe we could drive down by the river and take a walk?"

"Sure." She reached out to hug me, nestling against my chest.

I breathed in her scent, the mixture of coconut and pineapple instantly soothing my nerves.

"Is everything okay?" She pulled back, her forehead furrowed in question.

"We need to talk." It wouldn't do any good to put it off. I would only make things harder on myself...harder on her. That was the last thing I wanted to do.

"You're scaring me, Cole." She cocked a hip and put a finger under my chin, tipping my head up to force me to meet her gaze.

I stared into her eyes, recognizing the same kind of vulnerability I felt deep down inside. "How about that drive?"

Her smile faded and she let her hand fall away from my face. "If there's something you want to say to me, just say it."

"Danica, I..." I didn't want to do this here. Didn't want to do it at all, but it was better this way.

"You what?" The glint in her eyes hardened, challenging me to tell her the truth.

"I don't think it's going to work out between us." I closed my eyes as I forced the last couple of words from my mouth.

"You don't think? When did that occur to you?" Her tone was deliberate, measured. I didn't picture her as the kind of woman to work herself into an emotional frenzy, but the lack of emotion in her voice was almost worse than having her burst into tears.

I opened my eyes and stared at my feet, my hands, my chest... anything to keep from seeing the accusation in her eyes. "I'm sorry. Last night was my fault. I should have been there."

"Wait. You think the fire at the distillery was somehow your fault?"

I let out a sharp breath and finally met her gaze. "Yeah."

"You were in Knoxville when it started. That doesn't make any sense."

"Exactly. I was in Knoxville. With you." I rested a palm against the hood of my truck, the feel of the warm engine under my hand a reminder that I could still feel something. Every other part of me was numb.

"How could it be your fault?"

She didn't get it. How could she when she'd never had to

deal with the fallout of a mistake like the one I'd made all those years ago?

"Harper had a new guy running the still over the weekend since she'd been out of town. I should have been there keeping an eye on things. If I had, I would have known what to do. Instead, I was driving you back to Knoxville." I'd forgotten myself for a while. I'd let her distract me from the things that mattered most. It wasn't fair for me to be selfish and try to find my own happiness while the future of the people who depended on me hung in the balance.

"You took a night off." Her lips pinched together while she waited for me to acknowledge her point.

"And now the distillery will pay for it." The way I saw it, I was solely responsible for the fire. I might not have started it, but I should have been there when it happened instead of hundreds of miles away.

She shook her head while she waved her hands in the air. "Are you listening to yourself? Do you have any idea how ridiculous you sound right now?"

"That seems to be one of your favorite words to describe me." She'd used it often enough. "Maybe I am ridiculous. Maybe it's time I stop trying to be something I'm not. Stop reaching for things that aren't meant to be mine and focus on the things that I do have control over."

"You know what it sounds like to me?" Her eyes narrowed as she poked a finger into my chest. "It sounds like you're willing to sacrifice yourself for everyone else so that you don't have to put yourself out there."

I held my ground, fighting off the urge to wrap my hand around hers and draw her against me. "Sounds like you don't know what the hell you're talking about."

"Fine. Keep telling yourself that. It's easier for you to hide behind all of your obligations to others. Where were your brothers and sister when the fire started? Do you think it's their job to be personally responsible for everything that goes on here? Why are you the one who has to take the heat on this?" She flattened her palm against my chest. The hurt in her eyes made my heart crack into pieces. I wished I could be everything she needed, but I couldn't.

"I don't expect you to understand." I circled her wrist with my hand and gently tugged it away, breaking contact with my chest.

"Well, good, because I don't get it. I thought we had something special, Cole." She shook her head. I could almost see the cloud of defeat settle around her shoulders. "I really thought you were different."

"I'm sorry I—"

"Don't." She put her hand up, palm out, the universal sign for shut the fuck up.

"Danica—"

"Seriously. Stop."

"At least let me drive you back to the bed-and-breakfast." I sounded like a douchebag, even to my own ears.

"Don't bother. I can handle myself from here." She spun around and started walking down the gravel drive to the main road.

It would take her an hour to walk the four and a half miles back to town. I went back inside and found my phone. There was only one person I'd trust to help me out in a situation like this.

Vaughn answered on the first ring. "Hey, what's going on? Did you hear anything from the fire inspector?"

"Nothing confirmed, but he doesn't suspect foul play. I need a favor, though. Can you pick Danica up and drive her back to town? She just left my place and is walking back to the bed-and-breakfast."

"Yeah, sure. Want to tell me what's going on?"

"Not yet. But be careful. Make sure she knows it's you and not me, or she might not get in the truck."

"I'll pick her up and take her to town, but then I'm heading over."

My chest loosened a little at the tone in his voice. Danica was wrong. I did have someone else I could share the burden with. We already shared the same DNA. Grateful he was on his way, I flipped open my laptop. It was time to pull out all the stops and figure out how to save my family's business.

CHAPTER 30
Danica

LESS THAN TWENTY-FOUR hours after I'd left my apartment in Knoxville, I walked back up the sidewalk. The sight of the scraggly bush by my door brought on a fresh wave of almost-tears. No matter how much I hurt, I wouldn't let myself cry.

Cole Bishop wasn't worth it.

I flung my apartment door open and stepped inside. The scent of the cologne he'd worn last night hung in the air. Had it really only been last night that we'd flirted with each other right here in my living room?

My head spun with everything that had happened in the past twenty-four hours. I'd gone from feeling on top of the world to being buried under so much heaviness that I wondered if I'd ever be able to dig myself out.

I slumped onto a couch cushion and cradled my head in my hands. Of course I'd dig myself out. That's what I always did. Though I'd never mix work with my personal life again. I should have learned my lesson the first time around. Silly me. I'd thought Cole was different.

Thinking about him only made me feel bad about myself.

I'd never been one to wallow. The three-hour drive home had been my allotted woe-is-me time slot. I needed to update my presentation so I could send it over to Davis before our meeting tomorrow. Though Cole had blindsided me by ending what had never even really started between us, I wasn't going to let that affect my recommendations for the distillery.

I hadn't had a chance to finish my presentation last night at Pappy's, so I flipped open my laptop to log in. While it booted up, I went to the kitchen to grab a glass of water. The bottle of whiskey Cole gave me sat on the counter next to the refrigerator. I flipped open the small card hanging from a gold ribbon.

Here's to honoring the past while keeping an eye on the future.

Yours,
Cole

My heart hiccupped. Dark amber liquid filled the heavy, clear container. Devil's Dance Distinct. Cole told me he only had a couple of bottles left of the hard-to-find whiskey.

Though part of me was honored he'd chosen to share it with me, some collectors had paid upwards of five thousand dollars per bottle for it. I couldn't keep it. He'd given it to me when things between us were different, when there'd been hope for a future.

Before I gave in to the shoulda-known-betters that threatened to suffocate me, I filled up a glass of water and gulped it down. It didn't matter how I felt about Cole—I'd do the job I'd been hired to do by Davis, even if it did mean changing my initial recommendation to incorporate a nod to the history of the distillery.

I ignored all the reminders of Cole being in my apartment the night before and focused on my laptop sitting on my kitchen table. In desperate need of someone who could help me figure out a plan, I pulled up Jolene's number. Hoping she wasn't in the middle of one of her big family brunches, I hit the call button.

"Hey, how did the big date go last night? Are you ready to move to the mountains and make gorgeous brown-eyed babies with your whiskey man?" My bestie laughed at her own joke.

"Not exactly." I tried to keep the tremor out of my voice, but she knew me well enough to be able to tell I wasn't okay.

"What happened? Did he stand you up? Did your mom do something at the party? Tell me, Danica."

If she'd give me a chance to speak, I'd be happy to fill her in on how miserable the past twenty-four hours had treated me. "Last night was great. Until it wasn't."

"What happened?"

"Where should I start?" I filled her in on the fire, the drive back to Beaver Bluff, and the big break up scene.

"What a bastard. You're better off without him. You know that, don't you?" Jolene used her boss babe voice—the one we'd modeled after listening to an inspiring motivational talk J. Lo had given.

I pressed my fingers to my temples, where a headache threatened. The kind that required silence, a cold washcloth on my forehead, and complete darkness. "Maybe Peter was right. Maybe I am a fuck up who won't be able to make it on her own."

"Cut it out. You know you were his number one. He just couldn't handle you doing things better than him. Don't let him get in your head."

It was too late for that. What if he was right? What if I didn't have what it took to handle every aspect of the business? It hadn't even been a month yet, and I was already failing.

"Danica…" Jolene said my name in a sing-song voice. "Talk to me, girl. What are you going to do?"

"I don't know yet, but I'll figure it out." I'd made it this far. I couldn't let this derail me.

"Let me know if you need to vent. You've got this. I know you do."

"Thanks." I was grateful for her faith in me. She seemed to be the only one who still had any left.

I pulled my notebooks out of my backpack and got to work. The distillery needed to change to stay viable in today's landscape, but their best bet at striking a chord with new customers was to tell their story. It was the same story Cole had been telling me all along.

How his ancestors had joined forces with a few neighboring families to charter a new opportunity and forge ahead to create a new life. How the distillery had survived fires, floods, wars, and Prohibition.

My mind played through the experiences we'd shared, like watching a movie in my head. Conveying the history of the product would create that emotional bond for the customer. Devil's Dance was in prime position to take advantage of its current market share and drive customers to try new expressions, new experiences, and new varieties without losing sight of their history.

I poured everything I had into that presentation. When I was done, I saved the file one last time. I was tempted to call in for the meeting. Driving back to Beaver Bluff for the second time in twenty-four hours didn't seem like a necessary move.

But I had bigger plans in play. Not only did I want to blow Davis and Harper away with my recommendations, I also wanted to talk to Cole and show him what I was proposing. He'd taught me more in the past two weeks than just how to taste whiskey. He taught me I needed to stand up for myself and not let others keep me from going for what I wanted.

I wished I'd been able to teach him a thing or two as well. Like he shouldn't have to keep paying the price for what happened when he was a kid. He'd let the guilt suffocate him, but he needed to learn the only one who could set him free was himself.

I wanted him to be a part of my life.

And if he'd let me, I was fully prepared to do whatever I needed to do to make that happen.

CHAPTER 31

WHEN DANICA TOLD me she was heading back to Knoxville, I assumed that meant she wouldn't ever come back to Beaver Bluff. But Charity said she'd walked into the office like she owned the place and took a spot in the conference room, right across the wide table from Davis and the rest of the Stewarts. I wasn't invited to the meeting of minds, but that didn't stop me from finding reasons to pace the hallway outside.

Vaughn was onto me. "You keep that up and you'll wear a groove in the floor."

"What do you think is going on in there?" He was the only one I could talk to about what went down between Danica and me, and I hadn't even given him the whole scoop.

"They already had the door closed by the time I got here this morning, so I can't say for sure." Vaughn poured the dregs at the bottom of the coffee pot into the sink. "But it doesn't sound good."

My gut felt pulled in all directions, like one of those machines that stretched saltwater taffy had gone to work on it.

"How's our presentation coming?" he asked.

"It's fine." I was almost done putting the finishing touches on the twenty-plus page report. He'd have it by the end of the week, which would give him a few days to look it over before we had to run it in front of the board.

He filled the pot from the tap, then poured it into the water reservoir. "Do you have any idea what she might be recommending?"

I studied his expression, looking for some hint that might indicate Pappy had told him about the USB drive. Unless my twin had figured out how to fool me, he clearly had no idea.

"No. She told me she appreciated learning more about our history, but I don't know if she's actually going to use any of that in her suggestions."

"All that time you spent together, and you didn't get any sense of her plans?" His lips pinched together, one of his tells that he was pissed.

"We didn't do a lot of talking, okay?" I spread my arms out, anger and frustration swirling together inside my chest like a toxic cocktail that could have negative consequences if it spilled over.

Vaughn dumped several scoops of ground dark roast into the filter. "You really screwed the pooch on this one, didn't you?"

He wasn't saying or thinking anything that I hadn't already thought of myself. Yeah, I fucked up.

Again.

But I owned it. Shut down the chance of anything happening between me and Danica over it. No matter how bad he made me feel, it wouldn't come anywhere close to how disappointed I was in myself.

"It'll be fine." If I continued to tell myself that, maybe it would come true.

While we stared at each other from opposite sides of the break room, the door to the conference room flew open.

Harper poked her head around the corner of the break room door. "Hey there, Cole. I figured you'd be close by. Davis was wondering if you could join us for a few minutes."

I shot a quick glance at my brother. He shrugged. Obviously, he had no idea what was going on. "What's this all about?"

Harper cocked a hip against the doorway and examined her nails, like she had all the time in the goddamn world. "Davis thought your girlfriend might need some backup."

"My girlfriend?" Anger clouded my vision, but I held it in check.

"Yeah,"—Harper shrugged a slim shoulder—"we heard she flipped sides on us while we were gone. He thought you might want a chance to say goodbye before we send her packing."

Fuck. They'd found out we'd been seeing each other. But how? We'd been careful. I'd never meant for her to lose her job over this. I clenched my jaw, glared at Vaughn, and stalked out of the break room and across the hall.

Danica sat in a chair at the far end of the conference room. She was holding herself together… barely.

My gut instinct told me to go to her, but I didn't want to make the situation any worse before I figured out what the hell was going on. Davis held court at the head of the table. While our eyes met, he calmly lifted a mug of coffee and took a sip.

"You wanna tell me what's going on?" I fired the question at him, the need to level him surging inside me like a hunter who had a buck in the crosshairs.

He leaned back in his chair and crossed his arms over his chest. "Have a seat, Cole. I was just about to ask you the same question."

With protecting Danica as my goal, I sat down a few chairs away from her and mimicked his body language. "Satisfied?"

"Hardly." Davis sneered. That's the only way to describe the look that passed across his features as he shifted his gaze from me to Danica and back again.

"Are you okay?" My voice softened, and I looked at the woman who still held my heart in her hands. I might have ended things, but that didn't change the way I felt about her, or my need to shield her from whatever Davis was plotting.

Danica barely looked at me. She kept her eyes trained on the head of the table, but I saw the tremor in her hands as she clasped them in front of her.

"That's sweet. Checking in on your girlfriend to make sure she's okay?" Davis stood and shoved his hands in his pockets.

It took every bit of self-control I possessed not to stand up and deck him on the side of his chiseled jaw. "Cut the bullshit. What's going on?"

"Evidently, the two of you had quite the time while we were away. Tell me, Cole, when did you target the consultant we hired? I heard rumors the two of you met before she even came to town. Did you look her up and pick her out of all the women at the hotel bar that night, or was it just a coincidence?"

I drew my brows together. "What are you talking about?"

"They know we met in Knoxville." Danica spoke, but avoided making eye contact. "Jolene said something and Harper put two and two together. Yes, Cole and I met before I came to Beaver Bluff, but we met as strangers. We didn't mean to get involved, it just happened. I can assure you, though, my association with Cole has nothing to do with the plan I put together. If you'll let me go over the details with you, you'll see it's—"

"We've gotten what we need from you, Ms. Watson."

Davis's voice was cold enough to set off another Ice Age. "I have no interest in hearing about a plan that favors the Bishop family. Especially since they went behind our backs and were trying to separate themselves from the business."

My throat went dry. How did he know about that?

"That's right, Cole." Davis's lips curled up in a smirk. "You might have gone to Knoxville in your search for an attorney, but did you forget that's where I went to school and got that degree in Forestry? My roommate might have failed out sophomore year, but not before I met his daddy, who happens to be a high-powered corporate lawyer."

"You were pulling away from the distillery?" Danica finally faced me, her features a mix of confusion and hurt.

"I can explain." I put my hands out, trying to calm down the situation before it spun out of control.

"We'll leave the two of you to your lover's spat." Turning toward Danica, Davis shook his head. "I had high hopes for your plan, Ms. Watson. I think it goes without saying that we're relieving you of your service to the Devil's Dance Distillery. We'll be moving forward with the original ideas we talked about."

"We'd also like to relieve you of the laptop we provided." Harper held out a hand. "According to our contract, we own the rights to everything you created for us during your time here."

Davis watched over Danica's shoulder while she shut down the computer and handed it over.

"I'm sorry it came to this." Jaw tight, his features a mask of cool, collected fury, Davis didn't look sorry at all.

Danica shoved her notebook into her bag. She might be fooling Davis and Harper, but I saw the way her hands shook and the rise and fall of her uneven breaths. We needed to talk. I never meant for any of this to happen.

"I'll call that company you used to work for to see if they have someone available to help us finalize the plan we're going to present," Davis said on his way out the door. "We can't tolerate this level of incompetence."

The hairs on the back of my neck rose at the insult. Danica and I might not be on speaking terms, but she wasn't incompetent. She was smarter than the lot of us put together. And there was no way in hell I'd let her old boss step foot on distillery grounds. Not after she told me what he'd done.

Danica followed, not bothering to look at me as she fled the conference room. I tried to catch up to her before she got into her car. "Hey, wait up. We need to talk."

"What's there to talk about?" She finally met my gaze, but her eyes had lost their shine. "You tried to double cross the Stewarts. We both lied. I deserve this."

"No, you don't." I reached for her, but she slipped inside the car and pulled the door shut. Pressing my palm to the window, I leaned down. "I'm sorry, Danica. Please, let me make it up to you."

She covered her face with her palms. For a moment I thought she might open the door and give me a chance to help her figure out next steps. But then she started the car.

I barely jumped back before she pressed on the gas and reversed out of the parking spot. A few seconds later, she was gone. Her taillights blinked once as she pressed on the brakes before turning out of the lot.

I felt like someone punched me in the gut and knocked the wind out of me in one smooth move.

Vaughn met me by the front door with raised brows. Composing myself, I lifted a shoulder in a half shrug in response.

"What the hell was that all about?"

"I don't know." Stepping into the building, I ran my fingers through my hair, like that would jumpstart my brain into figuring out what to do next.

He knew just as much as I did about what was going on, though I intended to change that as soon as possible.

"Sounds like your girlfriend's in some trouble."

My head jerked up at the comment. "Cut that shit out. She's not my girlfriend."

"But you wanted her to be." The way he said it held no judgment. Just fact. A fact I couldn't argue about because it was true.

"We don't always get what we want, do we?" He knew that better than most. I felt like a dick for bringing it up.

His expression changed and the light in his eyes went out, like someone had pulled the shutters and made everything go dark. I'd gone too far.

"Sorry, man." I held out a hand in a gesture of apology, hoping he'd take it. I couldn't afford to have my strongest ally pissed off at me. Not when it looked like we were about to head into battle.

The moment stretched. Vaughn eyed me like he couldn't decide whether to make peace or deck me for reminding him of everything he'd given up. Then his hand gripped mine. "We're in this together."

"I've got to tell you something."

"What?"

He let go of my hand and I led the way back to his office. If I was going to help Danica save her reputation, I needed to come clean with my brother first. "I've got a copy of her presentation."

"How did you—"

"It fell into my possession. Doesn't matter how."

Vaughn evaluated me through narrowed eyes. "What did she recommend?"

"I don't know." Every second I spent caught in Vaughn's intense glare should have sent my pulse into triple digits. Knowing I was doing the right thing brought on a sense of calm I hadn't felt in... maybe forever. "I haven't looked at it, and I don't intend to."

He scrubbed a hand over his chin—the same move I always made when I needed to think about something. "What's your move then? I don't get it."

"I don't know what she suggested, but I'm confident I've done everything I could to convince her to consider our position." In a moment of clarity, I realized that might be what scared me the most. She could see things from an unbiased point of view. If she thought moving in Davis's direction was best for the company, maybe I needed to consider listening.

"So?" Cole studied me. For the first time I could remember, he couldn't read my mind.

"I think we should hire her to make our case to the board."

"Are you fucking kidding me?" A smile hovered at the corner of my brother's lips. "She was working for Davis. I know you're drawn to the woman, but—"

"I don't have any idea what her plan entails. For all I know, she's going to recommend we shut down the whiskey operation and start making fruity vodka." Even saying it out loud made my chest tie into knots. "Now that we're down a still, we're going to have to be very deliberate about how we use the resources we've got until we can fix it or buy a new one."

"It's up to you. I know you must have talked while you were together because of the two of us, you're the one who never shuts up. Do you trust her to have the best interest of the distillery at heart?"

"I do." At that moment, everything became clear. I'd been fighting Davis for so long that I'd lost sight of what would be best for all of us. In our short time together Danica had taught me that the most satisfying success comes from compromise. Though I didn't know what was in that file, I trusted that she had the best interest of Devil's Dance at the core of it. "There's only one problem. The USB drive... I didn't want to be tempted to look at it, so I tossed it."

He checked his watch. "What time do they pick up your garbage?"

"Any time. They're not exactly consistent."

Vaughn clapped me on the shoulder. "Then go do what you need to do."

"Thanks." My keys were in my pocket, so I headed straight for the parking lot. If I hurried, I might beat the truck and only have to sort through my own trash to find the drive. I should have set it aside when Pappy gave it to me instead of tossing it. No time to feel sorry for myself now.

I sped toward home with laser pointed focus.

Get the trash.

Retrieve the USB drive.

Find Danica.

If I could get the file, we could go over it together and make sure the plan we presented next week would be in the best interest of Devil's Share Distillery, not one family or the other.

I was so lost in my own thoughts that I didn't see the squad car parked in the median until the red and blue lights flashed in my rearview mirror. Fuuuuuuuuck.

Deputy Hurley adjusted his hat as he walked toward my window.

"Where's the fire?" he asked as he leaned into the window.

"Ouch. Isn't it a little too soon for fire jokes, Hurley?"

His forehead crinkled. "Sorry. I wasn't thinking. It's a damn shame what happened down at the distillery the other day."

"Yeah, it is." I kept my hands on the wheel and turned my

gaze forward. "I'm kind of in a hurry. If you're going to give me a ticket, can we get it over with so I can get a move on?"

"Where you headed?"

"Home." I glanced over, noting the regret still clouding his eyes. Maybe I could use it to my advantage, though he'd let me off the hook before, so he might not be as willing this time. "I've got to get there before the truck shows up to pick up the trash. Any chance you can give me a warning and I can be on my way?"

"You're doing sixty-two in a forty-five because you forgot to put out the trash?"

The longer it took to explain, the less likely I'd be to beat the truck to my trash bin. "No. I accidentally threw something away and need to get it back before they pick up."

"What'd you throw away?" His eyes lit up like he was settling in for story time.

"It's a flash drive. Are you going to give me a ticket or not?" I usually didn't like to provoke people who had the ability to make my life more miserable. Despite how misplaced his power was, Hurley definitely fell into that category.

He leaned farther in the window. "I feel bad about the fire crack. What if I provide an escort to your place? Will that make up for being insensitive?"

"That would be great. Thanks, man."

He tipped his hat. "You bet. Stick tight to my rear bumper, and I'll have you there in no time at all."

True to his word, Hurley raced through town and covered the distance to my place in half the time it would have taken if I'd paid attention to the speed limit.

We both screeched to a halt in front of my drive. The trash bins sat where I'd left them. Blue for garbage and green for recycling. The service picked up with two different trucks, so just because the green lid stuck up a little from the cardboard

I'd tossed inside, didn't mean the truck hadn't been by to pick up the trash yet.

"Did we make it?" Hurley yelled from the open window of his squad car.

I reached for the lid of the can, hoping the kitchen bags would still be stuffed inside.

Empty.

"Dammit." My chest tensed like someone had tied a bunch of knots in my muscles and pulled them tight all at once. I shook my head as I glanced down the road. Maybe I could catch up to the truck.

"Get in." Hurley reached for his radio. "I'll call ahead and see if we can locate the truck."

I looked from the flushed excitement on Hurley's face to the empty trash bin. What did I have to lose? Unless I found the drive, I wouldn't have anything to work on with Danica. Before I let myself think about it too much, I walked around the squad car and reached for the handle of the front door.

"Oh, not up here." Hurley jerked his thumb toward the back seat. "I'll break some rules for you today, but nobody gets to sit up front with me. You'll have to ride in the back."

Eyeing the partition between the front and back seat, I hesitated. I'd only been in the back of a squad car once, and that hadn't ended well.

"You're wasting time, Cole." Hurley put his hands on the wheel. "What's it going to be?"

With a sinking feeling filling my chest, I pulled open the door and slid onto the vinyl seat. "Let's go."

CHAPTER 32
Danica

WELL, that meeting had gone over about as well as a bull biding time in a china shop. I wrapped my hands around the steering wheel and tried to fight off the tears that threatened. Starting my own business after leaving my last position under murky circumstances was one thing. Getting cut loose from my first solo gig without a recommendation wouldn't just take the wind out of my saggy sails, it would rip them to shreds.

I swallowed the goose egg of anxiety that seemed to lodge in my throat. That presentation had taken me weeks to put together and now it was gone.

My phone rang, pulling me out of the dark fog of self-pity.

Cole.

Again.

He'd called a few times since I pulled out of the parking lot. I sent him straight to voice mail. He'd lied to me. All the time I thought I was trying to come up with a plan to honor the history he loved so much, he was trying to cut himself loose. I'd never figured him for someone who'd walk away from something he loved. Though I didn't seem to be the best at judging a person's character lately.

Even my bestie had failed me. She must have known I was thinking about her because my phone rang again and her number flashed on the screen. I might not be ready to talk to Cole, but I wanted to hear from my best friend how long it had taken her to betray my trust.

I answered the call on speaker. "What do you want?"

"I just got off the phone with Harper. She said you got fired. What happened?" Worry laced her tone.

"What happened? That's rich." I couldn't keep the sarcasm from leeching into my voice.

"What do you mean?"

"You told her I was seeing Cole. They figured my loyalty was compromised and fired me on the spot before they even let me run through my presentation. Why'd you do it, Jo?" The anger gave way to hurt.

"Oh no. I didn't. I mean, I guess I did, but I didn't mean to." I could picture her chewing on her lip—a move she always made when she was nervous. "She asked a few questions about your personal life and how you knew so much about whiskey. I might have said something about running into Cole in Knoxville before you knew who he was. Crap. I'm a horrible friend. I'm so sorry."

Her betrayal stung, but I'd known her long enough to recognize the sincerity in her voice. I believed her when she said she had no idea what she was doing. Why would she? She didn't know Harper well enough to be privy to the complicated layers of relationships that made up Devil's Dance Distillery.

"It's okay. I know it's not your fault." The anger dissipated and I let it out on a long sigh.

"What are you going to do?"

"I don't know, but Davis said he's going to call Peter's firm to come in and save the day. No telling what he's going to present to the panel, but I guarantee it won't be good. Plus, once Peter knows I botched my first client, I bet I'll never be able to find a marketing job in the state of Tennessee."

"It won't come to that," Jo promised. "Where are you now?"

"I'm on my way home and hopefully by the time I get there, I'll have something figured out." The sound of a horn in the background came through the phone. "Where are you?"

"En route. You left the first man you've slept with in years and lost a job you were counting on to launch a new career. I'm on my way to your place. I'll be there in an hour. We'll figure this out together, I promise."

"Okay." Even though I was alone in my car, I nodded to myself. I could do this. With Jolene's help, I could come up with a plan.

An hour later, she knocked at the door. I pulled it open, and she wrapped her arms around me, pulling me into a freesia-scented hug.

I hugged back, my heart letting out a huge sigh of relief that someone still cared.

She let me go, holding me at arm's length while she gave me a once over that saw beyond the carefully applied makeup and shellacked hair. "I came to save you from drowning your sorrows in cinnamon rolls and spiked coffee."

"I'm not eating my feelings." At that moment, the microwave dinged.

Jolene arched a perfect brow.

"Okay, so I brought home one tray of Jackie Jay's cinnamon rolls from Beaver Bluff." I tugged her into my living room and shut the door behind her. "You've got to try these, though. They literally melt in your mouth."

She followed me into the kitchen, where I pulled a big mug down from the cabinet and filled it with coffee for her.

"How's the plan coming along?"

"So far, so bad." I cupped my hands around my own mug and avoided her gaze. "I'm mad as hell at Cole, but I really think my idea for moving forward is his best chance at getting everyone on board."

"And they made you give up your laptop?" she asked.

"Yes. I should have used my own, but Davis insisted I needed a company-issued computer if I wanted access to their network. I wish I'd grabbed my notes from my office at the distillery." Had I realized I was getting a big boot in the butt, I would have packed my things and taken them with me. "I've thought about sneaking back to Beaver Bluff to grab them, but they probably won't let me near the front door."

"Looks like we're road tripping, then. Go get dressed and I'll drive." Jolene reached for the plastic-covered plate of cinnamon rolls sitting on my counter.

"I don't think that's such a good idea." I hadn't just burned the bridge between me and everyone in Beaver Bluff, I'd detonated it.

"I'll go in. Just tell me where they are and what to grab." Jolene licked a glob of frosting from her lip. "Wow, these are good. I might drive all the way back there just to pick up more cinnamon rolls."

"I don't know what to do, Jo. Davis is going to present the version of my plan that shuts out everything Cole wants to do. It's what he asked for, so it's what I originally was going to propose."

"What do you think is best for the distillery?"

I rested my butt against the counter. The bottle of Devil's Dance Distinct caught my attention. "They need to compromise. I think Cole realizes that now, but it might be too late."

Jolene shook her head. "Do you love him?"

"What?" Her question caught me off guard. Neither of us had mentioned the "L" word. The idea of love hadn't even crossed my mind. Had it?

I pictured him, his arms crossed over his chest like he was trying to protect himself from getting hurt. He hid his sensitive heart under layers of attitude and brawn. But deep down inside, at his core, he was the kind of man I could fall for. Not just the kind of man, I corrected myself. The man.

Jolene gave me that look she always did when she'd already crossed the finish line and I was struggling to catch up. "Do. You. Love. Him?"

"I think I do." The feeling had snuck up on me. While I'd been trying to do the job I'd been hired to do and plot against him, my emotions had been sabotaging me from the inside out.

"What are you going to do about it?" Having inhaled her cinnamon roll, she thrust her hands on her hips.

"I'm going to tell him how I feel." I had to. As long as there was still a chance for us, I had to make a stand.

"That's my girl. When do we leave?"

I bit my lip, trying to figure out the best way to approach this. "They have to present to the board on Monday. That gives me three days to recreate my plan and convince him to present it."

"I guess you'd better get started. What can I do to help?" She nodded toward the dining room table where I'd set out my personal laptop.

"We're going to need caffeine. Lots of it."

Jolene jiggled her keys in her hand. "I'm on it. Anything else I can pick up while I'm out?"

Before I had a chance to respond, my phone rang. My

mother had the worst sense of timing. I held up a finger, signaling for Jolene to wait while I answered. "Hey, Mom."

"Danica, thank goodness I reached you. Your father and I need you to come home this weekend."

"I'm already home. I drove back this morning." She didn't need to know the details, and I wasn't eager for her to spread the word about my failure to half of Tennessee. That's exactly what would happen when she found out about my botched attempt to start a business of my own.

"Wonderful. We're hosting a charity event at the mayor's residence on Thursday night. It's a small affair, just a couple hundred people. We're raising money for families in need and I thought it would be nice if we attended as a family as well."

"That sounds like a very worthy cause." I braced myself for the reaction my next words would incite. "I'm sorry I won't be able to join you."

Her haughty laugh didn't surprise me. "Of course you'll join us. You already said you're home."

"I am right now, but I'm heading back on Friday morning. "

"That will be fine. You can attend the event with us on Thursday night and have Friday all to yourself." She thought it was settled. That I'd continue to put her needs above everyone else's.

"I'm sorry, but I can't. I need to have time to prepare for my meeting."

"Don't be silly, Danica. It's the mayor's mansion." She stressed the word "mayor," drawing it out three times as long as necessary. Maybe she thought I hadn't heard her right the first time.

"I get it. I'm sure the mayor has a lovely home, but I won't be there to see it. There are a few things I need to deal with in Beaver Bluff."

"How long do you plan to stay?"

That was a tricky question, but I wanted to answer as truthfully as I could. "I'm not sure yet, Mom. If all goes well, I might never come back to Knoxville."

Jolene grinned—a smile so wide that it made her eyes crinkle. She made a fist and bumped it against mine. Her encouragement fueled my confidence.

"Is there anything else? I have a lot of work to do and need to get started."

"Well, I…"

"Love you, Mom. Have fun at the mayor's house, and I'll give you a call this weekend to fill you in on my plans."

I waited for her to reply, but the phone remained silent. For the first time in my life, I'd rendered my mother speechless.

"Who the hell are you and what have you done with my friend Danica?" Jolene eyed me with a mixture of wonder and joy.

"I figured it was about time I started standing up for myself." I gestured toward the door. "Don't just stand there gaping. Weren't you about to go get coffee?"

"Yes, ma'am." She practically bounced through the door.

I watched her go, my attention snagging on the freshly shorn bush Cole had attacked when he'd been at my apartment. I loved him. Loved everything about him. From his growly expressions to the scars covering his back. From his stubborn streak to his kind heart. Now I just needed to find a way to show him before it was too late.

CHAPTER 33

"FOR FUCK'S SAKE, how much trash do the good people of Beaver Bluff create in a given week?" I eyed the edge of the dump where the trash truck had just emptied its load.

Hurley had done his best to track down the truck that picked up in my neighborhood, but by the time the dispatcher identified the route and we caught up, it had already backed up to the edge of the dump.

"You want me to answer that, or is it one of those rhetorical questions?" he asked.

"Never mind. Can you let me out of here?" Being locked in the backseat of the squad car made my stomach churn.

He took his time getting out from behind the wheel. Even made sure his hat sat squarely on his head before he reached for the handle to the back door to set me free.

"Thanks." I took in a full breath, grateful to be standing in the sun instead of trapped inside the car. The smell of garbage filled my nose. I coughed, suddenly hyper aware of where we were. The sounds of heavy machinery moving tons of trash around filled the air.

"What are you going to do now?" Hurley asked. "You're not going to go dump diving to find your trash bag, are you?"

My gaze swept over acres of discarded waste. The only other time I'd been out here was years ago when my dad had to dispose of some outdated equipment we'd replaced at the distillery. I didn't remember the gag-inducing combination of smells or whether being out here had made my eyes water like they did now.

"If the truck that picked up my trash dumped here, it should be in this general vicinity, shouldn't it?" I took a few steps toward the most recent addition to the piles of trash. A bulldozer approached. If I wanted to try to find that USB drive, I needed to do it now, before the bags and bundles were pushed deeper into the pile.

"I suppose." Hurley took a toothpick out of his pocket and flipped it into his mouth.

"Any interest in helping?" I already knew the answer, but figured it didn't hurt to ask.

He smiled and adjusted his hat. "You ain't even got half the brain of a slug if you think I'm going to climb into the county dump with you."

"What if I made it worth your while?" I racked my brain, trying to figure out something I could offer Hurley to get him to help me. "I'll let you pick a barrel and fill up a whiskey bottle with your name on it if you find the bag before me."

He shook his head. "It's going to take more than that if you want me to risk getting someone else's shit on my just-shined boots."

The bulldozer bumped over the uneven ground, heading closer. "What'll it be, Hurley?"

His mouth ticked up into a grin. "Got any more of that Devil's Dance Distinct?"

I turned toward the pile of white kitchen trash bags. All of them looked exactly the same. "Half a bottle if you find the bag before me."

"Not enough, Cole. I get the whole bottle if I find it before you. If you find it before me, I still get half to compensate me for my effort." He clamped his hands to his hips.

"Fine." I was running out of stock of Devil's Distinct, but I'd promise him my firstborn son if he'd find the damn bag. Even though the temperature hovered in the high sixties, a drop of sweat rolled down my back as I walked closer to the edge of the dump.

I pictured Danica's face—the lazy look in her eyes when she first blinked them open in the morning, the way the light hit her irises, bringing out every shade of green. She deserved better than losing out on a job because of a family feud we hadn't been able to get under control. I put a foot on a bag at the edge and tentatively reached for the tie.

"You might want to use these." Hurley tossed something in my direction and, without thinking, I snagged it out of the air. "I keep a stash in the trunk. You never know what the hell you'll come across out in the middle of nowhere."

"Thanks." I slid my hands into the heavy-duty rubber gloves. Thank God someone was prepared.

He didn't waste any time wading into the sea of bags and ripping the first one open. "If you want me to help, I need to know what I'm looking for."

"It's a flash drive. About two inches long. Black with a silver button." I pushed a few papers around in the bag I'd pulled open. Some kid's math homework had been wadded up into a ball, guaranteeing that bag wasn't one of mine.

"What kind of trash did you throw away with it? Anything I can look for to make sure we've got the right bag before I start digging around inside?"

I hadn't been hungry after Danica left on Sunday, so I'd

heated up leftovers for dinner. Then I'd gotten distracted by the hockey game and burned it to the skillet. "I guess you can look for burned trout."

"Burned trout?" Hurley stood. "That's downright sacrilegious."

I didn't bother to provide an explanation. The sooner we found my trash, the sooner I could get cleaned up and head toward Knoxville. I planned on delivering the drive to Danica myself and asking her to help me present her ideas to the board.

She probably didn't want to see me, and I didn't blame her, but I needed to clear the air between us. Thinking about life without her made me realize how different my life had been with her in it. It might take me a while to learn how to shift from my all-or-nothing mentality when it came to the family business, but I was ready to try.

Ready to try with her.

She got me—understood my fascination with the past and accepted it. I couldn't say the same about a lot of people, especially the Stewarts. With her help, I'd started to see that it didn't have to be all or nothing. I wanted more of that in my life. Actually, I needed it.

"I think I got something." Hurley held up a bag in his hand. A huge cat-got-the-canary grin spread across his face.

Eager to get this nasty task over with, I headed his way. "Be careful. You don't want to accidentally lose it in the crap underfoot."

"I've got it." He pulled a pocketknife out and sliced the bag down the side, carefully spreading it open like it was a precious package of breakables instead of someone's garbage.

One glance at the contents told me that bag wasn't mine. Wads and wads of tissues filled the bag, along with a few pieces of junk mail and several empty cans of tuna fish.

"That's not my bag." The smell of tuna made me want to gag. I would have pinched my nose, except that would have meant touching my skin with the gloves I'd used to sift through the trash. Instead, I trekked back to where I'd been working before, eager to put some distance between me and the evidence of someone else's lonely life.

"Well, I'll be." Hurley held up a postcard. "This is Pappy's stuff. Wonder what he did with all those tissues."

Squinting up at the sun, I tried to bargain with the universe. If I could find the bag in the next five minutes, I'd apologize to Danica on my knees and beg her to take me back.

The next bag I grabbed showed promise. Scent of burned trout? Check. Wrappers from Jackie Jay's takeout? Check. I rolled it around in my hands, trying to spread out the contents and see through the sides. My fingers felt something that fit the dimensions of a flash drive. With every cell in my body begging for this bag to be the answer to my prayers, I pulled the bag open.

Pieces of charred fish fell onto my shoes. Dammit. I righted the bag and thrust my gloved hand inside, searching for the item I'd felt through the plastic. I'd almost given up hope when my fingers closed around it. Cautiously optimistic, I pulled my hand out of the bag and flipped the item into the palm of my hand.

There it was. Covered in a mixture of something that smelled so much worse than fish, it sat in the center of my glove.

"I found it!" Wrapping my fingers tightly around the drive, I shoved it into the air.

Hurley dropped the bag he'd been flipping through and stomped toward me over a path of trash bags. "Let's get the hell out of here."

He didn't have to make the suggestion twice. I let the bag fall to my feet and scrambled toward the squad car.

Hurley snapped off his gloves and tossed them onto the pile of trash. "We're riding with the windows down on the way back."

"Fine by me."

"Are you really going to give me half a bottle of Devil's Dance Distinct?" His forehead creased and his eyes narrowed like he wasn't sure whether or not he could trust me.

"I gave you my word." It would hurt to part with some of my dwindling supply, but if offering Danica the drive would help me earn a place back in her heart, it would be worth it. In that moment, I would have given up my entire inventory... my share in the distillery... nothing I had meant a damn thing without her.

Hurley nodded. "You're good people, Cole Bishop. You can sit up front."

I pulled open the passenger side and slid onto the seat.

"It's just this once. Don't let it go to your head, and for God's sake, don't you dare tell anyone I was digging through garbage for you this afternoon. If you do, I'll find some reason to arrest you and hold you without bail. I'll even frame you myself if I have to."

"You got it."

If Hurley thought I was good people, maybe there was still a chance that Danica might feel the same way.

CHAPTER 34

I'D UNDERESTIMATED the amount of time it would take to recreate as much of my presentation as I could from memory and get myself ready to face the folks of Beaver Bluff. There were major holes in my document, and I needed the files in my desk drawer in Beaver Bluff to help me fill them in.

As Jolene navigated onto the highway to take me back to Beaver Bluff not even twenty-four hours after I'd left, my heart tightened into a series of complicated knots. I'd been back and forth to Beaver Bluff so many times in the past two days that I'd lost track. This was the trip that would count. All I needed was to get my hands on my notes so I could finalize my presentation and convince Cole to take a look.

"Tell me exactly what happened with the hot whiskey guy." Jolene tightened her hands on the wheel. She'd been asking me for details, but I hadn't had a chance to update her yet.

"He doesn't think he can have a personal life and manage the family business at the same time." It went much deeper than that, but Cole's issues could be distilled down into that key concept.

"And you told him to get his head out of his ass?" she asked.

I stared out the window at the scenery flying by. "Not in those exact words."

"What was his response?"

"His response was to shut down any chance of something happening between us." I squinted at her, wishing I'd thought to grab my sunglasses.

"The man clearly doesn't have his head on straight. We can fix him after we get your notes and update your presentation." The way she said it—like it was just a matter of time before it happened—loosened the knots in my chest.

"You think it will be that easy?"

She shifted her gaze away from the road for a second. Just long enough to meet mine. "Yes, I do."

Her confidence filled me with hope. Maybe I was the one who'd been overthinking things. Once Cole saw my presentation—how I'd incorporated the history of Devil's Dance into the marketing plan I wanted to pursue—maybe then he'd realize he didn't have to decide between business and family. We could work together to take the distillery into the future while honoring the past he cared so much about.

Jolene filled the rest of the drive, talking about another upcoming business trip. I couldn't wait for the day when I could run my own place and bring her on board to help. We'd focus on helping female entrepreneurs who'd been screwed over by their male counterparts. I'd create an entire network of boss babes who would rise up and put a stop to douchebag bosses who expected more from their employees than giving it their all at the office.

We pulled into the parking lot at Devil's Dance in the early afternoon. I scanned the vehicles left in the lot, relieved to see Cole's truck in his usual spot.

Jolene pulled a stocking cap out of her center console and tucked her hair up inside.

"What are you doing?"

"I'm going incognito. I don't want anyone to see who I am in case I end up working with them on a project later." She tapped her finger against the side of her head. "Smart, right?"

"It's seventy degrees out. If you go in dressed like that, they probably won't let you past the reception desk." I peered through the tinted window at the front door. "I think this is something I'm going to need to do alone."

"Are you sure?" Jolene asked, already shoving the hat back in the console and slipping her arms out of the long trench coat she'd shrugged on.

"Yes, I'm sure." I wrapped my fingers around the door handle.

"Ooh, duck. Someone's coming out." Jolene slithered down in the seat.

I glanced over in time to catch Miller leave the building. Good. One less body I'd have to worry about running into.

"Get down." Jolene pulled at my sleeve.

"He can't see us from here." I waited until he backed his truck out of his spot across the parking lot and turned onto the main road. Then I got out of the car and eyed the door. "If I'm not back in ten minutes…"

"What? Call 9-1-1 because one of the families decided to throttle you?" Jolene joked.

"I guess come in and try to find me." It shouldn't take more than a few minutes to walk to my office, grab the files, and see if I could find Cole. If they even let me past the front desk.

"Good luck." Jolene squeezed my arm.

My shoes crunched across the gravel parking lot as I made my way to the front door. I just came to collect the rest of my personal belongings. There was nothing to be nervous about.

Then why was my heart beating triple time? Why were my palms so sweaty I was worried my fingers might slip off the door handle? Why did my breath not seem to fill up my lungs?

The scent of wood and whiskey washed over me when I opened the door. I inhaled deeply, instantly reminded of Cole. Forcing my feet to carry me past the empty receptionist's desk, I swiped at my nose. I didn't want the reminder, not now. Depending on how things went, maybe not ever.

Confident he was somewhere in the building since I'd seen his truck outside, I took the shortcut past his office to reach mine. The door sat open, and I glanced over as I passed. He sat behind his desk, his eyes snapped to his laptop screen.

Until I walked by.

His gaze lifted in extreme slow motion, like someone had pressed a button and slowed everything down by at least half.

When he saw me, his eyes widened. At the same time, his brows lifted. My heart sped up even though my feet felt like they were barely moving. Our eyes met and heat shot through me. Time instantly fast forwarded.

We both spoke at once, talking over each other so that neither one of us could hear the other.

"You go first." I stepped into his office, not sure what kind of reception I'd receive.

"What are you doing back here?" He'd gotten up from his chair and reached for my hands as he rounded his desk.

I slid my fingers against his. As I did, a feeling washed over me, like everything in my life had just snapped into place. "You told me I needed to stand up for myself and fight for what I want."

He nodded. The scruff on his cheeks was longer, darker. The lines around his eyes looked deeper than they had the last time I'd seen him. "That's right."

"I'm here. I want to fight for Devil's Dance. Davis took my

presentation, but I pulled together what I could from memory. The notes in my office should be able to fill in the gaps. I think it's your best bet for moving ahead. If you'll let me walk you through it—"

The firm touch of his lips on mine cut off my words. His arms wrapped around me, pulling me tight against his chest—my very favorite place to be.

We broke apart a few moments later. "Does this mean you're still speaking to me?" he asked.

"I'd rather be kissing you than talking to you, but I'm up for both." I smoothed my palm over his cheek. How did I ever think I'd be able to turn my back on him?

"I need to show you something." He took my hand and tugged me toward his desk. "You might not need your notes to recreate your presentation."

He picked something up from the edge of his desk and held it out to me.

"What is it?"

"Pappy copied your file from your computer the night of the fire. He gave it to me, thinking I might be able to use it against Davis, but I didn't want to violate your trust, so I threw it away."

I flipped the flash drive over in my palm. "If you threw it away, how—"

"That's a story for another time." He pressed a gentle kiss to my temple. "Let's just say I hope I never have to visit the Shellacky County Dump again."

"You went to the dump for me?" My heart skipped a few beats, like it was playing hopscotch in my chest.

"I was actually about to head to Knoxville to track you down. I'd just stopped by the office to wrap up a few loose ends so I could be out of the office for a couple of days. I should have already been on the road, but I got caught up talking to Miller. Jack got into some trouble at daycare and, hell, it doesn't matter. All you need to know is that I'd go anywhere for you."

"Why?"

"Because you deserve a shot at following your dreams, and I think working with Devil's Dance is going to be the best way for you to take it."

"What about your dreams, Cole? If I turn in my recommendation, the board might decide to go in a different direction. I know how much honoring the history of distillery means to you. Why would you risk that for a relative stranger?"

He swallowed. Hard. Then he lifted his head and met my gaze. His eyes filled with the same softness I'd seen when he held me in his arms at the cabin. "I've been so caught up in trying to make up for the mistakes I've made in the past that I lost sight of the possibilities the future holds. After the fire, all I could think about was how I'd brought that on myself. That's why I pushed you away. But I was wrong."

There he was. The man I'd started falling for. He stood in front of me, vulnerable and willing. "What are you saying?"

"I'm saying I trust you." He reached for my hand. "With my business... and my heart."

Any lingering resistance I held melted away at the truth in his eyes. "That file's incomplete. I updated my plan to make sure the history of the distillery isn't forgotten. That's what I was working on the night of the fire. I know Davis hired me to come up with a brand-new direction, but you've taught me how important it is to make sure I honor both. That's what I was going to present to the Stewarts, but they never gave me the chance."

"You don't know how happy it makes me to hear you say that." He lifted my hand to his lips and kissed my knuckles.

Warmth swept through me. I wasn't so blinded by the light

in Cole's expression to think that he and Davis would be able to see eye to eye on everything, but maybe we could put a plan together they could both agree on.

"If I can take what you saved on that flash drive and fill in the gaps on what I pulled together from memory, would you want to present an idea together? Something that gives both families a little bit of what they're hoping for and incorporates everything the distillery needs?" My heart lodged in my throat while I waited for an answer.

"I think you're onto something. What would you say to sticking around and getting started right away?"

Relief flooded my system. He was in. "I'd say yes."

"Can we take tonight off and get started in the morning?" Heat replaced the softness in his eyes.

I couldn't say yes fast enough.

CHAPTER 35

Danica

"ARE YOU READY FOR THIS?" Jolene asked. She'd stuck around Beaver Bluff for the past few days, taking my room at the bed-and-breakfast while I stayed with Cole. The three of us had worked around the clock to finalize a presentation that would hopefully check off all the boxes for both families. Now Jolene and I were on our way to meet up with Cole.

"As ready as I'll ever be. I hope I can pull this off."

"You will. Davis Stewart is going to be so impressed he'll give you a contract to handle all of their marketing for the next fifty years."

I couldn't help but laugh at that. "I love your ridiculous optimism."

"Why, thank you!" Jolene batted her eyelashes at me as she adjusted the rearview mirror.

"Davis can't do anything without a majority. None of them can." I pushed my sunglasses farther up on my nose to combat the mid-morning sun. "That's why we need to blow them away with our plan."

"It's a great plan. They'd have to be idiots not to recognize it."

"Yeah, well, we're dealing with two families who would rather kill each other than sit down at the same table, so…" I didn't finish that thought. That might have been how they felt when I first met them, but Cole had come a long way in the short time I'd known him. He'd started by trying to separate his family's interest from the Stewarts, but over the course of the past few weeks, he'd realized how important it was for them to stick together.

"You think getting them on the same page with this plan will end the feud?" Jolene checked her GPS and turned onto a street lined with industrial warehouses.

"No." Ending a feud that had lasted over a century was too lofty a goal for now. But maybe, given enough time, the hostility would ease. "I'd settle for getting them to agree on a plan for next year."

Jolene turned into the parking lot of the party we were crashing. "I guess you've got to start somewhere."

Cole's truck sat in a spot out front. He was meeting us inside. Since Davis had fired me, he'd made good on his threat and hired the one man I'd hoped to never see again. Now the only thing standing in our way was Peter Peterson, my ex-boss, and the reason I'd found myself at Devil's Dance in the first place.

Based on what Cole heard through the distillery grapevine, Peter had invited the Stewarts to a launch party he was putting on for a new brand of vodka. Cole said Peter talked it up and hoped to do something similar for Devil's Dance. This was our last chance to get everyone on board with what was best for the distillery before Peter presented their plan, my original plan, to the board on Monday.

I could feel the bass from the speakers thumping through my veins the moment I opened the car door. Peter might not have very original ideas, but he didn't skimp on launches.

Knowing him, he'd hired some big-name DJ from the west coast to spin some tunes while women in skimpy costumes passed out fancy shots featuring the new vodka they were launching. His recipe for what he considered a successful event never varied much.

I hated to think what he'd do with Devil's Dance if he ever got his hands on their branding.

Jolene met me by the back bumper of the car. "Ready?"

I swiped on some lip gloss and tried to add a little volume to my hair. I wanted to avoid coming face-to-face with Peter, but if I couldn't, at least I wanted to look halfway decent. Wait a sec. That right there was part of the problem. Why did I feel like I had to impress a guy who'd fired me?

Because if he saw me looking like a wreck, he'd automatically assume it was because I'd lost my edge when he let me go. It was infuriating, but true. I didn't want him to think that I'd fallen to pieces since I left his company. It was frustratingly complicated being a woman sometimes.

I followed Jolene up the walkway to enter the event center where they were having the party. Women in bikinis greeted us as we stepped through the front doors. Peter had truly let his bad taste take the lead this time. He must have gone tropical with the theme.

"Looks like he's bringing the beach to Tennessee," I observed.

Jolene didn't bother trying to hide the eye roll she gave me. "Such an original idea. I bet he's got them serving sex on the beach with a side of naughty shots."

"Oh, it's not a tropical theme," one of the bikini-clad women said. "It's a launch party for Muddy Vodka. There's a mud wrestling pit inside."

"You're kidding." I hoped like hell she was, but I could tell by the confused look on her flawless face that she wasn't.

"No. They're raising money for the wildlife rehabilitation center over in Beaver Bluff. For a fifty-dollar donation, you can challenge someone to three minutes in the pit." She held out a tray loaded with shot glasses. "Care for a shot?"

Jolene glanced at me. "Are you sure you want to head into a mud wrestling party without some sort of liquid courage?"

"Yeah. We've got this, Jo."

The woman with the shots shrugged and walked away.

"I can't believe he brought in a mud pit," I said.

"Can't you?" Jolene asked.

We stepped through a set of heavy black curtains into the main event. The interior of the building had been decorated to look like a mountainside cabin. The windows were covered, so the only light inside came from dozens of lanterns hanging down from the ceiling. A faux log cabin housed the bar area where more bikini-clad young women filled shot glasses and mixed beverages.

Peter stood on the other side of the room on a raised stand. I couldn't see what sat in front of him, but as Jolene and I moved closer, I realized it was a large indoor swimming pool full of wet, sticky, dark brown mud. He'd gone too far this time.

"I'm going to walk around if that's okay with you?" Jolene asked.

I nodded, and she disappeared into the crowd, leaving me standing alone with a direct line of sight to Peter. He looked like he was about to speak—something I wasn't too keen on witnessing. Movement on the other side of the mud pit caught my eye. Cole stood half a head taller than everyone else—easy to recognize. His eyes lit up, and he smiled. I waited while he worked his way through the people in front of him, trying to close the distance between us.

"Hey, I was starting to think maybe you'd changed your

mind." The dull roar of dozens of conversations taking place around us, coupled with the beat from the music, almost drowned out his words. He had to lean in so I could hear him. The vibration of his voice rumbled through me, reaching all the places that had been sparked back to life by his touch.

"Now that I've seen what Peter has in mind for Devil's Dance, I wish I hadn't," I said. We'd planned on stopping by to find out what kind of tricks Peter had up his sleeve before we cornered the Stewarts at the office later and forced them to listen to our updated plan.

"The prodigal consultant returns."

I knew that voice. I hated that voice. I'd had recurring nightmares featuring that voice.

I turned as Peter approached. My skin crawled as he gave me a slow once over. He reached for my hand, but I crossed my arms over my chest instead. I'd never give him the satisfaction of touching me again.

"What do you want, Peter?" I practically spit the words at him, hoping for once in his life he might be able to take a hint.

Unaffected by my snub, he held out his arms and looked around. "What do you think, Danica? In spite of your attempt at sabotaging the Muddy Vodka job, I was able to salvage the relationship and think the party came together rather nicely, don't you?"

"Peter?" Cole's expression changed. His jaw tensed and his eyes narrowed slightly. "This is the Peter you used to work for?"

"Peter Peterson." Peter held out his hand to Cole. "And you are?"

"Cole Bishop." Cole crossed his arms over his chest, matching my stance.

"Of the famous Stewart-Bishop feud, I assume? Don't

worry, I'll try not to villainize all of your ancestors when we work the feud into our marketing plans."

"You wouldn't dare." Peter was low, but I couldn't believe that he would go that far.

"Wouldn't I? A generations-old feud? It's a marketer's dream. Your soft heart is the reason for your downfall, Danica." The look on his face reeked of self-righteousness.

I'd had enough. "No, the reason for my downfall was your lack of professionalism."

His eyes widened. "Lack of professionalism? That's rich, coming from you. We could have been invincible together, you know."

I couldn't listen to one more word. All I wanted was to shut him down for good. Seemed like Cole felt the same way based on the way his hands tightened into fists. It wouldn't do any good for him to start a fight and widen the rift between the families.

I gripped his arms and forced him to meet my gaze. "Don't bother. He's not worth it."

"Oh, it's like that between the two of you then, is it?" Peter's eyes took on a wicked glint. "I didn't realize Danica had continued her habit of mixing business with pleasure."

Cole lunged toward Peter, but I reached him first. Pain exploded up my arm from where my fist connected with his jaw.

"Danica, I didn't expect that from you." He staggered backward, then wiped the back of his hand across his mouth. "You should have hit harder the first time."

Before I could stop him, Cole hauled back. The crack of his knuckles across Peter's chin sounded louder than thunder.

Peter stumbled against the side of the mud-filled pool. "What the fuck was that for?"

"That was for being an asshole. Danica told me what you

did." Cole rubbed the knuckles of his right hand against the palm of his left.

"Did she? And what makes you think she told you the truth?"

My heart stopped beating at the look in Peter's eyes. He was like an animal in a trap who was so desperate to free himself he'd do whatever it took, even if it meant chewing off his own leg in the process.

Cole clenched his hands again, like he was preparing to take another swing.

"Wait." Peter straightened his suit jacket. "We could join forces, Mr. Bishop. I have a proven track record of launching successful brands. Think about it. Your whiskey paired with my know-how would guarantee a winning campaign. Trust me, you don't want to waste time on my sloppy seconds—"

The sound of Cole's fist meeting Peter's jaw prevented him from saying anything else. He was expecting it this time and grabbed onto Cole's arm. The two men struggled, knocking over a bar top table and sending bottles of Muddy Vodka crashing to the ground.

One of the servers standing next to me screamed and dropped the tray of shots she'd been holding. A loud crack came from my left. I turned just in time to see Cole and Peter stumbling into the side of the above ground pool that had been rigged to hold the mud.

While attendees in cocktail dresses and suits scrambled to get out of the way, the side of the pool split open. Mud coursed through the room, covering everything in its path.

Including me.

CHAPTER 36
Cole

MY FEET COULDN'T GAIN traction. I tried to stand, but they slipped out from under me. A wave of mud carried me past the tables and chairs, dumping me on my ass at the edge of the room. Dark brown liquid covered every inch of me. I grabbed hold of the edge of one of the drapes and wiped it across my eyes so I could try to figure out what happened.

Danica stood at the edge of the room, her eyes wide. A blob stumbled toward her looking like something that crawled out of one of the swamps nearby. It moved closer, and I launched myself at the form.

She shrieked, barely managing to avoid getting caught between us. This wasn't how I envisioned our afternoon going, but when that asshole opened his mouth and started insulting the woman I loved, I couldn't control my reaction.

"Get out of here, Danica." I pointed toward the exit with my finger, not that she could tell one piece of me from another in my current state.

"You ruined everything." My nemesis for the night tackled me into the mud and we rolled around, coating ourselves like a pair of chocolate-dipped truffles.

The music stopped. The overhead lights came on. The collective roar of dozens of voices ceased all at once.

A voice came over the loudspeaker. "Party's over. Make your way to the exits, please."

"Not you two." A hand grabbed the back of my shirt.

I twisted around to see Hurley hauling Peter out of the mud. He let go of him and Peter fell into a chair. Another deputy did the same to me. Peter and I faced each other across a low table that hadn't been swept away in the mudslide.

"What the hell was that?" Hurley wiped his hands off on the back of his pants, making it look like he'd just shit himself.

I couldn't even muster a chuckle. Not that any of this was funny. Okay, maybe the tiniest bit funny just because Danica's ex-boss finally got a heaping helping of what he deserved. I'd also discovered on the way over that he'd invested heavily in Muddy Vodka, making the implosion of his launch party extra sweet.

"I'm going to need to get statements from both of you, as well as any witnesses who are still around." Hurley put his hands out like he wanted to instill a sense of calm. "Stay here while I talk to a few people. I'll be back to deal with the two of you in a minute."

Peter waited until Hurley walked away, then leaned across the table. "Are you happy with yourself, you miserable piece of shit?"

I lifted the neck of my T-shirt up to wipe the mud away from my mouth. "Happier than a dog with two tails."

"I'm going to make sure they put you away for a long time for this." He shrugged off his suit jacket and ran the sleeve of his button-down shirt over his face. "You just cost my client a mint. Add in assault and battery and you're probably looking at actual jail time, asshole."

Hurley returned in time to hear the tail end of Peterson's threat. " Cole, you're free to go."

"What the hell?" Peterson stood. "You should be cuffing him and putting him in the back of a squad car."

"If that's the way you want me to handle this, I can." Hurley reached for his cuffs and my lungs seized. "I thought maybe you'd want to skip that part since the manager here told me you didn't pull a permit for the mud."

The breath I was holding seeped out, and I filled my lungs with air. Hurley was a miracle worker. I planned on telling him that. Soon. After I found Danica and made sure she was okay.

Peterson wasn't ready to give up so easily. "The man assaulted me. I have the bruises to prove it."

"I don't see any bruises." Hurley squinted. "Maybe if you wiped all of that illegal mud off your face, I'd be able to tell. How many gallons of mud would you say you brought in here? I need to know whether we should fine you by the gallon or the pound."

"But…" Peterson sputtered.

"But what?" Hurley prompted. "I'm sure the judge would be happy to hear all about it."

Even though I wanted to get outside to find Danica, I waited to make sure Peterson wasn't going to be an issue. I didn't make a habit of going around punching guys in the face, but he deserved it. Maybe this would teach him not to take advantage of others, especially women like the one I'd fallen for.

Danica could take care of herself when it came to this creep, but damn, it felt good to knock the shitty grin off his face.

"I suppose we can go our separate ways and consider this a valuable lesson for us both." Peterson's left eye twitched as he spoke. It wasn't like he'd waved an olive branch and offered lasting peace. More like he'd lifted a twig into the air, but I'd take it.

"Do you need me for anything else?" I directed the question to Hurley.

"Nope. I'll see you around, Cole. Try to stay out of trouble for a few days, will you?"

Between visiting the dump and bathing in mud, staying clean for a little while sounded good to me. "I'll do my best."

CHAPTER 37

Danica

GUESTS STREAMED out of the front door of the venue in various states of muddiness. The lucky ones only had a few splashes drying on their legs or pants. Others must have slipped while trying to get to the door or gotten swept up in the tide. Peter was going to have a mess on his hands—figuratively and literally. I couldn't seem to muster any amount of sympathy for the man who'd made the past couple of years of my life so miserable.

"There you are." Jolene called to me as she crossed the parking lot and pulled me into a hug.

I pushed off from where I'd been leaning against the car. "Did you see Cole? Is he okay?"

"Turn around and see for yourself." Jolene looked over my shoulder, her focus resting on something behind me.

That prickle of awareness I always seemed to get when Cole was nearby pebbled my skin. I turned around slowly, not sure what to expect. Cole stood there, covered in dark mud from head to toe except for a clear swath across his face where he must have swiped it away.

"Danica."

"Are you all right?" I reached for him, not caring that I got covered in mud in the process.

"I'm fine. How about you?" He lifted a hand like he wanted to smooth it over my hair but thought better of it. "Do we need to get some ice on those knuckles?"

"It hurts like hell, but it was worth it." I snuggled against him. "You didn't have to punch him. Is he pressing charges? I saw the deputy heading in when I left. I'm the one who started it."

"You might have started it, but I sure as hell enjoyed finishing it." Cole let out a sigh.

"Well, it's nice to see the happy lovebirds have reunited," Jolene joked. "Did either of you happen to talk to Davis while you were inside? That was the whole reason we crashed the party, wasn't it?"

Cole lifted his head from where his chin rested on my hair. "Dammit. I didn't even see him."

"I'm not sure he'll want to get very close to you in your current condition, but isn't that him over there?" Jolene pointed to a black SUV I recognized as Harper's vehicle.

"Let's see if we can catch him." Cole put an arm around my shoulder and matched my stride as we moved toward the Stewarts.

"I don't want any trouble." Davis put his palms out. "Stop right there, both of you."

"I don't want any trouble, either. This isn't the kind of vibe we want for Devil's Dance, is it?" Cole nodded toward the entrance of the warehouse where small groups of people milled around.

Davis shrugged. "You didn't leave me much of a choice after you turned my marketing guru against us."

"I didn't turn against you, Davis." I took a step forward. "Cole and I put together a plan we'd like you to take a look at.

All of you. It incorporates the vision you shared about expanding your offering to include other spirits and also honors the Bishop family's wishes of telling the origin story of Devil's Dance Distillery."

Davis's gaze shifted from me to Cole to the SUV, where his brother and sisters waited for him.

Sensing a weakness in his resistance, I pressed on. "We'd love to do a run-through back at the office. It would only take about fifteen minutes to get a high-level look, though if you're interested, we can deep dive into the details."

Davis turned to consult with his siblings. While we waited, Cole gave me a smile. My confidence bloomed. We were doing the right thing. For the distillery. For the Stewarts. For the Bishops. And finally, for me.

"Fine. We'll head back to the office now. I'm assuming you'll need a little extra time to clean up before you're ready?" Davis asked.

"Give us an hour." Cole slung his arm around my shoulders.

"One hour." Davis got into the SUV and pulled the door shut.

The tires spun, sending a cloud of dust into the air.

"Great. Now we really do need that shower." Cole turned his back to shield me from the dirt cloud heading our way. "Think we have time to wash each other's backs?"

"Only if we hurry." I wiped my fingers over his cheek, clearing a spot where I could press my lips.

"Let's get going then." He tossed his keys to Jolene as we made our way back to the truck. "Can you drive us back to my place? Just go slow since we'll be sitting in the bed."

"Not too slow, though, right?" I asked.

"Don't worry, baby. We've got plenty of time. I'm talking about the rest of our lives."

I took his hand and let him pull me onto the tailgate. "Well then, we'd better hurry."

"Why's that?" he asked as he pulled me down next to him and leaned against the cab.

"Because I can't wait to start spending the rest of my life with you."

Epilogue

COLE

"THAT'S IT?" Davis sat at the head of the conference room table. I'd figured giving him the seat of honor might stroke his ego a little bit. Despite the strength of the plan Danica and I had come up with together, we needed his buy-in before we could put it into action. If he gave a nod of approval, I had no doubt his siblings would follow his lead.

Danica closed her laptop. "I'm sure we'll refine the plan and make accommodations as we go, but yes, that's it."

She radiated confidence, and it was damn intoxicating. I enjoyed watching her toy with Davis's emotions, leading him through the same marketing narrative we'd use to tell the compelling story of the distillery's history.

"For what it's worth, I think y'all are fucking geniuses." Miller flipped to the page detailing the sales projections. "If your forecasts check out, we might set a record for growth over the next two to five years."

I caught the hint of a smile curve Danica's lips up. We had Miller. I knew he'd get a hard-on over those numbers. Now we just needed to get the rest of them on board.

"Everything sounds good to me," my brother Evan said.

"Just make sure you give me plenty of lead time to guarantee the warehouse is ready."

"The ideas you have for the year-long anniversary celebration are rock solid." Ruby shrugged. "Unless Sawyer can see any reason not to go along with it, I think we're in from a marketing and events perspective."

Sawyer shifted her gaze to the head of the table, checking for approval from her big brother.

Davis cleared his throat. This was it. The moment that would make us or… well, probably not break us since I'd learned Danica was a hell of a lot stronger than anyone gave her credit for. But if Davis wasn't all in, we'd have to go back to the drawing board or give him enough time to come up with an idea of his own to present to the board.

"As much as it hurts me to say it—and it pains me like a million tiny paper cuts—I think your plan might have potential." He grimaced as the words left his mouth, leaving me no doubt that it almost killed him to admit it.

Danica tucked her chin against her chest in an attempt to hide her smile.

"All in favor of putting this plan into action?" I asked.

Five Bishops, four Stewarts, and two Devines all nodded their assent. Pride filled my chest. Danica had done something others had been unsuccessful at for the past hundred years— she'd gotten us to agree on a common direction.

I had no doubt we'd have ups and downs as we navigated this new course of action, but with Danica gently steering—or possibly prodding the more reluctant ones—we might have a shot at a new level of success.

"Looks like we've made a decision," Vaughn said. "I'm assuming Danica will oversee things while we put the plan in motion?"

Another round of nods confirmed.

"Great. Should we get back together in a couple of weeks to check on progress?" Davis asked.

Just because Vaughn and Davis agreed as co-managers that we would start heading in a new direction, it would probably be a pretty rocky road. I didn't envy her having to wrangle the two of them, but I was looking forward to having her around more.

Everyone filed out. I stayed behind to help break down her laptop and congratulate her on the win.

"That went exceptionally well." She closed the door after the last person trailed out of the conference room. "I wouldn't believe it if I hadn't seen and heard it myself."

"What, that the Bishop and Stewart families actually agreed on something?" I slipped my arms around her waist and pulled her against my chest.

"Yes."

"It was all you, babe."

"Not all me. You helped."

I might have helped brainstorm some ideas and filled in a few gaps, but she was the mastermind behind the plan, and I wouldn't let her avoid taking the credit she deserved.

"You're amazing. Do you know that?"

Her fingers rested on my shoulders. "I don't mind hearing you say it."

"Then I'll say it again. You're amazing, Danica Watson." I pressed a kiss to her forehead, savoring the scent of coconut and pineapple that tickled my nose.

"You're pretty amazing yourself." She rose to her tiptoes and kissed me—a sweet peck on the lips that instantly made me crave more.

There would be time for that later. Assuming we'd be successful today, I'd arranged for a private celebration. Right now, since we'd passed the first step of putting our plan into action, there was something I wanted to ask her. "Looks like you're going to be spending an awful lot of time in Beaver Bluff over the next several months."

"Is that what it looks like?" she teased.

"Based on what we agreed to today, yeah." I reached up to tuck a few strands of hair behind her ear. "Have you thought about where you might stay while you're in town?"

"I'm so glad you asked. I heard there's a pretty sweet cabin in the woods not too far from here."

"Might be a little drafty." I still needed to get up there to replace the pane of glass I'd shattered that last time we'd been there together.

Her lips turned down. "Bummer. Do you happen to know of some alternate accommodations I could try?"

"Move in with me?" My hands tightened behind her, drawing her even closer against me. "We can make this work."

She pulled back and gazed up at me. "Are you sure?"

"I've never been so sure of anything. The plan, the distillery… none of it means a damn thing if you're not here to experience it with me. I love you, Danica."

Her eyes shone and her lower lids filled with tears. She let go of my shoulders to try to wipe them away, but I stopped her.

"Hey, it's okay. You don't have to say it back."

"You think my eyes are running like a faucet because I don't feel the same way?"

I kissed a shiny spot on her cheek where she'd smeared her tears. "It doesn't matter. If you don't feel the same way, I can handle it. I'll just keep proving to you every day why you ought to change your mind."

"I thought you Bishop brothers were supposed to be so smart." She pushed against my chest. "I'm crying because I love you, too."

"You do?"

"Of course I do. I love you, Cole. All of you. The way you wear your heart on your sleeve and are so protective of your family. The way you honor your history while still keeping an eye on the future. The way you make me feel like I'm the only woman in the world. I love it all."

"You are the only woman in the world. At least for me." I swept her up in my arms and swung her around. Her feet left the ground, and she shrieked before I sent both of us sailing into the wall.

A knock sounded on the door. "Hey, what's going on in there? Some of us around here are trying to work." Miller's voice held an edge of humor. One of these days, someone was going to come along who'd knock my baby brother off his comfortable rocker and open his heart up to love again. I couldn't wait to see that happen.

But not today.

Today was made for me and Danica, and I knew just how I wanted to spend it.

"What do you say to getting out of town for the weekend?"

She tilted her head back and gazed up at me, a glimmer of humor making her eyes look especially bright. "You have somewhere in mind?"

"As a matter of fact, I do. It's a remote slice of paradise. Just takes a little effort to get there."

"I'm only going if there's a chance we might get stuck and have to spend the night." Her lips split into a contagious grin that I couldn't help but match.

"I ought to warn you… there's only one bed."

"Who says we're going to be doing any sleeping?"

I followed her out of the conference room, hot on the heels of the woman who'd taught me so much about life and love in such a short time. Sometimes a man had to let go to move forward. Stop blaming himself for things he couldn't control to make room in his heart for what mattered. Danica had made me realize all that and so much more.

It was our time. Time for me to stop worrying about the past and start looking toward the future... with her.

THANKS FOR PICKING up this copy of **Drinking Deep**! For an exclusive bonus scene with Cole and Danica, subscribe to Dylann's newsletter: https://dylanncrush.com/drinking-deep-bonus-scene/

AND TO PRE-ORDER the next book in the series, Tasting Temptation: https://dylanncrush.com/tasting-temptation/

FOR A SNEAK PEEK at the next book in the Whiskey Wars series, turn the page...

Tasting Temptation

MILLER

"SHE DID WHAT?" I slid a bowl of instant oatmeal onto the table in front of my six-year-old son, Jack.

"She pushed me at recess. You told me not to hit girls, but I wanted to, Dad." His eyebrows bunched up, looking like two angry caterpillars over his dark green eyes.

"Did you tell the teacher?" I emptied the carafe of coffee into the travel tumbler my mom had given me for Christmas. Pictures of Jack plastered the sides. Yeah, I was the kind of dad who didn't mind if people knew how much I loved my kid.

He talked around the bite of oatmeal he'd just dumped into his mouth. "Mrs. Blessing says not to tattle."

"Jack,"—I unplugged my laptop and slid it into my computer bag—"if she's hurting you, it's not tattling." For the umpteenth time, I cursed myself for not holding him back a year. With a birthday at the beginning of September, he was always the youngest kid in his class. It didn't help that he'd inherited his mom's delicate bone structure, either. Some of the girls in his class towered over him, like Bettina Calbot, the one who'd been bullying him since last fall.

"If I tell, she'll just do it again." He continued to shovel his breakfast into his mouth. Oatmeal dribbled down his chin.

I stopped next to him on my way to add his lunchbox to his backpack and swiped my thumb across his face. "Where's your napkin, bud?"

He reached for the hem of the T-shirt he had on.

"Try again." I leaned toward the middle of the table, where a single paper napkin sat in a plastic holder. "Damn, how can we be out of napkins already?"

Jack's brows shot up at my choice of words.

"Sorry. Here, use this." I pressed the napkin into his hands as I glanced at the clock on the microwave. Late. Again.

"She called me puny and said if I worked out a hundred years, I still wouldn't have any muscles." He made a fist and flexed his tiny biceps. "Is she right, Dad? Will I always be a shrimp?"

My chest squeezed tight at the way his lips curved into a frown. I thought parenting a boy would be easy. Hell, I grew up with three older brothers. I figured my own childhood had been enough preparation for raising a son. But thanks to the stocky European gene pool my DNA pulled from, I'd never been the small kid who everyone picked on. My own brothers stopped teasing me by the time I'd turned ten since I outweighed them all. I didn't have any experience with being bullied, especially by a girl.

"Come on, clear your bowl. We've got to get going." I slid his chair in after Jack got up and shuffled to the sink, his favorite SpongeBob bowl in hand.

"It's true then." Shoulders slumped, Jack let out a huge sigh.

We should have left five minutes ago if I wanted to make it to the eight o'clock meeting my brother Vaughn had scheduled at the distillery. I'd lost count of how many times I'd told him I couldn't make the early morning meetings he favored. His lack of consideration was another reason I didn't want to take him up on the job he kept offering. The sooner they found a full-time accountant to join the staff, the happier I'd be.

"Get your shoes on." Sensing he needed a little inspiration, I grabbed his light-up sneakers from the bin and set them on the mat. "What did I tell you about Uncle Evan?"

With all the excitement of a cow on its way to the slaughterhouse, Jack took baby steps on his way to the back door. "That he used to be puny until he started working out."

"That's right. You keep eating healthy and playing hard, and I bet you'll be bench pressing Bettina Calbot by the time you get to second grade." I picked him up under the armpits and set him down on the stool by the door so he could pull on his shoes.

The bowl clattered in the sink. I looked up in time to see my dog Titus prop himself up on the counter with his front paws and lean into the sink to lap the last bits of oatmeal from Jack's bowl.

"Titus, get down!" I clapped my hands together, but the beast just lifted his brows in my direction while his tongue continued to clean the bowl.

Something in my life needed to give. The past few months, I'd been busier than a cross-eyed rooster on an anthill, trying to get Jack through the second half of the school year, keep the family business afloat, and stay on top of my full-time job. Even though I was pissed at Vaughn for scheduling our meeting so early, finding someone to take over the work at Devil's Dance Distillery would free up a huge portion of my time.

Guilt pierced my gut as I imagined what it would feel like to cut my ties to the family business for good. There just wasn't a place for me there. I'd known it all along, and it was about time I made it clear to my brothers. They'd been holding out hope I'd step into the role my mom had played for the past twenty-five years after she and my dad retired, but I couldn't.

Like Jack, I had my own demons to fight—the same ones that had been following me around for as long as I could remember. Unlike my son, no one had taken the time to try to teach me how to defeat them, so instead of leaving them in my past, they'd grown with me. Now they were too big and too strong to take down. It was easier to walk away and let them win.

I'd learned my lesson, which was why I kept after Jack to figure out a way past his current issue with freaking Bettina Calbot. I wasn't sure what bothered me more... the fact the pint-sized tyrant was making my son's life so miserable or that I stored so much hate inside my heart for a six-year-old little girl.

"Tell you what, Jack. I saw an email from Mrs. Blessing about needing volunteers for your Valentine's Day party next week. I'm going to sign up to help." I didn't have time to take an afternoon off, but my kid needed me. No matter what I had going on, he came first.

"You're gonna come to my school?" His eyes lit up, reminding me how little it took to make him happy.

"Yeah, bud." I bent down to tie his shoes. We were still working on perfecting that skill, and though he could do it, we didn't have time for the multiple attempts he'd have to make to get the job done.

"You promise this time?" He looked up at me, his eyes wide with hope.

The last time I'd said I'd volunteer at his school had been right before the holidays. An emergency at the distillery had popped up, preventing me from being there to help him make a gingerbread house out of graham crackers. My sister Ruby had gone instead, and the masterpiece they created together won second place. I still felt the sharp pang of regret when I looked at the red ribbon he'd hung on his bedroom wall.

"I promise. Now grab your backpack, we've got to get." I stood and ruffled his hair before I planted a kiss on the top of his head. Nothing would prevent me from following through this time. I needed to see Miss Bettina Calbot in action so I could help Jack formulate a plan to end her bullying once and for all.

HEAD back to Devil's Dance Distillery when you pre-order Tasting Temptation now! (https://dylanncrush.com/tasting-temptation/)

TO STAY "IN THE KNOW" about upcoming books, giveaways, and all of Dylann's other author news, sign up for her weekly newsletter here! (www.dylanncrush.com/signup)

Acknowledgments

Cheers! I don't think there's a better way to celebrate the release of a book about whiskey than to raise a glass and toast to the many folks who had a hand in helping me bring Drinking Deep, the first book in the series, to life. The Whiskey Wars series has been taking up space in my head for a long time now and wouldn't be possible without the following...

Special thanks to Pennington Distillery, especially Jenny and Chris. Not only do they make amazing Tennessee whiskey right in the middle of Nashville (seriously, check them out!) that I enjoyed many times while doing my research, but their staff answered so many of my questions about the distilling process and the operations side of the business. Huge thanks!

I had the opportunity to chat with several hardworking whiskey enthusiasts and tour a few distilleries while I was working on Drinking Deep. Thank you to the folks at Panther Distillery in Osakis, Minnesota, Old Tennessee Distillery in Sevierville, Tennessee, Brushy Mountain Distillery in Petros, Tennessee, and Deadwood Distilling Company in Deadwood, South Dakota for letting me peek in on your fascinating world. Any errors are mine alone.

This book would never have come into existence without the keen eyes of L.A. Mitchell, Donna Alward, Shasta Schafer, Carrie Rushing, and Serena Bell who provided editing, proof-reading, and first passes. Enormous thanks to Sarah Paige at

The Book Cover Boutique for designing the drool-worthy cover.

All my love and endless Crumbl cookies to Aidy Award, Claudia Burgoa, JL Madore, ML Guida, and Bri Blackwood who helped me brainstorm ideas, pushed me when I got stuck, and made sure I kept my butt in the chair to get the words out on the screen.

To my cheerleaders who provided lots of encouragement while this series consumed me: Christina Hovland, Brenda St John Brown, Serena Bell, LeAnn Bristow, Megan Ryder, and all of the other author friends who touched this book in some way.

Love and hugs to Mr. Crush, HoneyBee, GlitterBee, and BuzzleBee who reluctantly toured whiskey distilleries with me, waited (somewhat) patiently in the car while I chatted with distillers about mash bills, and didn't complain (much) when deadlines kept me busy.

And last, but most importantly, ginormous thanks to YOU for being a romance reader... for supporting authors like me and letting us write the stories we love. XOXO

Also By Dylann Crush

WHISKEY WARS SERIES

Drinking Deep

Tasting Temptation

TYING THE KNOT IN TEXAS SERIES

The Cowboy Says I Do

Her Kind of Cowboy

Crazy About a Cowboy

LOVEBIRD CAFÉ SERIES

Lemon Tarts & Stolen Hearts

Sweet Tea & Second Chances

Mud Pies & Family Ties

Hot Fudge & a Heartthrob

HOLIDAY, TEXAS SERIES

All-American Cowboy

Cowboy Christmas Jubilee

Cowboy Charming

THE LOVE VIXEN SERIES

Getting Lucky in Love

STANDALONE ROMANCES

All I Wanna Do Is You

About the Author

USA Today bestselling author Dylann Crush writes contemporary romance with sizzle, sass, heart and humor. A true romantic, she loves her heroines spunky and her heroes super sexy. When she's not dreaming up steamy storylines, she can be found sipping a margarita and searching for the best Tex-Mex food in the Upper Midwest.

Dylann co-hosts Romance Happy Hour (https://www.romancehappyhour.com/) with live episodes every 2nd and 4th Thursday of each month and is the founder of Book Box Babe (https://www.BookBoxBabe.com) where readers can find hand-curated, romance novel themed subscription boxes, and specialty items.

Although she grew up in Texas, she currently lives in a suburb of Minneapolis/St. Paul with her unflappable husband, three energetic kids, a clumsy Great Dane, a lovable rescue mutt, a very chill cat, and a crazy kitten. She loves to connect with readers, other authors and fans of tequila.

You can find her at www.dylanncrush.com.

Made in the USA
Middletown, DE
13 June 2022

66979098R00179